I'm living my nightmare.

Sue wanted desperately to snatch Max and run, but she simply stood, imprisoned in this awful scene.

"How about it, Max?" asked Blackjack, smiling down at the little boy. "How'd you like to copilot a plane with me?"

"Yeah!" Max exclaimed. "Okay, Mommy?"

Sue watched Blackjack's face carefully— watched as Max's words registered the fact that Sue was Max's...

"Mommy?" whispered Blackjack. His bright, carefree smile began to slowly fade away from his face. Blackjack looked down at Max. "How old are you, son?"

"I'm five."

Blackjack's stunned gaze turned to Sue, and she saw the truth clear as day in his eyes. *He knows.*

Dear Reader,

Ever wonder what it would be like to meet not one but *four* fabulous handsome hunks? Well, you're about to find out! Four of the most fearless, strong and sexy men are brought to their knees by the undeniable power of love—in this month's special VALENTINE'S MEN.

Meet Rodger ("Blackjack") McConnell in *Flyboy* by Rosemary Grace.

Rosemary Grace grew up a quarter mile from a small county airport outside Pittsburgh, Pennsylvania. She remembers countless Saturdays when her dad, an air force veteran, would take her up to the airfield to watch the planes, or play a game called "pilot-to-copilot" with her on their back porch rocking chairs. Now a writer and editor in New York City, Rosemary still lives close to an airport, but the sound of jet engines seldom bothers her. It reminds her that miracles do lie within the scope of human vision. It also reminds her of home.

We don't want you to miss out on any of these sexy guys, so be sure to check out *all* the titles in our special VALENTINE'S MEN.

Regards,

Debra Matteucci
Senior Editor & Editorial Coordinator
Harlequin Books
300 East 42nd Street
New York, New York 10017

FLYBOY

ROSEMARY GRACE

Harlequin Books

TORONTO • NEW YORK • LONDON
AMSTERDAM • PARIS • SYDNEY • HAMBURG
STOCKHOLM • ATHENS • TOKYO • MILAN
MADRID • WARSAW • BUDAPEST • AUCKLAND

This book is proudly dedicated to my father, Antonio A. Alfonsi, a man who served his country and his family. Thanks, Dad, for showing me how to use my imagination. You were right. I *can* fly without a plane!

Special thanks to Marc Cerasini for knowledgeable advice, shared enthusiasm and general sexiness. I couldn't have done it without you.

ISBN 0-373-16619-2

FLYBOY

Copyright © 1996 by Alice Alfonsi.

Prologue

TO: CAPTAIN RODGER MCCONNELL

FROM: PRESIDENT OF THE UNITED STATES,
WHITE HOUSE, WASHINGTON, D.C.

CLASSIFICATION: PRIORITY ONE

CC: GENERAL T. GORDON EVERETT,
COMMANDER, 336th SQUADRON, FOURTH
TACTICAL FIGHTER WING, SEYMOUR JOHNSON
AFB, NORTH CAROLINA

EFFECTIVE 0600 HOURS, AUGUST 9, 1990

ALL TACTICAL FIGHTER PERSONNEL ARE TO
REPORT TO CENTRAL COMMAND MOBILITY
UNITS FOR IMMEDIATE TRANSFER . . . TO
DHAHRAN, SAUDI ARABIA, FOR DUAL-ROLE
DEPLOYMENT ... DETAILS AND FLIGHT PLAN TO
FOLLOW. FIRST BRIEFING ON FAST
DEPLOYMENT IS SCHEDULED FOR 0800,
AUGUST 7.

GENERAL MICHAEL J. DUGAN
CHIEF OF STAFF, USAF

August 8, 1990
Seymour Johnson Air Force Base, North Carolina

She had waited long enough.

Lieutenant Sue Rigger rose from the beautifully set luncheon table, leaving her plate of perfectly grilled swordfish and tender new potatoes practically untouched. She had no appetite.

Like an unerring radar beam, the light brown gaze of the pretty, blond-haired twenty-five-year-old swept the large Officers' Club banquet room until… There he was. Captain Rodger "Blackjack" McConnell. With characteristic exactness, Sue studied the powerfully built officer.

He looked at attractive as ever.

She tried not to linger on this thought. Or how the combination of his dress blue uniform and midnight black crew cut brought out the striking electric sapphire of his eyes—as startlingly blue as Maryland's choppy Chesapeake Bay on a crisp fall day, an ironic reflection of the serene color above it.

But Sue wasn't in Maryland now. And, like the choppy Chessy, Blackjack, with his cocky laugh and go-to-hell temper, was nothing close to serene. He was a top-gun fighter jock, the most daring and dangerous kind of pilot there was. The son of an Air Force general, McConnell was a prodigy who'd graduated with honors from the Air Force Academy. He'd no sooner aced his Red Flag tactical training than he'd won the Air Force's William Tell top-gun competition, solidly ranking him as one of the best fighter pilots in the country, if not the world.

Sue watched Blackjack's trim, strong form rise from his table and walk toward the VIPs at the head of the room. She was hardly surprised when he easily charmed the small group of powerful men. Within minutes, the four Pentagon officers and even the vice president of the United States were laughing and talking, clearly impressed with the thirty-one-year-old captain.

Today was the official send-off. Tomorrow most of the pilots in this room would be on their way to the Persian Gulf. The orders had come down only two days ago. Sue remembered the morning Blackjack had received them, and the passion they had shared that very same evening.

She wished she could change everything that had happened since then—or even since a few months back, when she had first become romantically involved with the handsome pilot. She should have listened to her brother's warnings.

Now it was far too late for regrets. It was not, however, too late for revenge. For Sue had discovered firsthand that when it came to women, Blackjack's tactics closely reflected his fighter training: the man could not only be unpredictable, but a dangerous and ruthless son of a bi—

"Sue," a voice called.

Will Rigger, Sue's older brother, was smiling as he stepped past a large potted palm. "If looks could kill, we wouldn't need tactical weapons where we're going," said the lanky young captain. "All we'd need is you."

"Thanks," said Sue dryly.

Sue's brother shared her high cheekbones and fair complexion, but his handsome face had a stronger, squarer chin, his blond hair was a bit darker and his eyes were a deep green rather than light brown like his sister's.

Will smiled. "I'm just glad I'm not the one who's on the receiving end of that glare of yours."

She turned toward her brother and gave an amused laugh. "Well, there's no reason *you* would be. *You're* a decent guy."

"Women don't always think so."

Sue agitatedly combed her fingers through her short cap of light blond hair. "You may have your bad days, but you're not capable of the kind of crap Blackjack pulled on me."

She knew that her withering, emotional glare was *not* her M.O., not even close. She was a research scientist, a competent pilot and, above all, serious, somber and careful. But for the first time in her life, Sue actually wanted to act on pure emotion—not on the coolly calculated outcomes of probability theories, but on a simmering need for some payback.

Her brother turned to look across the room. "I know it's hard to believe. But Rodger has his reasons for acting the cad," he said, then paused a second. "Don't be too hard on him."

Another laugh, not so amused this time, escaped Sue's lips. "*Me?* Hard on *him?*" She felt her breath quickening. "Are you telling me that he can dish it out but he can't take it?"

Will eyed his sister. "What's going on in that much-too-active brain of yours? Don't tell me sparks are about to fly."

A slight smile spread across Sue's face. "Don't worry. I'm just getting the idea that two can play the game of Blackjack."

Another pilot called Will's name. Her brother turned to go, then stopped and looked back a moment. "Remember, Sue," he said, raising a cautioning finger, "I did warn you about the guy."

Sue's eyebrows rose. Will had raised that same finger at her when she'd been a child in blond pigtails. She nearly stuck out her tongue in pure reflex.

"Get a grip, Rigger," she told herself. "You're in uniform."

As the formal luncheon drew to a close, the pilots began to assemble. Although the vice president's visit was last minute, the protocol officer had pulled together every detail of this function down to the final salute.

The VP had come to bid the men in blue godspeed on their show-of-force mission—a "dog and pony show," Will called it. No one, least of all Sue Rigger, thought there'd be a war in the Persian Gulf. These men weren't going to combat, she kept trying to assure herself; it was more like an extended tour in the desert.

The vice president was already standing by the door now. He was flanked by a Pentagon general and the base's commanding officer. Just as the protocol officer had planned it, each of the pilots of the tactical wing began to walk down the line. One by one, each donned his cap, saluted the VP and moved out.

Sue's heart beat faster as Blackjack, now clutching his dress cap under his arm, approached the vice president. Jerry "the German" Bruckman, Blackjack's backseater, had already saluted the man and moved on. Next came Will.

Now it was Blackjack's turn.

Sue's gaze was fixed on the pilot as he snapped to attention and saluted the Pentagon general, then he turned, took a few more steps and faced the vice president of the United States. Again he saluted with military precision.

Sue felt her whole body tense as a voice inside her wondered, *What if this mission isn't just a show of force? What if it turns into something much more dangerous?*

Despite herself, confusing emotions welled up in Sue's throat. She thought of the men and women being sent overseas, possibly into a war situation. She thought of the families they left behind. All the people who cared about them, who loved them—

Sue closed her eyes, trying to block her thoughts and fears.

When she opened them again, the vice president had already returned Blackjack's salute. The pilot was now pivoting to make his exit. She watched as he approached the doorway. His wide shoulders, draped in dark dress blues, were starkly silhouetted by the bright glare of the midday sun.

Damn him, thought Sue as she watched his lean, powerful form disappear down the outside stairs. No one had ever made her *feel* anything so strongly.

She forced herself to remember how cruelly he'd rejected her. How he'd made certain that she saw him with another woman. The anger came back to her, and she clung to it, letting her fists clench—as if she could crush every tender feeling for Rodger McConnell in her bare hands.

"Time to dish a little back out," she whispered, swearing that Blackjack would never again think of her as the naive little sister of a friend—a woman gullible enough to begin falling in love with him, then stupid enough to tell him.

She'd show him—and her brother, too.

Trying to remain calm, Sue watched as the last pilot in the receiving line saluted the VP and the official entourage of uniforms and dark suits exited. She followed with the rest of the personnel. The humid heat of August hit her immediately as she stepped from the cool air-conditioning, but she barely noticed. She was too intent on her plan.

The vice president was already quickly passing through the precise corridor of military uniforms outside. Sue spotted Blackjack at attention. She descended the stairs, trying to remain hidden within a small crowd until the official cars sped off and the pilots were dismissed.

As the group began to disperse, she finally stepped forward, ready to do her deed and make a hasty disappearing act. She planned to remain invisible for the next fifteen hours, until Blackjack was long gone from the base.

Her own route would take her out of North Carolina, as well. She was due to head north in three weeks anyway. Back to Maryland and the think tank where she'd finish her doctoral research on the use of virtual reality in fighter aircraft. And that would be that. She'd never have to see Blackjack again.

"Oh, Captain McConnell?" she called out.

Blackjack was speaking with Will and Jerry among a small group of pilots. His face turned, and when his electric blue eyes caught sight of her, it seemed to Sue that he was actually happy to see her. Then suddenly his eyes changed— as if the flame burning inside them had quickly been doused.

"Yes, Lieutenant?" he asked in a careful, emotionless tone.

"I've got something for you. Before you leave."

Sue sighed with anxiety as she stepped up to the tall, powerful form of the square-jawed warrior of the skies before her.

Don't lose your nerve, Rigger, she warned herself.

Blackjack's eyebrows rose. "What've you got for me, Rigger?"

Sue smiled tightly. "Just a little something to remember me by."

She watched him, making certain he was off guard. Then she moved with lightning quickness.

In a flawless jujitsu move, she took Blackjack's right arm, revolved beneath it with fluid power and levered him over her right hip. A crowd of pilots watched as their cocky comrade flew through the air and landed on his backside.

For a moment, a shocked silence came over the crowd. Then a roar of laughter broke the tension. Pranks were SOP in the military—Standard Operating Procedure. Blackjack's fellow pilots knew his reputation with women, and they knew that he probably had this coming for a long time.

Sue's stomach knotted as she released him and quickly turned to make her exit.

"Nice move!" shouted German Bruckman at Sue's fleeing form.

"Just call my sister 'Sparks' Rigger," said Will.

"Yeah, when she's around, sparks fly, and so does Blackjack—without an airplane!" joked German. Again the group of pilots roared with laughter.

That remark earned German Bruckman a withering glare from Blackjack, who quickly shook his head clear and shot to his feet. Sue was fast in making her exit, but Blackjack was faster.

In no time, she felt the iron band of his hand around her upper arm. *Dammit,* she thought, suddenly remembering why it was that wise people never acted on their emotions: emotional people never thought about *consequences.*

Blackjack's piercing blue eyes glittered like a feral hunter's. His hat had been knocked off in the jujitsu flip, and his jet black crew cut was slightly damp with perspiration. He smiled—a dangerous, threatening baring of teeth.

"Let me go, McConnell—you had it coming!" Sue warned in a pathetic attempt to make her panicked voice sound intimidating. She twisted and pulled in his grasp, trying hard to break loose.

"Let . . . me . . . go!"

But it was no use.

Slowly, inexorably he pulled her toward the crowd of pilots, who were still hooting and hollering.

"Whooee!...Give it to her, Blackjack!...She got you good, yeah!...Look at that!...Whoo! What're ya gonna do?"

Sue felt her fair skin flushing every shade of pink as he pulled her into the middle of the group. She caught her brother's eye and sent him a pleading look, but he shook his head.

She could almost hear his answer in that damned innocent-bystander look. *You got yourself into this, little sister,* he seemed to be saying, *now it's time to take what* you *dished out.*

Sue sighed in frustration. "I'm warning you," she said to McConnell while digging her heels into the dusty ground.

He just bared more teeth, tightened his grip and pulled harder. When he finally stopped, they were smack in the center of the sea of Air Force blue.

"Aren't you going to kiss your flyboy goodbye, sweetheart?"

"I'd rather suck on the tailpipe of an F-4, you bast—"

But he'd cut her off, pushing her smoothly into a dramatic dip, bending over her and planting his lips against hers.

She was mortified and tried to break loose, but he held her firmly. She could only pray that he would pull away after a quick few seconds of this vulgar show. But instead his lips remained, harsh and firm, their angry line pressing hard— an unrelenting punishment for humiliating him.

Or for loving him, an inner voice whispered.

But something was happening as he prolonged their intimate position. Sue felt him changing; the harshness of his lips began to soften, to caress. The hoots and hollers faded to her ears as the hand that had been firmly gripping the back of her head now lowered to lightly massage the back of her neck.

She tried to resist, but the heat of his mouth, the play of his soft, full lips, was quickly disarming her—as he had melted her so many times before. But this time Sue realized that Blackjack's own anger had been disarmed, as well—and suddenly the kiss became more than a payback prank, much more.

It became a tender goodbye.

What if this is the last time you'll ever see him? that voice inside her asked once more. But no answer came. There was nothing she could do, even if it was.

Finally, after what seemed a very long time, he released her. His head rose. His breath was as labored as hers, and Sue blinked in confusion, her mind wondering about this so-called hard-hearted lady-killer.

Could she really have as much of an effect on him as he had on her?

His glittering blue eyes met hers for a fraction of a second and answered her question. She gasped with the knowledge—unable to believe or even accept it.

He looked away in the next moment and quickly slapped a cocky grin on his face, a practiced mask. He stood erect, pulling her fully back to her feet again.

"Now, *that's* how a fighting man should be sent off, sweetheart. Have you learned your lesson?"

As his buddies applauded, Sue felt her face flush again with indignant anger. She automatically pulled her hand back—not for a sissy slap, but an all-out roundhouse punch. He ducked in time to shove a shoulder at her middle and stand again, her body draped over his like a sack of potatoes.

"Dammit! Let me down!"

The hoots were even louder as he coolly walked her to a nearby hangar where a large oilcan sat, half-filled with greasy rags. He dumped her squirming, screaming body into it, then turned and walked away.

Sue made a vow then, in the fifteen seconds it took her to tip the oilcan over and crawl out. She promised herself that if she ever *did* see Rodger McConnell again, she'd never, ever fall in love with him.

As she got to her feet, she frantically reached for the first possible projectile she could find. *Perfect.* Now she could give McConnell something else to remember her by....

She let the sopping paintbrush fly through the air.

It hit him square between his shoulder blades.

But Blackjack McConnell never looked back.

Chapter One

February 14, 1997
Flatlands Air Force Testing Base, Nevada
Thirty Thousand Feet Up

It felt good to be in Reeva's arms again.

Rodger McConnell was content, too comfortable to move, to think...he was happy just to wait and to listen. To *her* voice. That all-too-familiar voice—sexy, soft and feminine.

"I missed you, Rodger."

"I missed you, too, Reeva."

"You're tense today."

Tense? Maybe...she'd certainly know better than him.

"Just relax. Pull me closer."

Rodger did; he could almost feel her arms around him.

A few moments passed. Rodger heard only his own breathing, magnified by the confining headgear. He felt his pulse rate slow, his whole body, his entire *being* relax in Reeva's embrace.

Just as he seemed to be dozing off, Reeva began to question him. With eyes closed, Rodger forced himself to concentrate.

"Do you feel my movements?"

Rodger felt for a moment, then answered, "Yes, I feel it...."

"I'm moving faster now, can you stay with me?"

"Yes, Reeva, it's fine...."

Rodger could feel himself moving with her, faster and faster. His pulse rate shot up along with his blood pressure. His breathing was labored, but he was doing it. He was controlling this fighter aircraft. Through this sweet-toned virtual-reality program, he was able to fly this baby through his voice commands and, slowly but surely, through his thought commands.

"Are you having trouble breathing?"

"No, Reeva, no. Don't stop."

"We're up to speed now, Rodger... I'm not hurting you, am I?"

"You're not hurting me, Reeva."

"All right, Rodger, we're going to try to turn...."

Rodger tried to relax. He tried to just let go—let it happen.

"Tell me when you are ready, Rodger."

Rodger swallowed. In the distance, he heard wind whistling. The familiar weight of gravity pressed hard on his chest. He ignored the noise and discomfort, focused on her commands.

"Tell me when you are ready, Rodger."

"I'm ready, Reeva."

"Good. We are going to turn now, to the right. Slowly."

Rodger felt a momentary stab of panic... he didn't want to fail now... he didn't want to fall out of sync. He could feel the weight on his chest increase as they both began to turn. Slowly. Agonizingly slowly. But something wasn't right. It seemed too slow. Rodger felt the sudden need to speed up, to take control.

That was his undoing.

"Wait, Rodger...you're turning too fast...."

From far away, alarms started to sound. Rodger could feel consciousness returning. He was floating to the surface of his mind as the noise increased to deafening intensities. His breath rattled in his dry throat.

Again Rodger heard the fading voice of Reeva—the Reality Emulation and Enhancement Virtual-reality Adapter. Programmed with that oh-so-familiar voice from years ago.

Sue Rigger's voice.

As her presence again disappeared, he whispered to her, "Reeva, I'm sorry...."

Then she was gone.

Rodger felt hollow, emptied. A void opened inside of him, as it always did when Reeva left him. For a few moments, Rodger felt disoriented. Then he recognized the usual force of gravity mashing the oxygen mask against his face and pressing the virtual-reality helmet down on his head.

A blast of static crackled in his ears, and Rodger heard his backseater's voice, calm and reassuring but laced with regret and frustration. "Sorry, Blackjack...I had to take control. We almost went into a spin...."

Again.

Flexing his fingers, Rodger reached up and pressed the helmet-release buttons on each side of the VR unit. With a loud snap and a rush of air, the helmet popped open. Rodger blinked and squinted as the harsh sunlight flooded his vision. Wiping the moisture from his brow, he asked, "How long?"

"Fourteen minutes. You were doing fine until the turning maneuver, then you lost it...ah...sorry, Blackjack."

Rodger's shoulders slumped, and he reached out to his plastic squeeze bottle of Ibuprofen-laced water. He gagged down a huge gulp, feeling an ache begin at the back of his skull.

He peered out of the bubble canopy of the modified F-15E Eagle attack fighter at the Nevada desert rushing below. Taking another squeeze from the plastic bottle, Rodger listened absently as his backseater spoke with the control tower at Flatlands Base.

He took no comfort in the fact that this was only a test, that no one expected him to pull off a miracle. He had *failed* again. He had *failed* the program, he had *failed* himself and he had *failed* Reeva.

Sue Rigger had nothing to do with this—other than her voice. A voice that had been prerecorded back in some research lab. So why was it that Colonel Rodger Blackjack McConnell had a dark, deep sense that somehow he had failed her, too?

His eyes, as piercingly blue as the cloudless sky surrounding them, continued to stare straight ahead. But all he could see were the images that had haunted him for years— a young, pretty officer with short-cropped blond hair and intelligent brown eyes. The one woman with whom he'd ever truly felt a deep connection.

Like a projector stuck on the same few slides, his mind replayed the images over and over again. Sue laughing and talking. Sue stimulating him with her ideas, arousing him with her touches, challenging him with her temper. And then came the last slide. Always the last one—Sue simply staring at him. Lost and hurt—completely and utterly heartbroken.

Blackjack had always thought the memories would fade over time. But he'd used them too often, he supposed, for comfort in lonely stretches of long flight hours and in times of self-doubt—one of which was now.

The years hadn't weakened the images of Sue Rigger. If anything, they were becoming more potent with time's passing, reminding him of what he'd left behind.

Blackjack didn't like being reminded of losses. Or failures. It made him more than unhappy. It ticked him off.

Tightening his shoulder harness reflexively, he sighed with bitter resignation as his backseater brought their jet fighter in for a landing.

Less than thirty minutes later, Colonel McConnell was sitting in the mission-debriefing room with a dozen personnel assigned to the Reeva-Horizon project's testing staff.

Still wearing his gray Nomex flight suit, Blackjack sat back in the uncomfortable folding metal chair. With crossed arms, he listened as his backseater recounted their latest test flight on the modified F-15E.

Blackjack hated these debriefings about as much as these chairs, but they were standard procedure.

"Thirteen minutes and fifty-three seconds into the experiment, I heard the warning Klaxon and took control of the aircraft. I checked on the status of Colonel McConnell and brought the aircraft home," finished Lieutenant Colonel Jerry the German Bruckman.

Fingering the gold band on his left hand, Bruckman leaned back in the folding metal chair, then smoothed his brown mustache with his thumb and forefinger.

Blackjack could feel all the eyes in the room on him. He exchanged a knowing look with German, then crossed an ankle over a knee in an overtly casual gesture. Slowly he uncrossed his arms and reached a hand into his breast pocket.

After retrieving a small pink rectangle, Blackjack took his time unwrapping it, glancing absently at the Bazooka Joe comic. Then he stuck the bubble gum in his mouth and began to chew.

His straight black hair was damp with sweat despite the cool temperature in the debriefing room, and he ran a hand through it to keep it off his brow. When he looked up again, his blue eyes locked with the hardened black gaze of an older man wearing three stars on his shoulders—Lieutenant General Russell Simpson, the commanding officer at Flatlands. As usual, the CO's stony expression was as unreadable as the best poker players in Vegas.

Dr. Raspail, the civilian scientist, on the other hand, was as easy to read as an engine warning light. The disgust and anger at yet another failure were obvious on his pale, fleshy features.

"It's got to be a software glitch," Simpson said, shaking his head. The lieutenant general's salt-and-pepper crew cut looked more gray under the fluorescent lighting.

"It's not the software," Raspail snapped. Withdrawing one of his many pens from his plastic pocket protector, he pointed it at Blackjack like a loaded side arm. "It's your man, he just can't interface with the program—"

"I'm sorry, Doctor," countered Simpson, "I just don't buy that...he's the only pilot we've tested who's ever gotten this far with Reeva. We were lucky to get him."

Raspail threw up his hands in exasperation, letting the ballpoint fly through the air and bounce along the table. It rolled to a stop in front of Blackjack.

"The software's fine," insisted Raspail in a clipped, superior tone. Reeva is the first VR system able to allow a pilot to fly the plane through his thoughts. The general scientific community is thirty years behind us! But if we can't get any valid data, any proof that it will work, then Washington will cut our funding."

"Dr. Raspail, don't you think I know that?" barked Simpson.

"Mark my words...if this project does not go forward here, it is because the *pilot* is inferior! I don't need to remind all of you that careers are on the line—"

"And you're *out* of line, Doctor," Simpson interrupted, cutting the engineer off in midsentence. "I'm telling you the problem is not on our end."

The tension hovered in the air for a moment more, then Dr. Raspail hefted his heavy frame off the rickety metal folding chair. "Excuse me," Raspail said, sighing with impatience. "I have postflight checks to conduct—"

Raspail stooped at Blackjack McConnell's swift and unexpected rise to his feet. The watery hazel eyes of the scientist met the cool blue gaze of the pilot. Slowly Blackjack walked to stand in front of Raspail. Raising his hand, he presented the scientist with his discarded pen, pressing the pointed tip of the pen's cap lightly into the man's solar plexus.

"You...forgot...something...." said Blackjack in a staccato threat, each word punctuated by a stab of the pen against Raspail's lab coat.

Wheezing, Raspail snatched the pen from Blackjack's hand and left the room. The rest of the testing staff filed out, too.

Lieutenant General Simpson exchanged glances with Bruckman. Both men looked at McConnell.

Simpson shifted. "What have you got to say, McConnell?"

Blackjack's gaze met his commanding officer's, his low voice drawing out the words. "Looks like we're stalled out, sir."

"Well," Simpson said, a grin forming from ear to ear, "then it's a good thing I went behind Raspail's back." Picking up the reports scattered on the table, the lieutenant general rose.

"I put in a call to General Bradford at the Pentagon and requested the original software designer for Reeva to fly in tonight."

Immediately Blackjack's muscles tensed. "*Who* exactly is flying in, sir?"

Simpson flipped a page on his clipboard, "Rigger."

Blackjack's jaw worked a moment. "Which Rigger?"

Simpson's eyebrows rose. "You know more than one?"

"Oh, Rodger knows more than one, all right," German said, chuckling heartily till Blackjack's murderous glare silenced him.

"Brother and sister, sir," explained Blackjack. "I served with Will Rigger during Desert Storm—great guy, actually. If he's the man coming in, we're home free."

Simpson waited. "And? The sister?"

After a moment of silence, German spoke up. "Sue Rigger's a computer science genius like her brother—they work together. She's a pilot, too. Right, Rodger?"

Blackjack nodded.

Simpson looked at Blackjack. "You got some kind of *problem* with the sister?"

Blackjack glared a warning at German, then turned back to the lieutenant general. "Who's flying in tonight, sir?"

"You're in luck, McConnell, it's your old buddy. Washington says Colonel William Rigger, Ph.D., is the software team leader. He was to be contacted this morning and he'll be flying civilian. Due to Las Vegas at 19:00 hours on a commercial flight."

Blackjack's relief was visible. "Are you sending a sergeant to pick him up?"

"Well, Colonel, since you served with the man, why don't you do the honors? Bring him up to speed on the project before Ras-*pale* gets his ear. Might want to grease the wheels a little."

"Right, sir."

German waited until Simpson left the room. "So, the lovely Sue won't be with us—"

"Don't start with me, German." Blackjack moved to the door.

"I'm not starting a thing," taunted German, right on his heels. "But you sure do look like a convict who's just gotten a last-minute reprieve from the governor."

Blackjack stepped into the whitewashed hallway, where a few enlisted men were milling about. "I'm just happy I'll be seeing 'Wild' Will Rigger again. It's been years."

German nodded. "Gonna stay in town a night, loosen him up?"

Blackjack laughed, blew a pink bubble and popped it. "If memory serves, Wild Will wasn't the Rigger who ever needed any loosening up."

The two men turned and began to walk toward the base showers. "Yeah," continued Blackjack, "I think Will might like a good meal and a few drinks."

"And a few show girls if I know you."

"Oh, you know me, German. Too well."

TO: CAPTAIN SUSAN RIGGER, PH.D., BONDERANT CENTER FOR MILITARY RESEARCH, MARYLAND

FROM: GENERAL MARCUS BRADFORD, PENTAGON

PRIORITY: CLASSIFIED

CC: LIEUTENANT GENERAL RUSSELL SIMPSON, FLATLANDS; COLONEL WILLIAM RIGGER, PH.D., USS EISENHOWER

EFFECTIVE IMMEDIATELY

REEVA-HORIZON PROJECT IN JEOPARDY. DIAGNOSTICS REQUIRED. COLONEL W. RIGGER UNAVAILABLE. REPORT TO FLATLANDS VIA COMMERCIAL FLIGHT. BASE PICKUP TO BE ARRANGED. FIRST BRIEFING AT DISCRETION OF FLATLANDS CO

GENERAL MARCUS BRADFORD, USAF

After reading her orders again, mainly out of boredom, Captain Sue Rigger pushed the papers back into her leather purse and stared vacantly into the bustle of the airport terminal.

Suddenly her wandering gaze stopped. It had just passed over the silvery metal of a—

She looked again, not quite believing her eyes.

Yes, she reassured herself, she was looking at a shiny metal slot machine. It stood with two others in a line next to a bank of pay phones, a cigarette dispenser and a soda machine. Lost in thought, Sue brushed at her bangs—her light blond hair was much longer these days, falling well past her shoulders.

Now, what was a slot machine doing in an airport?

"Well, of course," she murmured, the realization hitting her. This was Nevada, after all...*Las Vegas*, Nevada.

Her older brother, Will, would surely laugh at her for taking so long to make the obvious connection. Strange as it seemed, Air Force Captain Sue Rigger, active pilot and Ph.D., could spot infinitesimal glitches in complex software programs, but often failed to see the big picture.

Like now.

She hadn't once considered the casinos, the garish neon lights, the gambling. She'd been so intent on getting to the top secret Flatlands Air Force Testing Base, she never before this moment noticed the tourists rushing off to Vegas for vacation—if you could call gambling your life savings away a vacation.

Except for taking one stupid chance in her past on a cocky bastard of a pilot, Sue had never gambled. Or taken risks. Not anymore.

Well, that wasn't entirely true. Parking briefly in a loading zone, sending Christmas gifts after December 20, doing her own income taxes—these risks she did practice.

What she never did was take any *impractical* risks. This included her work and most aspects of her life—especially her love life.

Still, the slot machine beckoned. And no Air Force sergeant had yet shown up to claim her. Placing her large carry-on bag down, Sue fished in the pocket of her dark green suit for a quarter. She had worn civvies for the flight— her uniforms were packed in the garment bag on her shoulder.

Pulling her hand from her pocket, she came up with bad news—five pennies and a dime. Oh, well. Gambling was a waste anyway. Must be fate, she thought, until a man's deep voice sounded from just behind her—

"You need this?"

Sue stopped. That voice. Every muscle in her body turned stone-cold upon hearing it. She'd swear her heart stopped beating.

Her gaze shifted to see a quarter resting in the palm of a masculine hand. Then slowly, after a deep breath, she lifted her head. There they were. Just as she remembered them. The bluest eyes she'd ever seen—as blue as the skies he lived in. Unfortunately they were set in the square-jawed, handsome face of the man she all but loathed.

"Rodger McConnell," she breathed in sheer disbelief.

"Blackjack," he said. "But you can call me *Colonel*."

Sue couldn't believe it. She knew he was stationed out west as a test pilot—Will had mentioned it in passing. But after over six years, she never expected to cross his path again. She tensed at the mere sight of his arrogant features and that tall, rock-hard physique made all the more masculine by the tailored fit of his dress blue uniform and the campaign ribbons on his chest.

"What's the matter, Rigger," goaded Blackjack, "software glitch cripple your tongue?"

Sue bristled. "No, McConnell. I just didn't recognize you *standing*—I believe you were on your backside the last time I saw you."

"Your memory's faulty. Wasn't it *you* in the compromising position?"

Sue allowed a tight smile. "Come to think of it, seeing you in *any* position is a shock to me. I thought you would have gambled your life away by now."

"On the contrary," he returned coolly, "until I saw you, I was having quite a winning streak."

Sue's fists clenched so hard she felt the cold edges of the coins she held cutting into her palms. "Well, by all means, don't let me spoil your fun." Shoving the coins back into her pocket, she picked up her carry-on bag and strode toward the gate's seating area. "I'd say it's been a pleasure—"

"But, as I recall," said Blackjack cutting her off with a slight, cocky smile, "pleasure was something you needed to learn a lot more about."

Ignoring his last gibe, Sue pushed past a crowd of retirees and made a beeline back to the gate's waiting area. Sitting down in a plastic orange chair, she crossed her long legs with agitation and swore when she heard her stocking snag.

Where the hell was that sergeant? she thought, stretching her leg to check for a run.

Sue knew the flight had been on time, and most of her fellow passengers had already departed for the baggage claim. Could her escort have been delayed in traffic?

"Leaving so soon?" Settling into another plastic orange chair across from her, McConnell leaned back and casually crossed an ankle over a knee, his gaze fixed on her long, shapely legs.

Sue looked at her watch, then pointedly glared at Blackjack. "I'm waiting for the standard base pickup, not that it's any of your business."

"Oh, but it is, my dear Captain."

Sue's questioning look brought her an odd answer.

"Wild Will," said Blackjack.

"What about him?"

"What do you mean, *what about him?* Where is he? I'm here to pick him up—and brief him on Reeva. You're a liability I hadn't been warned about, although I should have known better—that you'd tag along, I mean. But there's plenty of room at the hotel suite to accommodate the three of us."

Sue paused a moment. Then it hit her like a C-130 Hercules loaded to capacity. "Oh, no."

"Where's Wild Will, Captain?"

"You mean to say *you're* the test pilot on our Reeva?"

McConnell uncrossed his legs and slowly stood, his tall, powerful frame towering over her. Then he reached down, gripped each of Sue's upper arms and pulled her to her feet.

As he bent his head toward her, his eyes flashed with dark blue fire, and Sue caught the faintest wisp of an outdoorsy after-shave. She was nearly nose to nose with him, and the proximity unnerved her.

Oh, God. She'd forgotten. Forgotten how powerful an effect this man had on her senses—on every nerve in her form. She blinked in surprise, and Blackjack paused for a moment, as if taken off guard. But he quickly regained his resolve.

"Captain, I want to know *where* your brother is?"

Sue blinked again. "I...uh...I would guess he's about fifty fathoms under."

"Under what?"

"The Atlantic Ocean."

"What!" The look on Blackjack's stunned face was priceless, and Sue savored the uncharacteristic loss of his cool.

"My brother is unavailable, Colonel. He was called to troubleshoot a classified project. It could take weeks."

Sue shook herself loose from McConnell's slackened grip, then angrily brushed at the wrinkles on her sleeves. "And since I'm the cocreator of Reeva," she continued, "as far as the Air Force is concerned, when it comes to reviewing the test at Flatlands—"

"Oh, no," murmured Blackjack.

Sue nodded her head. "*I'm* your man."

Chapter Two

Sue's brown eyes widened in fascination behind the passenger window of the black Range Rover. She pressed the button on the armrest to roll down the glass between her and the passing scene.

Rushing in on a burst of cool, dry desert air came the sounds of the large and most garish carnival she had ever seen in her life. The blare of tinny music, car horns and laughter blended with the wailing bullhorns of gaming-house barkers and screaming sirens of slot machines hitting their jackpots.

Sue gaped in fascination at the unending line of signs flashing a spectrum of neon above sidewalks swarming with crowds. Casino after casino passed, vaunting vulgar architecture—each more spectacular than the next in its bold abandonment of anything remotely resembling taste.

Here was a sixty-foot neon cowboy, there a lighted, bikini-clad figure of a woman winking and waving customers in. Over there a life-size Indian chief, and here a rainbow horseshoe sign boasting Live Table Games and a thing called Keno.

So this was the world-famous Las Vegas strip.

"Decadent beguilement," remarked the deep voice beside her. "Isn't it great?"

Sue turned toward Blackjack, relaxed behind the wheel. His hat sat on the seat between them. She looked up to his head. He was wearing his jet black hair longer now. It came down just past his ears, slightly curling at the collar in back. A big change from his gung-ho, crew-cut days just before the Gulf War.

The longer hair suited him better, thought Sue, so did the crow's-feet at his eyes. Both softened his harder edges. On the other hand, they made him look much more rakish.

Sue wasn't going to be fooled. Maybe Blackjack Mc-Connell appeared a little less dangerous as a warrior these days—but she would bet anything he was even more deadly as a lover....

Just sitting next to him was making her remember all too well the days when their lovemaking had nearly consumed her completely. But she wouldn't remember—she couldn't.

She had a job to do here; that was all. Everything else was history. Over—except, of course, one very important part of her past. And though that part would never be over for Sue, she had vowed six and a half years ago to keep it a secret from Blackjack forever. That alone was enough of a reason to keep her emotional distance from this man.

"This place? Great?" she said aloud, finally responding to him. "It must be the biggest, most vulgar circus in the world."

"It's fun, Rigger."

"Fun." Sue glanced back into the chilly February night. The streets full of people—their faces on the hunt. Possessed. Obsessed. "Maybe while you're winning. But what happens when you lose?"

Blackjack gunned the engine through a green light. "No, Captain. You don't get it."

"Get what?"

A wan smile touched his lips as he continued down the strip, glancing at the passing structures. "It's simple," he said as he turned the Rover into a curved driveway of a hotel-casino called the Gold Strike.

"'When the One Great Scorer comes to write against your name, he marks not that you won or lost—'" Blackjack paused to stop the Range Rover and throw it into Park "'—but how you played the game.'"

"Shakespeare—or Bazooka Joe?" she asked sarcastically as he turned toward her.

"Grantland Rice...as quoted by Granddaddy McConnell, anyway." Then, with a cocky wink, Blackjack grabbed his hat and jumped out of the car. A valet suddenly opened Sue's door.

"Good evening, ma'am, welcome to the Gold Strike."

Confused, Sue awkwardly unsnapped her seat belt, grabbed her purse and stepped down from the Rover.

"McConnell!" she shouted, searching out his form and spotting it at the back of the vehicle. "Why are we here? Are you picking someone up?"

Ignoring her, Blackjack unlocked the hatch and watched as the valets picked up her two pieces of luggage along with one other bag from the back.

"McConnell? Where are they going with my luggage?"

Tipping the valet, Blackjack strode from her and onto the red carpet leading to the double glass doors of the hotel. She watched in horror as her luggage disappeared inside the building and the Range Rover took off down the guest-parking ramp.

Standing in the middle of the driveway, Sue fantasized for a moment about once again using her jujitsu to throw McConnell. How she'd love to put the arrogant bastard flat on his back right in the middle of one of this town's blackjack tables. The thought made her smile, then a blaring horn made her jump.

Storming out of the driveway, she burst through the double doors. Her gaze swept the room. There, beyond the fake marble pillars in the spacious lobby, her gaze locked on to McConnell's dress blues. He was standing by the registration desk—predictably, the object of an attractive woman's attention.

Sue stepped across the plush burgundy carpeting and stopped at the squared blue shoulders of McConnell, then tapped him—none too gently. But before she could utter a word, he turned from the slender brunette in a tuxedo dress and spoke to Sue.

"We're staying here, Rigger. One of the Gold Strike's owners is a retired Air Force officer. He's especially good to pilots when they come through town. I've got a suite here whenever I want it. And I want it tonight. Right, Nina?" he finished with a glance back to the brunette.

The woman smiled pleasantly, and, it seemed to Sue, flirtatiously. "Of course, Blackjack," she purred in a sweet Western drawl. "You and your guests are always welcome at the Gold Strike. Call on me to find anything you'd like...anything...." She nodded, then departed for the nearby entrance to the hotel's adjoining casino.

Blackjack turned toward Sue and searched her guarded face. "Nina Rowen is the Gold Strike's hostess," he explained. "It's her business to make guests feel...comfortable."

"How comfortable?"

Blackjack raised an eyebrow. "Let's just say she was prepared to make your brother and I *very* happy."

Sue shook her head and exhaled with loathing.

"What's the matter, Rigger? Jealous?"

Sue studied the cool blue eyes before her, sparkling now with mirth. Jamming her hands on her hips in fighting fury, she tried not to notice the slight dimples at the edges of his upturned lips.

"Don't flatter yourself, McConnell," she retorted. "There've been plenty of men since you, you know."

"But I'll lay fifty-to-one odds—" he paused and flashed a cocky grin "—that none have measured up."

"Up to what?"

"To me."

Sue's scoffing laughter belied a twinge in her gut—the twinge of her own hypocrisy. Though she'd rather eject from an F-15 with a bum chute than admit it, Blackjack would easily win his bet.

She had been to bed with other men, but not one had come close to the wild and hotly erotic ministerings of this bastard of a pilot. Unfortunately for her, it was true: in both the cockpit and the bedroom, Blackjack was unsurpassed in the pleasure of performing.

But pleasure has its price, Sue warned herself.

Still, some little devil inside her made her wonder if it would be the same way between them—

"C'mon," he said, taking her arm and guiding her toward the elevators. "Nina took care of the check-in. Let's go to our room."

"*Our* room?" she asked, her elbow firmly imprisoned in his grip as they walked.

"Suite, Rigger. It's very big, and there are two separate bedrooms. Don't worry, your virtue is protected."

"Don't get cute with me, McConnell. This is ridiculous, I'm here to do a job. I demand you take me to Flatlands tonight."

"Forget it," he said, pushing the elevator Up button. "I outrank you."

Sue lightly rubbed her temple in thought. Every fiber of her body wanted to bolt right now, but her mind overrode her emotions. What could she do? Flatlands was a top secret installation, probably two hours' drive from the city. She couldn't very well call a cab when no civilian map listed the place, and she herself didn't even know exactly where it was.

She could call Flatlands and ask for a pickup, she thought as the elevator doors opened and McConnell firmly guided her inside. A well-dressed Japanese couple and a stocky man in jeans and a cowboy hat stepped in after them.

Sue glanced at her watch—22:00 hours. Ten o'clock. If she called the base for a car now, an airman wouldn't get here until midnight. Then two more hours to drive out. That would mean she'd arrive at Flatlands at five in the morning Maryland time. She could stand putting off sleep that long. Anything was better than a night with McConnell.

The doors opened onto the tenth floor, and the man in the cowboy hat stepped out. McConnell seemed to be studying her, but she ignored him, watching the flickering numbers instead—14, 15, 16...

On the twentieth floor, the penthouse, the Asian couple stepped out and walked down the hall. McConnell and Sue followed until he suddenly halted her. He waited until the couple turned the corner, then he spoke.

"Okay, Rigger. Spill it."

"Spill what?" Sue did her best to look innocent.

"Come on. It may have been years since I've seen you, but I still remember that look. What scheme are you cooking up?"

"Cooking?"

With a sigh of frustration, he reached for her wrist.

She reacted automatically: pull, lever, flip.

The long, empty hallway had plush carpeting, and that was lucky for the flying body of Colonel McConnell. He landed on it with a soft thud. Sue watched him blink for a second in confusion as he stared at the cut-glass light fixture in the ceiling above him.

She moved her furrowed brow into his line of sight.

"Great. Just like old times," he remarked dryly, rubbing his neck.

"Uh . . . sorry," she managed. "Reflex. It's that hand-to-hand training. Remarkable how it really stays with you."

"Shame on you, Rigger," he said, staring up at her from the floor. "You should save that stuff for the enemy."

"Dammit, Blackjack. You *are* the enemy."

He sighed and sat up. His shoulders slumped in a dejected posture, his blue eyes searching her face. "Am I?"

Sue felt something twist inside of her. *No matter the past, he is still a decorated combat veteran and he saved your brother's life. Besides,* warned her inner voice, *you've still got to work with the man.*

"Look, McConnell, just promise not to manhandle me," she stated.

"What?"

"Promise me, and I'll call a truce."

She held out a hand and he took it, rising to his feet. He held it a moment, then smiled. She recognized that feral gleam a split second too late.

In a flash he'd pulled her against his solid chest, swept her legs out from under her in a classic martial-arts maneuver. Then he followed her down to the floor.

With a hard "Umph!" she landed on her backside. A split second later, the weight of the infamous lady-killer was pinning her.

He's also deceitful, and you should never, ever trust him again!

"I should have known—" she groaned.

"Yep, you should have, Rigger. I *never* make promises I can't keep."

That she should have remembered. He never had promised her a thing six and a half years ago. The more fool her. Sue's brown eyes glared at the man as she squirmed under his weight.

She watched his blue eyes darken with interest.

"Get off me, you idiot, before I have to straighten you out."

Blackjack laughed—a short staccato burst. Then he smiled. "You talk about not being 'manhandled,' *Captain*, but yet you told me at the airport you're the best *man* for the Reeva job? I think you'd better straighten *yourself* out."

His mouth was close to hers, and Sue felt his breath warm on her cheek. She felt her own breath quickening, her body responding, traitor that it was.

"Of course, no red-blooded male in his right mind could *ever* mistake you for a man," he whispered with a teasing smile.

She opened her brown eyes and saw his mouth begin its descent. At first she thought he was going to kiss her, but in the last moment, he'd turned his head to brush his soft, warm lips against her ear.

"Mmm...you still wear the same perfume...sweet..."

"And you're...still shame...less," she charged between labored breaths. She tried not to notice the feel of his mouth so close to her skin, the tickle of his hot breath at her ear.

"How about it, Sue?" he said in a husky murmur. "I'm not so battle fatigued I don't know a good thing when I see it—"

"Well, now, excuse me—" came a nearby female voice.

Blackjack was off Sue in a millisecond and gallantly pulling her up behind him. She came to her feet with surprise, watching in amazement as Blackjack's ever-ready charm locked right into place faster than a heart-seeking missile.

"No, no, excuse us," he smoothly announced to the heavyset maid standing before them, her arm propped on a hip.

Blackjack tipped his officer's hat to her and flashed his heartbreaker dimples. "We were just looking for the lady's...ah...earring."

"Looks to me like she's wearin' both of 'em," the maid remarked dryly with a raised eyebrow that said *I'm nobody's fool.*

"That's right," Blackjack said as he put his arm around Sue and began edging them down the hall. "We found it."

"Sure, sure...just watch yourself, Officer," teased the maid, "we don't want 'nother o' those Tailhook things goin' on 'round here."

Sue's face, pink with embarrassment, now reddened in mortification.

Rodger McConnell just smiled and winked. "Oh now, if you recall, that was the Navy, ma'am," joked Blackjack. "We don't do that sort of wild partying in the Air Force."

"Oh, su-u-u-re you don't!"

But they were already turning the corner and, in another minute they burst through the double doors of their suite.

Sue's eyes widened after Blackjack flipped the lights on. Compared to this suite, the garish sight of the Las Vegas strip twenty floors below was tasteful. He hadn't lied when he said the room was big—this place was huge. It was also red...from the velvet sectional sofa in the sunken living area and the textured paper lining the walls, to the lamp shades and plush carpeting.

"Nice place, huh?" Blackjack stated dryly.

"It's...ah...very red." Sue noticed a framed oil painting on the wall—apples, grapes, cherries. Red, of course.

"Yeah, I know, but it's got a nice view," Blackjack offered as he motioned her over to a large sliding glass door.

The night was crystal clear, as only nights in the desert can be, and the view *was* spectacular—a carpet of rainbow-colored neon spread out below them. She watched Blackjack flip the lock on the glass door then slide it aside.

A balcony extended out of the room, and they both stepped onto it. It was chilly and breezy, but the air felt refreshing. Sue wrapped her arms around herself and took in a deep breath.

"The strip is six miles long," said Blackjack, his forearms leaning on the railing. "That's not even counting Glitter Gulch, downtown. See, it's over there—"

Sue stepped timidly closer. "You're not going to throw me off, are you?"

"I could ask you the same question." Then he smiled. It was warm and genuine, and Sue tried not to look at it too long.

"C'mon, be brave," he coaxed. "Besides, we need you for the Reeva project. God knows."

Sue was surprised, even a little flattered, at this concession. She moved closer and peered into the night. They stood side by side for a few silent minutes, listening to the muted sounds of traffic, sirens and ringing jackpots floating up to them on the dry air of the desert night.

"Must be a million lights," she murmured.

"Two million...and forty-two miles of neon tubes."

Sue looked askance.

"That's what it was a few years back, anyway."

"What do you do, live in the casino?"

"No. My mother used to work in the city—that's how she met my dad. *He* was the gambler."

"I thought he was a fighter pilot."

Blackjack just laughed. "He was."

"Then why are you laughing?"

He shook his head. "Because all fighter pilots are gamblers, even if they never touch a card."

Sue stared into the night sky for a moment. "Not *all*."

Blackjack looked down at her, his blue gaze meeting the uneasy blinks of her pretty brown eyes. She felt her heart begin to beat annoyingly faster again. She ordered it to stop. There would be absolutely *no* fast heartbeats around this pilot. Ever.

A knock sounded at the door inside—their suitcases.

Blackjack took charge and had the bellboy put her two pieces into the larger of the two bedrooms. His went into the second room. Then he dug into his slacks for a bill.

"Thanks, Colonel McConnell," said the young man with a broad smile, transferring the bill to his own pocket. "Nice to see you again, enjoy your stay in the Valentine Suite." Then the bellboy turned to add in a lowered voice, "And, Colonel, as always, if there's anything else I can get you...you know..." Sue noticed the young man wink suggestively.

"That's *all*, Joey, thanks," he managed to say, practically pushing the kid out the door.

McConnell turned and strode back into the main room.

"Valentine Suite?" she asked.

Blackjack shrugged. "I guess that was Nina's doing, for some reason...."

Sue glanced at her digital watch. February 14. She hadn't even realized. *Oh, my God,* she thought. *I'm actually spending my Valentine's Day with Rodger McConnell.* The idea of it made her neck muscles knot. Was she the victim of a sick joke?

"I'll just wash up. Why don't you freshen up, then we'll have some dinner, get some air." He recited this like a military itinerary. In fact, he was so sure of himself that he hadn't even slowed his stride through the main room; he'd walked right past her and toward his bedroom door.

"No." It was simply and plainly said.

She watched his back stiffen, and her arms crossed her chest in automatic preparation for the onslaught.

"What did you say?" he asked, still facing the bedroom door.

"I've humored you this far, McConnell, because you're a combat veteran. And you're my brother's friend. And we're on this project together. But I'm not about to stay here with you."

She watched his hands go to his waist in an obviously irritated posture. He had yet to turn around, though, and Sue continued talking to his stiff back. "I'll wait in the room only until my ride gets here."

She walked to the phone on the wall, lifted the receiver and pressed 9 for an outside line. Then she began to dial the main number for Flatlands. But she only got four numbers pressed—

A large hand depressed the silver hook and cut her off in one blunt move.

"What did you call me? A *veteran*. What the hell's the matter with you?"

Sue was suddenly mute, surprised by his reaction. She must have struck a nerve.

"Do I look retired?" He grabbed the receiver from her hand and slammed it back on the phone. "Do I look like I'm finished? Washed-up?"

"Calm down, will you. I only meant—"

"I'm on active duty, Captain. Do you want me to prove how active—and potent—I still am?" He stepped closer and she stepped back.

"Don't you threaten me, McConnell—"

"Or what?"

Sue eyed him a moment. "Look, Colonel," she began slowly, "it's not personal."

"Like hell. It's personal, all right, Rigger. And I'll be happy to get personal with you—" He took another step closer, and again she stepped back. But this time she found her body flush against the scarlet-colored paper on the wall.

"What are you doing?" she blurted as the warmth of his strong body seemed to close in on her.

He didn't answer. Instead, he slowly moved his hands to rest on her shoulders. Then he used his right thumb and forefinger to play with the silky edges of her long blond hair.

"There's only one reason you want to run so fast tonight, Rigger," whispered Blackjack.

"Oh? And why...is that?" Sue managed to ask between increasingly labored breaths.

He used his thumbs, as he'd done years ago. Slowly he moved the soft pads up, along the muscles of her neck—the ones that always tensed terribly on her. *Does he really remember that about me?* she wondered as he positioned his thumbs just behind her ears and began that erotically slow massage of small, easy circles. His eyes, piercing and hungry, seemed to hold her spellbound in a trap of shimmering blue heat.

Then he leaned in, his mouth dangerously close to her own.

"Because things haven't changed that much in all these years. You still want me." His gravelly voice was thick with desire, his breath warm against her upper lip. "Admit it."

She inhaled the clean, fresh scent of his after-shave and swallowed, but she couldn't keep the shakiness from her whisper. "Not in ten million years."

Then he smiled, ever so slightly, and his lips brushed hers in the lightest of touches.

Ten thousand volts of electricity shot through her body as her mind reeled in disbelief. It *wasn't* the same as it had been years ago.

It was much, much better.

But though every nerve in her body seemed to have been sent into the stratosphere with that utterly arousing touch of his lips, her mind hadn't stopped working. It played back her own words, echoing them through her mind like a warning Klaxon at thirty thousand feet: *Pleasure has its price.*

Chapter Three

"Blackjack," Sue whispered against his lips.

But Rodger ignored her. He was too busy contemplating the sweet curves of her body and the petal-soft skin of her neck. Her light, sweet perfume brought him back years, and he was mesmerized by the feeling.

Sue Rigger was six and a half years older and more sexy than he recalled. He found himself even more attracted to her than he'd been years ago. Oh, she still had that same way of goading him. That hadn't changed. No other woman had ever been able to stand up to him, to challenge him the way Sue could. It drove him nuts sometimes, but he admired her for it.

Tonight, though, seeing her again after all these years, he sensed something different about her. She had more confidence in herself, more pride and self-awareness. And there was definitely more worldly-wise wariness in those big light brown eyes.

Sue Rigger had matured. And he was attracted to this older woman. Very much. There was something else about her, he realized, something in the way she looked at him, that he couldn't quite define. One thing he did know, though, was that he would have to stay in control or he'd go too far, too fast with her—and this was a delicate situation, to say the least.

Then again, Blackjack knew women. And he knew this one enough to know that she was very much turned on by him. So he'd just have to persuade her to see things his way and face the facts of their temporary fate—

"Admit it," he whispered against her mouth. "I'm as good as ever."

"Dammit, Blackjack!" Sue closed her eyes in frustration, pulling her mouth away from him. "You haven't changed at all."

"Thanks," he said. "That's admission enough."

"What I meant was, you're still a snake," she snapped, breaking from him and stepping away in agitation. She began brushing at some invisible wrinkles in her green suit.

He wasn't fooled by her pretense that she was unaffected by his touch. He could hear the trembling of arousal in her voice, and her cheeks were the color of the Valentine Suite's wallpaper. His mouth stretched slowly into a terribly cocky smile, and his arms crossed over his powerful chest.

"Maybe I am still a snake," he admitted. "But I made my point, didn't I?"

"Listen, one kiss from you is not about to change my mind. You can't keep me here," said Sue calmly. "I'm going whether you like it or not." She walked to the phone and again lifted the receiver.

"Please don't, Sue."

The anger was gone. The sexual teasing was gone. Blackjack said the words sincerely—one officer to another. He could see it caught her off guard, and she slowly put the receiver down.

"McConnell," she said, looking up to meet his gaze. "Give me one good reason I should stay."

"Look, Sue," Blackjack began, then stopped. *Here it is,* thought Blackjack. *The moment of truth.*

He knew how brilliant this woman was. There'd be no charming his way around her when it came to their work. It was time to risk being completely honest with her. His arms relaxed to his sides, and he turned from her to gaze out the window.

"We have to work together," he said in a low voice. "The project's in trouble, and we need ... *I* need your help."

Finally he turned to risk facing her. His cocky grin was gone. Her face was stoic, unemotional.

"I'm here for diagnostics," she said softly. "Not to help ... anyone ... in particular."

"I know," he said. "But I thought that with our history ... you and I ..." He didn't know what else to say. An awkward minute passed as he sighed and rubbed the back of his neck. "Look," he said, trying again, "why don't we just get some dinner and try to work out our ... personal problems tonight? Get it over with."

"Get *what* over with?"

Blackjack eyed her. "That depends on you."

Sue gazed at him, and he tried not to notice how she still pursed her lips slightly when she was thinking. He tried not to remember how she hated that cute dusting of freckles at the bridge of her nose. And he tried not to think about how much her decision to stay tonight suddenly meant to him— and how it had less to do with Reeva than with his own curiosity.

"I'll stay," she said suddenly, "provided that the 'problems' that we're going to work out tonight will *not* include the bedroom!"

"Fine," said Blackjack, though he'd bet that her resolve could easily be changed later this evening. "Glad you see the sense of it. Now, as I said, if you'd like to freshen up, we can grab a bite at the hotel's restaurant. Okay with you?''

''Fine,'' said Sue, her tone suddenly colder as she turned from him and walked toward one of the bedrooms. ''But do me a favor and don't touch me again.''

''Why should I do you any favors?''

The slam of her bedroom door was the only answer he got.

TWO HOURS LATER, Sue found herself finishing a sumptuous meal in the hotel's finest restaurant. The conversation had been easier than before, mainly because they kept it impersonal. They'd discussed the Reeva project a bit, and Blackjack gave Sue some background on the lay of the land at Flatlands Base.

She then filled him in on how her brother was doing.

''So, he's still 'Wild Will,' then?'' asked Blackjack, pulling the last bit of tender meat from his grilled T-bone. ''That boy had quite the appetite for women, as I recall,'' he said, placing the thick piece of red meat into his mouth.

Sue raised an eyebrow, watching the man chew with gusto. She nearly pointed out that there'd never been anything wrong with Blackjack's appetite, either.

''Oh, he's as wild as ever,'' she remarked instead. ''Though he's slowing his pace a bit. In fact, I'd say he's just about ready to settle down and find the right woman. *He'd* never admit it, but I can see it in his eyes when he's around—'' Sue stopped herself a moment. She almost blurted out *my son.*

She swallowed uneasily. The image of Max's little blue-eyed face and slight dimples assaulted her with surprising force. She hated being away from him, and she knew *this* was by far the biggest danger of being near Blackjack McConnell again. If she slipped and let him know she had a son, there would be questions, maybe lots of them. And Sue wasn't about to volunteer answers. The trouble was, evasion just made a tirelessly aggressive man like Blackjack even more determined to pursue the truth.

"Around?" prompted Blackjack.

"When he's around...kids," she finished awkwardly. "There are a lot of kids at my apartment complex in Maryland," she explained. "Will's so good with them, and I think that he wouldn't mind having a few of his own."

Sue looked up but noticed that Blackjack wasn't quite following her. He was staring off, distracted.

"Blackjack?"

He met her gaze and smiled. "Sorry," he said. "I was just...thinking. About kids. Jerry Bruckman—you remember him, he was my backseater at Seymour Johnson. He's a lieutenant colonel now. He was stationed in Japan for a time before Flatlands. Actually he's my backseater on Reeva."

"Of course I remember Jerry the German. Lanky, dark blond hair—still have that mustache?"

Blackjack nodded. "He has two kids, if you recall. You should see them now, they're so big."

"How old now?"

"Ten and twelve. Me and German play two-on-two basketball in their driveway—German and the twelve-year-old against me and the little one. It's hilarious."

Sue smiled, unable to imagine him playing with children. Then an image came to her: Blackjack playing with her young son. *Stop it,* she cautioned herself. Yet she found herself haunted by it still. Feelings of guilt began creeping around her nervous system, and she stared at her nearly empty dinner plate.

"Dessert?" he asked.

Sue's large brown eyes looked up at the man sitting across from her. The table's flickering candlelight reflected in his eyes, making tiny bright stars dance within the deep blue color. She watched him rub his chiseled, freshly shaved jaw.

"Or if nothing on the menu interests you—there's always me," he said, flashing that brilliant, sexy smile of his, flanked with those lady-killer dimples.

Here we go, thought Sue. *I knew he'd get around to this again.* The whole idea of Blackjack trying to seduce her once more made her more than a little uneasy—and that made her more than a little testy. Oh sure, when they'd arrived in the formal restaurant, she hadn't missed the turning heads of a dozen admiring females. Those women had openly followed his tailored dress blues across the room, and she supposed any one of them would have gladly melted at such an offer from this man.

But Sue Rigger wasn't any woman.

"No, thanks," she said, smiling tightly at her dinner companion while shooting him a withering glare. "The cost for enjoying that particular delicacy was always much too high."

Blackjack's eyes glittered fiercely at Sue's gibe. She knew what effect her goading had on him—it was more than annoyance. Her brother had told her that Blackjack had once admitted something as the two were sharing a drink after an exhausting ten-hour flying mission. Blackjack said that he'd never before met a woman who could hold her own with him—never before Sue. It turned him on.

She never forgot that. And she had to admit that she liked having such an effect on the man sitting across from her. It was quite a switch, her having the power.

"Hmm," he returned. "Maybe there's something we both can do about that," Blackjack said as he slowly reached for the half bottle of Bordeaux. He refilled her glass, then emptied the rest of the light, dry red wine into his.

"About what?" asked Sue.

"The cost."

"Of dessert?"

He nodded his head as he brought the French wine to his lips. His blue gaze raked the length of her possessively, then returned to her wide brown eyes.

Sue brought her own glass to her lips. She had to concentrate to swallow. He watched her as she took a drink then licked the edge of her mouth.

"I don't know what you're talking about," she said.

"I think you do."

"I think you don't—think, that is," challenged Sue. "Not a very good characteristic for a test pilot, Colonel."

Sue knew she'd hit a raw nerve the moment she said it. Blackjack was as cool as they came, but every so often, she found just the right frequency to jam him up. She watched the muscles in his jaw tense; his hand tightened around the wineglass.

Then he smiled tightly. "And I think that when Sue Rigger *lets* something cost her once, then she's too afraid to ever try it again. Not a very good characteristic for a pilot, *or* a self-respecting scientist, Captain."

She took a deep, angry breath. He was the only man who could send her blood pressure through the roof. "Only fools repeat their past mistakes!"

"I agree."

"What?" Sue blinked in surprise. "So...you understand?"

"Yes. But I doubt *you* do."

In confusion, she fell silent a minute, turning her attention to the napkin that was slipping from her lap. Her hands fixed the white linen square back into its proper place, then with brusque, highly agitated strokes, she smoothed it free of every last wrinkle.

By the time she looked up again, the busboy was clearing their table. Except for the rattle of plates and tinkling of glasses, a tense silence descended over the two dinner companions. When the dishes were finally gone, their waitress approached. "Would you like to have dessert?" she asked.

Blackjack's blue gaze smoldered as he studied Sue's face. "That's up to the lady."

Sue pursed her lips, still annoyed. She looked up at the waitress. "Yes, I *would* like dessert," she said, then turned her flashing eyes to directly meet his stare. "I'll have something from the *menu*."

SHE WAS STILL AGITATED when they returned to the Valentine Suite. After dinner, Blackjack had been the perfect gentleman, escorting her on a pleasant stroll. She was glad they bypassed the loud and crowded casino. Instead, he led her through the lobby and along a glass-enclosed hallway toward the back of the hotel, where the hotel pool was lit for the evening and café tables were set up along the edge of a large winter garden.

Their talk had returned to the Reeva project for the most part—the Air Force's expectations for it, the many future uses.

Reeva could be the solution to finally giving the hard-to-handle stealth aircraft faster maneuvering. And with Reeva, pilots of high-performance jets would no longer have to wait for their hands to tell the plane their mind's orders. Reeva would allow them to maneuver any plane as fast as the speed of their thoughts.

With supersonic fighter jets growing more and more sophisticated for pilots to fly, Reeva would not simply allow split seconds of time to be saved, but lives, as well. Accidents in battle, in training and in bailouts would be greatly reduced.

Reeva was not just a gadget—it was a revolutionary new concept in flight. And it meant everything to Sue and to her brother. *But does it mean as much to Rodger McConnell?* she wondered. *Or are the setbacks at Flatlands somehow because of him?*

Sue already knew what Dr. Raspail thought. He'd filed reports concluding that Blackjack was the glitch, that *he* was the whole obstruction to the project's progress.

Sue feared this could be true.

So far, Blackjack had been the only pilot capable of using Reeva in an actual fighter aircraft. But many other pilots had been successful in lab simulators. Perhaps it was time to bring in some fresh blood. Younger blood.

Perhaps, reasoned Sue, it was time to fire McConnell from this project.

On the other hand, Will had always thought highly of his buddy. No surprise there; after all, the man had saved her brother's life. For that, Sue would always be grateful, although with her mixed feelings toward him, she doubted she'd express it out loud.

As far as Will was concerned, though, if any pilot was brave enough and intelligent enough to push the envelope on a new flight system, it was Rodger McConnell. He was one of the top pilots in the Air Force.

Then again, thought Sue, even top pilots lost their edge.

A slight drumming began in the back of her skull. This back-and-forth thinking felt just about as tiring as whacking a tennis ball across a net—and right now her head felt like a tightly strung racket.

She closed her eyes a moment and massaged her temples.

Above all, she decided that she wanted to be professional—and that meant being fair to Blackjack, no matter the past. She'd simply have to wait and see the tests for herself.

"Headache?" asked Blackjack, tossing the room key on the bar of the Valentine Suite.

"Just a touch," she answered. "It's mostly tension."

"Would you like a nightcap?"

Sue walked to the red velvet sofa and collapsed. She sighed as she kicked off her shoes, noticing the little heart-shaped coasters on the coffee table. "Oh, brother."

Blackjack smiled as he watched her. "I take that as a yes?"

She returned his smile. "Just something mild."

He removed his uniform jacket and draped it over a chair, then he rolled up the sleeves of his dress shirt and unbuttoned his collar. He filled two shot glasses and brought them to the sofa.

Sue inhaled the sweet scent of orange and was about to sip the Grand Marnier when Blackjack's hand stilled hers. He sat beside her and touched his glass to hers with a gentle clink.

"To... new beginnings," he said. "Starting over."

He lifted his glass to his lips, then stopped when he saw Sue hadn't moved a muscle. She was staring at the glass-topped coffee table and the little red heart-shaped coasters. Some had little dried rings around them, marks where they'd been used.

His breathing grew sharp and shallow with agitation at her obvious rejection of his toast—and him. For a long moment, they sat like stones.

"What did you mean?" she finally asked carefully. "Back at the restaurant... you said that you doubted I understood." Sue's long lashes lifted, and her brown gaze met his tense blue stare. "What don't I understand, Blackjack?"

"The cost," he said. "You're too concerned with it."

Her eyebrows rose.

"Sue, fate has thrown us together again," he contended. "Why fight it?"

"I already told you. Only fools make the same mistake twice."

"So don't make it. Our past only cost you because you *let it* cost you. This time, just don't let it."

Sue closed her eyes. Strange, half-hysterical laughter came bubbling up from her throat. *If you only knew the truth of what happened between us all those years ago,* she said to herself.

Blackjack watched her carefully. "Well?"

She took a deep breath, then met his gaze. "Well what? Don't fall in love with you, you mean?"

Blackjack nodded.

"You know, of all the arrogant, cocky bastards that ever flew a plane, you've got to top the list."

"Thanks," he said without a moment's hesitation. "I don't have to tell you that confidence is what keeps pilots alive." He took a sip of his Grand Marnier, then stretched an arm across the back of the sofa, letting his fingers play with a few silky strands of her blond hair. "Of course, there's a very good reason for all this protesting."

"Oh, and what's that?" asked Sue, trying to pretend his nearness wasn't affecting her.

"Maybe you never got over me."

"Ha!" The sharp sound burst from Sue's throat. "You flatter yourself, Colonel. Maybe *you* never got over *me.*"

Blackjack reacted with a laugh of his own, but his was deep and threatening, like the rumble of thunder before an unstoppable storm. His determined gaze never left hers as he took another sip of his liqueur, then set it down on the coffee table. Leaning toward her, he used the backs of his fingers to brush the smooth ivory of her cheek. A shiver slipped across her skin, and she silently cursed herself. She could do nothing to stop her insides from churning with that old potent yearning.

"So soft," he whispered.

"Are you challenging me?" she asked, her own gravelly voice betraying his effect on her.

His mouth turned into a tense smile. "Face it, Captain, you want to enjoy yourself—but you're scared to death."

"Of what? Falling in love with you again?" Sue scoffed. "I say again, Colonel, you flatter yourself."

Blackjack moved closer. He lifted the glass from her hand and placed it beside his own. In another moment, he was turning toward her, leaning his body in, placing a hand behind her neck, his long fingers massaging the always-tense muscles there.

"So?" he murmured low.

"So?" she asked between uneasy blinks of her large brown eyes. She tried not to betray how she felt. But she was becoming intoxicated by his nearness—the sharp mind; the strong, powerful body; the brave, confident spirit; and those blue, blue eyes.

"So...I have something to say to you, Captain," he murmured, his breathing shallow, his mouth moving dangerously close.

Sue licked her lips, just waiting as his gaze caressed her face. The scent of orange liqueur was pungently sweet on his breath, and the feel of his warm masculinity was drenching her senses.

"What?" she managed to say, her voice barely there.

"Happy Valentine's Day," he whispered on a slight smile, then he brushed his full lips across hers.

Once again it was a high-powered connection, and it sent Sue soaring.

But one touch was not enough for Blackjack. Like a pilot practicing landings and takeoffs, his mouth was coming back for a touchdown again. First his lips would land, and then they'd lift. Ever so slight and teasingly gentle, he began to create a highly arousing tension within her.

Sue felt her head spinning with the erotic rhythm of his kisses. A voice inside of her still had some sense. *Push him away!* it screamed. *Are you out of your mind?*

She tried to listen to the voice of reason. But her arousal was drowning out that voice. She *did* want him again. Wanted to feel his arms around her, wanted to enjoy the kind of lovemaking she hadn't experienced in well over six years.

Part of her was curious. Would it be as good? And part of her was plain angry. While it was true that she did desire his body, she swore that she would *never* fall in love with this man again. And she burned to prove it to him.

It did occur to Sue as he kissed her, as she felt his hands caressing the back of her neck, that maybe, deep down, Rodger McConnell actually *wanted* her to fall for him again—

But why? So he could play his little power game and cruelly dispose of her as he'd done before? That seemed a waste of time. But then Sue knew her limitations—understanding men was definitely a course she'd never passed.

Anyway, she thought, there was really no danger of falling in love with Rodger again. She'd grown up—and wised up—plenty in the last few years, ironically due to him. If anything, this time it would be Blackjack who would fall in love and Sue who would crush his heart in her hands as she walked away.

So go ahead, then, she told herself. *Let go. Do what you really want. Enjoy yourself.*

Suddenly she broke away from him and rose to her feet. She heard him take a deep, shaky breath as he turned his face up to her. *He wants me just as badly,* she thought. *Good.*

"Giving up the challenge so soon, Captain?" goaded Blackjack.

"On the contrary, Colonel," said Sue. With renewed purpose, her hands went to her clothes. She removed her dark green suit jacket and flung it across the sofa back. Next her fingers went to the top buttons of her white silk blouse. She unbuttoned one, then another, and a third, her long-lashed brown eyes meeting the unwavering stare of the man sitting before her.

When she finished, she pulled her blouse from her skirt and flung it, too, over the sofa back. She stood defiantly now, her thin ivory lace bra the only barrier between them. A small strand of pearls glistened against the creamy skin of her neck.

"What's the matter, Colonel?" she teased. "Did I call your bluff?"

Blackjack let a slow, dangerous smile spread across his face. His blue eyes smoldered. "Be *very* careful, Rigger. I'm about to call yours."

"It's no bluff," she said, propping a hip in frank temptation. And when she looked into Blackjack's face again, she nearly gasped at the sight of the raw desire now in his fiery blue eyes. They burned with an alarming heat that she had never before seen in him—or any other man.

Slowly Blackjack stood. His hot gaze raked the creamy mounds of her lace-covered breasts then met her wide, dark eyes. Silently he unbuttoned his own shirt, pulled it from his slacks and flung it away, his intense stare never wavering from hers.

Sue felt her breathing grow shallow and rapid as she watched him revealing the powerful chest she remembered so well. It was a prime specimen of masculinity—heavily muscled and superbly sculpted, with a fine dusting of curling black hair.

Sue started slightly when she noticed something new. Two scars. One short, shallow scar bit a line into his right shoulder. Another, much deeper, stretched from his left shoulder to just above his washboard stomach. They were the only flaws in his otherwise masculine perfection.

Her hand reached up. With two soft fingers she touched the edge of the larger scar. She felt Blackjack's sharp intake of breath. Lightly she drew her fingers across his chest, tracing its long length.

Her questioning eyes searched his blue gaze. "The Gulf?"

He shook his head. "Test flight. Two years ago."

The second Sue's brow began to wrinkle in concern, she felt a powerful grip tightening on her hand.

"I survived," he snapped, almost bitterly, pushing away her concern for him as he leaned his body closer.

Sue felt the warmth of his skin as his hard, muscular chest leaned toward her. Despite her mild annoyance with his biting tone, a stream of molten lava began to flow through her veins.

"My scars are not the business at hand, my dear Captain." His voice was gentler as it breathed into her ear. Then his mouth was on hers again, but this time his kiss was not a teasing touch-and-go. This time it was hot and demanding.

As his lips moved hungrily over hers, she began to remember Rodger McConnell's consuming, overpowering kisses from years ago. Beneath the taste of sweet orange of the Grand Marnier, she also tasted Blackjack. She could never forget that dark, rich, masculine flavor that was all his own.

But memories weren't always sentimental...especially when they weren't all good. Suddenly she needed some breathing room. This was all happening too fast—

"Sweet Sue," growled Blackjack, his hands caressing her back. "I've missed this."

"Missed this?" she murmured. "How could you have missed anything about me?"

Sue didn't understand. Why was he saying this. To be cruel? If he had *missed* anything about her, ever, in all these years, he'd made no effort to remedy it.

After that day on the tarmac of Seymour Johnson, she hadn't gotten one phone call. Not one letter. Nothing to even remotely suggest he had wanted her back in his life.

"I have," he said, his lips finding her neck. "I've missed this...."

It was a lie. And she didn't believe him. In fact, she found the words so completely phony and utterly insulting that she immediately felt herself stiffening in his arms. It was as if he'd slapped her.

Before Sue even had time to think, her body reacted.

One moment she was simmering in the warm, strong arms of a potently masculine man, and the next, she was striding across the chilly hotel suite, walking into her room and slamming the door behind her, throwing the lock for good measure.

Damn him.

She leaned back against the cool wood of the door, waiting for some kind of explosion to erupt in the next room. She waited for him to come after her—to pound on the door and curse her. Or maybe...to try to change her mind.

But there was only silence. So Sue quietly undressed and climbed onto the king-size bed that had already been turned down by the night maid. As she crawled between the starched white sheets, her hand hit something small and hard on the pillow. She flicked on the bedside lamp and saw that the maid had left something. It was a little red foil heart.

"Happy Valentine's Day," she read on the heart.

Miserably she peeled back the wrapping and took a bite of the dark chocolate. Now it was official, she decided. Life *was* playing a sick joke on her.

Clicking off the light, she settled down into the sheets. She was alone again. With no one and nothing to comfort her but the unsettling ghosts of memories past and the even more unsettling memory of tonight's hungry kisses.

If only she could get that echo of Blackjack's voice out of her head. *I've missed this....*

The echo of a lie, she thought, dozing off. *Or was it?*

Chapter Four

"What time is it there? . . . Well, that's after your breakfast time, isn't it? . . . So what did you eat?"

Blackjack heard a muffled female voice in his dream. Then slowly he realized she wasn't in his dream but in the next room.

Yawning, he propped an elbow underneath himself. He glanced at the clock: 6:00 a.m. Yawning again, he began to recall the images from the night before. . . .

A slow smile stretched across his handsome face as he remembered how Sue had stood in front of him and stripped off her white silk blouse. He could still see her standing seductively in front of him, inviting him to unfasten her lacy bra and take her to his bed. He rubbed the raven black stubble on his chin and glanced across the starched white sheets. They were empty.

Empty?

But he remembered making love to Sue. They'd been in each other's arms, doing things—passionate, wonderful, barely legal things. Blackjack blinked once, then again. He'd been dreaming, he realized.

Dreaming? That was all?

He rubbed his tired eyes and began to recall things more clearly now. Yes, Sue *had* seductively stripped off her pristine white blouse and stood temptingly in front of him, inviting him to make love to her. But then she'd bolted from him, pulled the rug out—ruthlessly flipped him from completely aroused to painfully frustrated in less than a millisecond.

Blackjack dropped back down onto the fluffy hotel pillow. Now that he thought about it, he'd have preferred her jujitsu.

Any day.

What a bluff, he thought, shaking his head. He'd fallen hook, line and sinker. Funny thing was, he wasn't angry. He must be losing his mind. But now he was even *more* turned on by her.

Why was it that no other woman could get to him like Sue Rigger? She was the only damned female who could make him crazy angry *and* crazy to possess her at practically the same time.

"What did you say?"

He heard the voice and realized that Sue was talking to someone in the living area of the suite. He heard her laughing, sweet and light. He'd always liked that sound.

Who is she talking to? he wondered. But he suddenly realized that he could hear her voice, but he couldn't hear another. It wasn't room service. He slowly sat up to listen closer.

"I knew it!" she said, then laughed again.

Suddenly he didn't like the sound of that laugh—because it sounded too familiar. Too—caring. *Who the hell is she speaking with?*

"Max, that's a really funny joke. Who told you that one?"

She was on the phone, Blackjack realized. With a *man*.

A streak of jealousy overcame him like lightning from a clear blue sky. He was disturbed by the feeling, yet unable to stop it.

He leaned forward, listening even harder, but her voice became softer. Immediately he pulled back the coverlet and bedsheets and moved to the slightly open door. Careful to stay hidden, he listened again.

"I miss you, honey.... I love you, too, Max. But I'll be home again soon. I promise.... I'll call again.... Yes, I know. I love you, too. Bye."

Blackjack stood for a moment in complete shock. He walked to the bed and sat down in a kind of daze. Rubbing his eyes, he stared unseeing for a long moment. Something—a fist, a bullet, a cannonball—had just rammed him in the stomach.

She loves another man.

Blackjack took a deep, shaky breath. It looked as if virtual reality wasn't the only thing Sue had mastered over the past seven years.

It seemed she had mastered the game, he realized.

The game of Blackjack.

AFTER A TENSE and silent ride with Sue up to Flatlands Base that morning, Blackjack disappeared for hours, into his on-base room and the pages of the technical manuals piled high on his desk there.

He almost lost track of the time, but by 14:00 hours he was heading toward the pilots' lockers. He and Jerry the German were schedule to take to the air again to run the most scrutinized test yet on the Reeva system.

After zipping up his flight suit, Blackjack sat down on the bench in the empty locker room. He watched his old friend grab his flight gloves from his locker and fish a stick of spearmint chewing gum from a pocket.

"German, can I ask you something?"

Jerry folded the gum into his mouth and began to chew. He eyed Blackjack a moment before speaking. "No."

"This is serious," stated Blackjack.

Jerry smiled as he chewed. "Then definitely not."

Blackjack's fingers drummed impatiently over the gray padded helmet in his lap.

"I dunno," said Jerry finally, "I don't recall you ever asking to ask me anything." He slammed the locker door and sat down next to his old friend. "What's up?"

Blackjack paused a moment. "You think I'm getting too old for this crap?"

Jerry eyed his friend. "Are you kiddin' me?"

"Look," continued Blackjack, "I've just been thinking. What have I got to show for my time in, you know?"

Jerry's expression was one of disbelief. "What the hell's got into you? I've never seen you choke before—"

"I'm not choking. It's just that—" Blackjack stood and paced to the end of the row of lockers, then he turned and looked at his friend. "I've been thinking...I'm thirty-eight years old. My father died at sixty-eight—that means thirty-four was the midpoint of his life. I'm *past* the midpoint of life and—"

"Blackjack—"

"No, I'm serious," said Blackjack, punctuating his words with the bang of his fist against a locker door. "My dad had my brother and me by my age already. He had a wife and two kids—like you've got. A family, something on the ground, you know?"

Jerry's gaze remained fixed on his friend. He ran a hand through his short brown hair, then, as his habit dictated, smoothed his mustache with thumb and forefinger. "Look, Blackjack..." Jerry paused a moment, looked down at his heavy laced boots, then back up again. "I've got three things to say. First of all—you may not die that young. You may live to be ninety. Ever think of that?''

Blackjack sat back down on the bench. "No."

"Second of all—the reason I got a wife and kids is 'cause I chose to have 'em. One day I decided that's what I wanted. See my drift?"

Blackjack's brow knitted in thought.

"Maybe for you that day's finally come," suggested Jerry.

Blackjack shook his head. "No, I—I can't go that route."

"Why the hell not?"

"Just . . . can't. I'm not cut out for it."

Jerry sighed in frustration. "Who says? You never *tried* it before. Why do you think you're holding on to that little ranch of your dad's, anyway?"

"I'm selling it."

"Like hell. Why did you start remodeling the house, then?"

Blackjack paused a minute. "Better price."

"Bull-loney."

Blackjack was silent a long moment. "I know what you're saying to me, German. But I don't . . . I just don't know how to do . . . what you're doing. I mean, I'd just screw it up somehow."

"Not with the right woman you wouldn't."

Blackjack sighed and nodded his head. "With the right woman . . . I might be okay. But then I've got another problem. I've seen what leaving someone behind can do to them. . . ." Blackjack's voice just trailed off.

Jerry chewed his spearmint gum in thought, eyeing Blackjack carefully. "You plannin' on buying it? In the sky?"

Blackjack wouldn't look at Jerry. "Come on—"

"No, I mean it, Blackjack. 'Cause if you're plannin' it anytime soon, then please let me know so I can line up another backseater for you."

"Come *on,* German. You must think about it—"

"Nope," said Jerry without a moment's pause, "I don't. When I'm alive, I'm living. When I'm dead, I'll be dead. What's the point of living for dying?"

"But...what about Peg?"

"She knows the risks. Always did. It's not always easy for her, but we've both made our life work."

Blackjack nodded his head. "You're lucky."

"Damned right. But, you know, Blackjack, *you've* always been the big risk-taker. Maybe...if you take a chance on the right woman, you could get lucky, too."

Blackjack glanced at his friend. "Maybe."

"Maybe's a good thing to think about," said Jerry, leaning over to tighten the loose laces on one of his boots.

Blackjack raked a hand through his dark hair. "So you only told me two things. Wasn't there a third?"

"Third thing...ah...that's a tough one," said Jerry, tying up the top of his boot.

"Come on—"

"Well...you know what they say. The day a pilot starts thinkin' 'bout mortality, he starts to...you know—"

Blackjack silenced his friend with a lethal glare. He rose from the bench and grabbed his flight gloves from his locker. "I'm *not* losing my edge, German. I'm just thinking about my life on the ground."

Jerry nodded. "I understand." Then he paused a moment. "This little conversation wouldn't have anything to do with seeing Sue Rigger again after all these years, would it?"

"Hell, no!" Blackjack returned a little too quickly. "Besides, you helped me make up my mind."

"How's that?"

"I've got nothing on the ground for one reason—because I always wanted it that way. And that's the way it should be."

"What! That's not what I—"

"No. That's the way it is. My life isn't on the ground—it's in the air," said Blackjack, picking up his helmet, then slamming his locker shut with more force than necessary. "And that's where it's going to stay."

SUE STOOD at the floor-to-ceiling window of the Flatlands Base Operations Lab. Looking out at the airfield, she marveled how the vast Nevada horizon seemed to go on forever. The West sure was a different place than the East. She was surprised how much closer she felt to the wide blue yonder. Even on the ground, she felt as if she was a part of the sky.

It did her heart good to be here. She smiled as she watched a supersonic jet fighter roar down a far runway and leap into the crisp, clear winter air.

Her gaze dropped to the ground near the hangars, and she noticed two men walking across the tarmac. She immediately recognized the confident stride of one of them. It was Blackjack, all right.

Seeing his trim, strong form in a flight suit brought Sue back years. Suddenly her heart was beating faster. She ignored it, telling herself it was merely her excitement at being on an airfield again.

Over the past few months, her work had kept her entombed in the fluorescence of underground computer labs. Naturally she was thrilled to witness her work being put to the test. But it wasn't just exciting... it was also nerve-racking. Testing her work in a lab's simulator was one thing.

That was a *controlled* environment. She had grown used to safe, no-risk environments.

But it was quite another thing to actually run a test in the *real* world. In the real world, things could go wrong. And there were much higher stakes.

Her gaze followed Blackjack's movements, and she swallowed uneasily.

Much higher stakes.

Sue watched as Blackjack and German Bruckman walked toward the silver gray modified F-15E Eagle. Blackjack climbed his short boarding ladder and settled into the pilot's front cockpit. German took the seat behind.

"...weather clear, visibility fifty miles. Temperature forty-three degrees..." the voice from the tower sounded over the communications console near Sue as Blackjack and German closed their canopies and began taxiing out to a runway.

She would be monitoring their flight from the operations lab, located just beneath the base's steep control tower. The large op lab had a spectacular view of the airfield, and its sophisticated monitoring equipment filled the room with a constant buzzing around the clock.

Right now the dozen or so scientists and officers who made up the Reeva testing group were listening to the radio communications between the jet fighter and the control tower.

"Blackjack, you are cleared for takeoff...." announced the tower.

Sue's heart was still beating rapidly as she watched Blackjack's jet roar off a runway and up into the bright blue desert sky.

"Well, Captain Rigger, we're ready to begin," said a male voice. Sue turned to find the base's commanding officer standing close behind her. Lieutenant General Russell

Simpson was a tough-looking, black-eyed warbird with a salt-and-pepper crew cut and a crusty warmth about him. At their briefing this morning, he'd been helpful and friendly to Sue as she reviewed the flight data on the five earlier tests.

"Good," said Sue. "Dr. Raspail, has the altitude been a factor in performance?"

"Ha!" barked Raspail, sitting at a nearby monitor, "this pilot has yet to give us *enough* performance to get close to measuring altitude effects."

Sue sighed at the man's rude tone, but said nothing. Dr. Raspail was the Flatlands technical director of the Reeva project. A civilian, he worked for the private company that had won the bid to implement the system.

The pale, bespectacled scientist had been less than cordial to Sue all day. But then, why shouldn't he be annoyed; she'd been called in to troubleshoot what could be his errors—though all of his reports blamed the pilot.

"...and you are clear in your assigned pattern," finished the voice from the control tower.

"Roger, Tower," came Blackjack's voice over the console.

Simpson moved forward and depressed a button. "Blackjack, this is Op Lab. How's everything out there? Normal?"

"Roger, Op Lab," said Blackjack. "All is normal-normal."

"Good. Engage Reeva at your discretion," said Simpson.

"Roger, Op Lab."

A few moments went by, and Blackjack's voice was heard again.

"Ready to rock, German?" he asked his backseater.

"Roger, Rodger. Play that funky music, flight boy," quipped German.

"Okay," said Blackjack. "Time for inter...ah... now, what was that *inter* thing called again, German?"

"I keep tellin' you, inter*face,* Blackjack. Inter*face.*"

"Roger, German. It's just that I have so much more fun with that other *inter* thing."

"Roger, Rodger."

A few of the staff were smiling at the pilots' attempt to break the tension. Sue was smiling, too. Dr. Raspail, however, was not. His nose wrinkled in supreme distaste. "Test pilots!" he sniffed. "You simply can't deal with such men."

Reeva's voice—Sue's own voice, recorded back in Maryland and integrated into the complex software—was beginning the sequence to interface with Blackjack's mind.

"Shh...relax. Pull me closer," purred the computer.

On the medical monitors, Sue noticed the sudden, extreme changes in his physical state.

"That's odd," said Raspail. "That's the first time we've seen that particular response in the pilot."

"What's that?" asked Simpson.

"He's—"

Sue held her breath. She knew exactly what those signs meant.

"He's excited," said Raspail. "Aroused. Sexually."

"What!" cried Lieutenant General Simpson.

Oh, my Lord, thought Sue, feeling her ivory skin begin to flush pink in utter embarrassment, *it's Reeva's voice arousing him!*

"Wait a minute," said Raspail suddenly, his gaze glued to the screen. "I was wrong. He's relaxing now. Back to normal."

Simpson spoke up. "Maybe it was just a glitch in the sensors."

"Yes, yes," said Raspail, impatient. "We'll run a check."

Miller, a lieutenant on the medical-research team, let out a grunt of skepticism.

Sue, on the other hand, let out a silent sigh of extreme relief. Her eyelids closed a moment in thanks to Blackjack for being in such control of his body.

After the full seven-minute relaxation-and-interface sequence, Blackjack's mind had fully linked into the system. The op lab group watched as Blackjack flawlessly executed the first stage of the basic flight pattern. With the help of Reeva, Sue could see that he was doing it. He was actually flying the plane with his thoughts.

She smiled, unable to deny the pride she felt for his abilities to get even this far. No matter what Raspail said, Sue knew that this alone was evidence of his superior skill.

"I'm moving faster, can you stay with me?" asked Reeva.

"Yes, Reeva, it's fine...." responded Blackjack's voice.

"All right, Rodger, we're going to try to turn now...are you ready to turn?"

Sue watched his vital signs with the dispassion of a scientist, but something inside her began to stir.

She knew the risks involved with this system. Even with German along, a crash was not out of the question. If Blackjack lost control of the interface, and if the system rejected manual override, then both men would lose control of the Eagle. They'd be forced to eject—an incredibly hazardous choice.

Sue shook herself back to reality. She was stunned that her attention had strayed from the test. She took a deep breath. It was shaky.

She was extremely worried about Blackjack McConnell. And she knew it went well beyond the decent human concern over any test pilot's life. This fear for him penetrated her much more deeply.

It disturbed her. She didn't *want* to feel this way.

"Turning sequence is beginning," said Lieutenant General Simpson. "Captain Rigger, this is where we have the trouble."

"It's the pilot," snapped Raspail. "I'm telling you, we need a better pilot."

"Quiet, Doctor," said Sue instantly and quite loudly.

Dr. Raspail simply sniffed and turned to his screens.

She didn't see Simpson's smile at their exchange, but she heard the very slight chuckle in his next intake of breath.

"I'm ready, Reeva," Blackjack's voice asserted.

"Good. We are going to turn now, to the right. But slowly."

A few seconds went by. Nothing but static over the air. But the observation screen showed that the Eagle was turning.

"Rodger, you're turning too fast...."

Sue felt herself holding her breath. Her gaze remained fixed on the display. Then she saw it. She saw the *completion* of the turn. He did it. He actually did it.

Reeva's modulated voice came over the console. "Maneuver complete. Very good, Rodger."

"All right!" cried Jane Cortez, a young lieutenant on the testing staff.

"Nice job," concurred another officer.

"Helluva pilot," murmured Miller.

Sue sat back in her chair and shook her head.

Knowing what she did about the test, Sue couldn't believe that McConnell had actually done it.

She simply could not believe it.

BLACKJACK WAS too wound up to sit in the folding metal chair of the mission-debriefing room. He stood instead, leaning against the back wall, his raven black hair still flattened from the helmet and damp from the sweat of the mission.

Though he'd completed the first two turns, he was unable to continue on to more complex maneuvers. The dreaded warning Klaxon had sounded thirty-three minutes in. As usual, German was forced into taking over the controls.

It was the longest they'd been up—but it was light-years from what the system was capable of in the simulators. The project was still in danger of languishing way behind schedule.

"...and I'd like to know where we should go from here," said Lieutenant General Simpson. His probing black eyes glanced at Blackjack, then skimmed over Dr. Raspail to rest on Sue Rigger.

Although he tried his damnedest, Blackjack could not continue avoiding it—her. He turned his gaze toward the woman sitting, erect and unruffled, in the god-awful folding chairs. He took in her shapely uniform: her crisp, light blue blouse and dark blue skirt, hemmed strictly, of course, according to Air Force regulations. His gaze swept across the features of her pretty face—her pert nose, high cheekbones and full lips. Her wide, long-lashed brown eyes, the color reminding him of melted caramel.

He admired the soft, shining silk of her light blond hair, and he remembered how she'd worn it much shorter years ago, cropped just above her collar. It fell well past her shoulders now, and today she'd swept it back in a soft, loose ponytail, knotted at the nape of her delicate neck.

He watched with interest as her eyes flashed in annoyance at something Raspail was saying. Keen intelligence glittered like sharp chips of priceless crystal in Sue's light brown gaze, and he admired it—and her. A smile touched the edge of his lips. He figured he was proud of her.

Sue was always able to hold her own with any man, including him. Maybe even especially him.

"I think we should bring in another test pilot. Perhaps one with a better understanding of the background—" said Raspail.

"All right, stop right there, Doctor—though I use the term loosely."

"Excuse me, Miss—" sniffed Raspail.

But Sue had shot to her feet and gotten into the large doctor's face in a millisecond. "*Captain* to you! I'll have you know that this test pilot—" her hand gestured wildly toward Blackjack "—is a full colonel with advanced degrees in aeronautical and electrical engineering, and he is more than capable of understanding the workings of this system, not that it would have helped him with the way your hacking has butchered the original design!"

"What did you say?" broke in Lieutenant General Simpson.

"Sir," began Sue, flipping open one of a half-dozen folders that she'd brought with her from Washington. "Take a look at these specs of my brother's."

"What?" asked Simpson, looking them over. "I've never seen these before." The other members of the testing staff leaned forward, eager for a look.

"I'm not surprised," said Sue. "It looks as though Dr. Raspail here took it upon himself to reconfigure the sensor pattern on the F-15E. That plane should have almost twice as many sensors as it does now!"

"I *streamlined* the project," Raspail sputtered. "Surely you understand—"

Blackjack couldn't believe his ears. He shot Jerry an angry look—one that Jerry returned. It seemed they'd all been had.

"What I understand, Doctor," said Sue, her voice full of barely controlled anger, "is that you've wasted this base's time and this Air Force's money, *and* that you owe this test pilot an apology. That he's already gotten as far as he has with this program is a damned miracle—and a tribute to his skills as probably the *best* damned test pilot in the Air Force."

Blackjack's jaw slackened in stunned disbelief. He'd already convinced himself that *he* was the screwup. He couldn't believe that Sue, of all people, was the one who'd come to his rescue.

Dr. Raspail sputtered and stuttered something about his company's providing the lowest bid on implementation, but Lieutenant General Simpson ignored him. Instead, he turned to Sue.

"Captain Rigger, how long will it take to install the required additional sensors?"

"I don't know," said Sue. "It depends on your ground crew."

"You tell me what you need, and I'll authorize it."

"But, sir," she began, "I'm not the one who should be taking over this project—"

"Oh, yes, you are," said Simpson. "As of this moment, you are temporarily reassigned as Flatlands' technical director of the Reeva-Horizon project. I'll have orders confirmed in forty-eight hours."

"But, sir—"

"No buts," said Simpson, walking to the door of the room. "And, Dr. Raspail . . . you're fired."

"You can't fire me! My company won the contract on this project and—"

"And you'll be lucky you don't get your company's ass sued off!" he barked, his finger pointing at the man like a loaded weapon. "Now, get off my base before I have you *thrown* off!"

Blackjack watched Simpson and Raspail continue their arguing as they left the room. Most of the testing staff followed.

One of the staff, a second lieutenant named Jane Cortez, stopped by to speak with Sue. Smiling broadly, the young woman chatted a few minutes, then shook Sue's hand and left.

She remained behind to gather her materials.

"Say, Blackjack," said Jerry the German as he rose from the table.

"What's that, German?"

"Looks like you've still got a life in the air."

Blackjack reached into a pocket and brought out a pink rectangle. "Want some gum?"

"No, thanks." Jerry turned his gaze to Sue, who was filing papers into a folder. "Say, Captain Rigger, do you like riddles?"

Sue glanced up at Jerry. "What do you mean?"

"I mean, here's a good riddle for you to solve—what does a pilot do when he's on the ground?"

"I don't understand?" asked Sue.

Jerry threw a glance at his friend. "Blackjack does."

"See you in the *showers*, German," said Blackjack pointedly.

"Sure," said Jerry, smiling broadly as he left the room.

Blackjack watched Sue as she began to collect the pile of folders. She seemed to be doing her best to avoid looking at him.

"What did he mean?" she asked, still staring at the table.

Blackjack fingered the pink rectangle of bubble gum. He slipped off the paper and popped the morsel into his mouth.

"It's just a discussion German and I were having. Before the test flight."

"Oh, I see."

"No. You don't."

Sue turned to face him, and Blackjack couldn't help admiring her attractive shape. A part of him recalled the night before all too vividly—and what lush treasures were hidden under that prim blue uniform. He tried to keep his breathing regular.

"Colonel McConnell, *one* thing, at the very least, is clear to me here. We are going to be working together for some amount of weeks on this project," said Sue. "I suggest we keep—"

"Each other company?"

"—our distance."

"Somebody back home?" he asked, trying to sound casual.

Sue blinked a moment, as if caught off guard. "What are you talking about?"

"Nothing, nothing . . . but look," Blackjack began as he moved by her, trying not to inhale the sweet, fresh scent of her hair. But she turned on him instead, and they now faced each other in an all too close proximity.

"I just wanted to say . . . thanks," said Blackjack.

"Not necessary, Colonel. It wasn't a favor," said Sue softly. "It was the truth. The truth matters to me."

"It matters to me, too," said Blackjack, finding he wanted to kiss those full, soft lips—kiss them hard and well, until he'd completely wiped out that man she'd left back in Maryland.

Sue nodded, as if she were afraid to trust her voice.

Slowly he brought his hand up and let the pad of his thumb brush under her full lower lip. It felt warm where he touched her, and he could see her response in her eyes. She wanted him—still.

He enjoyed watching Sue sweep her long eyelashes downward a moment, trying to compose herself. Then quickly her gaze was on him again—the serious professional.

"Distance, Colonel," she advised, turning from him with a sharp military pivot. "Distance."

Blackjack watched her depart without trying to stop her. Instead, he headed toward the base showers. He was going to need a cold one.

Chapter Five

"So, what's the name of this bar we're going to?" Sue asked her new friend as they sped through the cold desert night in a base jeep. She had cracked the window, and the night wind was whipping through her loose blond hair.

The refreshing air, along with the familiar fit of her worn blue jeans, cream turtleneck sweater and sheepskin jacket, was a nice Friday-night release from the past two weeks of work.

Behind the wheel, Second Lieutenant Jane Cortez, also in blue jeans and a sweater, smiled. "Afterburners. It's a hangout for base personnel, local pilots, even some bikers. It's your average desert dive, but it's got a first-rate jukebox."

Sue smiled at the pretty Air Force pilot beside her. Jane Cortez had a pleasant face, a quick mind and a warm, honest smile that always reached her striking gray eyes.

"So how do you like Nevada, Captain?" asked Jane.

"Just call me Sue."

"What's your call sign, you know, your nickname?"

Sue smiled. "Sparks, but no one's used it in years."

"Yeah, well, I like it. Suits you—especially after that scene with that jerk Raspail the day you arrived, *sparks* flying from you and all."

Sue laughed. "Yeah, I know, that's how I got it, all right. My brother said my eyes shot sparks when someone irked me."

"Your brother is Will Rigger, right?"

Sue nodded her head, "That's right. What's your call sign, by the way?" she asked.

"'Curly.' It's pretty obvious, I guess, how I got it."

Sue laughed. Jane always wore her curly chestnut hair in a tight bun on base, but tonight it hung down past her shoulders, looking a little wild in the cool night wind.

"You know," said Jane, "I studied some of your brother's work when I was finishing my master's at Stanford. He wouldn't be coming down here, would he?"

"It's possible."

"I wouldn't mind meeting him."

Sue raised an eyebrow, recognizing the level of female interest in her new friend's voice. Jane Cortez was just Will's type—and that meant she was also "the dangerous type."

For years she had watched her brother go after nothing but flashy, air-headed women. Women like Jane, on the other hand, who were smart and down-to-earth—they scared the living daylights out of her brother. Those he called the "dangerous" kind, because he could easily fall hard for them. And that was the *last* thing he wanted to do—or so he said.

"Curly, I hope you do meet Will," said Sue. "But it's only fair to warn you—he's a fighter jock at heart, and his call sign is *Wild* Will for a good reason."

Jane laughed. "Yeah, well, that comes as no surprise. There's not a whole lot of rocket science to figuring out a fighter jock's game plan when it comes to women—no matter how big his brain-pan."

In another few minutes Jane was pulling the jeep off the lonely two-lane desert road. "Here we are."

Sue studied the unimpressive building before them. The rundown wooden structure stood alone off the long, flat road. It was the only sign of civilization, other than a gas station and convenience store about fifty feet away. Beyond that, the road gave the impression that it stretched on into the bleak, empty darkness forever.

The lot around the bar was filled with every kind of vehicle. She even noticed a couple of small propeller aircraft in the distance.

"Cessnas sometimes use the road as a landing strip," explained Jane. "This place is a kind of unofficial bull station for private pilots flying between Vegas, Reno and Tahoe."

"How convenient." Sue automatically glanced up into the sky for incoming aircraft.

"Come on, Sparks, let me buy you a beer."

She followed Jane as she pushed open the wooden door and entered the bar. From the corner jukebox, the voice of Jerry Lee Lewis shook the crowded place.

Sue recognized a group of airmen and women from the base at one of the many crowded tables. Across the room, she noticed pool tables and pinball machines, all with small groups around them.

"C'mon," said Jane. "I see some open stools at the bar."

After ordering up two cold beers, the two women raised their bottles. "To the women of the Air Force," said Jane.

"Amen to that," said Sue, clinking glass with her new friend.

The beer tasted refreshingly good. Then a sudden roar of shouts came from across the room.

"The fighter jocks are at it again," said Jane on a laugh.

Sue's gaze found the group of men in the corner, where a dart game was heating up. She noticed hands exchanging bills.

"They bet on bull's-eyes," explained Jane, "especially against the local bikers."

A handsome young Air Force pilot with a reddish brown crew cut stepped up to the line and took aim.

"That's Captain Harry Garner," said Jane. "Great bod and a top pilot, but a total bonehead, if you ask me."

She glanced at Jane. "He make a pass at you?"

Jane took a sip of beer. "Do jets fly? He tried. He'll try with you, too. It's a sure thing. He's into leggy blondes."

"Ha!" Sue had never heard herself referred to in such terms. She smiled, kind of liking it. "Jane, how'd you get so wise, anyway?"

"My father was career Air Force. I got an early education."

"Wish I had," murmured Sue. "My folks were high school teachers." At least, her adoptive parents were. She never knew much about her and Will's biological parents, other than that they'd both been reclusive scientists, killed by some freak accident. Still very young, Sue and Will had been adopted by distant cousins of the Riggers', a wonderful and warm couple who'd never been able to have children of their own.

She thought of them now and smiled. Earlier tonight, she had spoken through the lab's computer videophone, talking to her young son, Max. Her parents were taking good care of him, but she missed him terribly. She hoped, in another few weeks, Lieutenant General Simpson would give her leave to fly home and see him.

A shout came from the corner again, and Sue's gaze found Harry Garner's young, broad back. His three yellow darts had just missed the bull's-eye. Green bills exchanged hands as a biker in a black jacket stepped up and Harry Garner looked their way.

"Oh, no," said Jane, "bogie at five o'clock."

"Bogie?" Sue repeated, smiling at the tactical term for an unidentified aircraft. "I would say he's more of a bandit— a *recognizably* hostile aircraft."

Jane laughed. "I guess you don't need radar to spot 'em, huh?"

"You're right," said Sue. "I've been burned by a pro. Ever since, I've known what to look for. Besides, most women could see through this guy at ten thousand feet."

"You can say that again."

Sue took another sip of beer. Then she noticed another pilot taking aim at the dart board, and her bottle froze in her hand.

"That's Blackjack," said Jane. "Of course, you know him."

"What do you mean?" she asked, her face suddenly pale.

"I mean he's our test pilot on Reeva," said Jane. "What do you think!"

"Oh, yeah, right."

They watched with silent interest as Blackjack took careful aim with a red dart, then let it fly.

"Bull's-eye," said Jane. "Every time. The odds on that guy must be getting pretty interesting by now."

"And what's his reputation like... with the ladies?" Sue asked carefully, her gaze fixed on Blackjack's powerful physique, now clad in blue jeans and a worn gray Air Force Academy T-shirt, one of his sharply defined biceps bulging as he took aim with another dart.

Jane shrugged. "Good man. And the best pilot I ever saw."

"That's it." Sue turned to her new friend. "You mean he hasn't made a pass at you?"

Jane shook her head. "No—and no other woman that I know of. He's all business when it comes to Flatlands. If he plays the field, it's way off the base. In fact, as fighter jocks go, I'd say he's of the officer-and-gentleman variety.''

Officer and gentleman? Sue's mouth was gaping at Jane's words. She could not believe her ears. Could it be, she thought to herself, that the infamous lady-killer was actually mellowing with age?

"Gee, Sparks, you're going to catch flies if you don't shut your mouth," said Jane with a laugh. "What is it? Do you have a history with that guy?''

"Sort of," she said in a low voice.

Jane held up two fingers for the bartender, but Sue barely noticed. Her mind was still reeling from Jane's words. She watched Blackjack make a second and third bull's-eye.

"Eagle eye," said a masculine voice just behind Sue. "Or more like F-15 Eagle eye. Right, Curly?''

"Hey, Hollywood," said Jane, using Harry Garner's call sign. "Yeah, Blackjack's on his usual roll, I see. How's it going?''

"Okay," said Garner. "Who's your friend?''

Jane shot Sue an I-told-you-he'd-be-zeroing-in smile. "This is Sue Rigger.''

Sue turned to see the handsome young captain flash her a hundred-watt smile. "Enchanted, Ms. Rigger.''

"It's Captain," she said. Garner was Hollywood handsome, all right, but he struck her as so wet behind the ears, she almost laughed. She supposed he figured that with his slick smile and hard body he was making her knees turn to jelly.

But he wasn't. He did do something else, though: he made her miss another, more-seasoned pilot. All at once Sue missed the crow's-feet at the edges of Blackjack's eyes. She missed his lightning-quick barbs, his sharp-eyed blue gaze, and even the two deep scars on his powerful chest.

"Sparks here is the new Reeva-Horizon technical director that Simpson brought in from Washington," said Jane.

"Well, well," said Garner, all the more interested. "Let me buy you two some beer."

ACROSS THE ROOM, Blackjack pocketed another ten after his sixth bull's-eye that night and turned to Jerry Bruckman.

"I still got it, German," said Blackjack. "When are you going to start betting on me?"

Jerry Bruckman laughed. "C'mon, Blackjack, the day I bet on you is the day you miss the damned board entirely. Drink up, buddy, Peggy'll be here soon to pick me up."

Blackjack smiled. Even after two kids and a mortgage, German and his wife managed to stay deeply in love. Every other Friday, Peg met German here for a few drinks and then the two of them went on a "date." Blackjack always ribbed his friend about it, but deep down, he thought it was a pretty nice idea.

His mind automatically thought of Sue. He brought his beer to his lips and took a long drink, hoping to douse thoughts of her with half a bottle of lukewarm suds. He drained the last dregs of beer, but it wasn't nearly enough to quench his thirst for that perfect ivory skin and sweet-tasting mouth.

The memory of their Valentine kisses in Vegas was still making him crazy. Sleeping was especially difficult, but his combat training had kicked in on the second night, and he'd forced himself to get the rest he needed.

Of course, it didn't stop his dreams from replaying the image of her standing there in her lacy bra, inviting him to take her in his arms and—

Blackjack shook his head. *I've either got to stop thinking about her…or else actually* do *something about her.* But in the past two weeks, every time he had tried to get close, she either iced up or fled like a startled rabbit.

The only thing Blackjack could figure was that she'd made a choice to stick with the guy back in Maryland. The idea of it grated. But he got the message. He wasn't about to become a poster child for constant rejection. Tonight he would begin to forget her—just as he'd forced himself to do years ago.

Trouble was, this time he wasn't flying halfway across the globe. This time he had to see her nearly every damned day.

"Hey, Blackjack," said German, interrupting his thoughts. "Isn't that Sue over there with Curly Cortez?"

At the mention of her name, Blackjack's glazed eyes blinked. He scanned the bar. There she was, all right, laughing and talking with Second Lieutenant Jane Cortez and—

"Looks like Hollywood's got her targeted already," said German. "He's about as fast as you were at his age."

"Thanks, German, you really know how to hurt a guy."

"Oh, touchy, are you? Can't take lookin' in the mirror. Or is it just Sparks that's got you in a nosedive?"

One edge of Blackjack's mouth turned up at the mention of Sue's call sigh. "*Sparks.* I'd almost forgotten. No chance you forgot how she got it?"

"No way, buddy, I remember it all too well—that perfect summer day, the blue of your dress uniform flying through the air and landing smack on the tarmac, that stunned look on your face. I think *that's* what really sent you."

Blackjack's gaze turned to his friend. "Sent me?"

"Over the edge. I mean, there's probably been a few dozen women since Sparks, wouldn't you say?"

Blackjack grunted. "So?"

"So...I still say she's the only one who ever made you *flip*," German said, laughing hysterically at his own joke.

Blackjack eyed his friend with a smirk. "Yeah, very funny, German. Be careful I don't sic her on you."

Across the room, a slow Elvis ballad began on the jukebox. Blackjack watched with interest as Hollywood flashed his toothpaste-commercial smile and held out a hand to the ladies. Curly shook her head no, but he noticed Sue give her friend a slight shrug, then stand up off the bar stool.

Sue's light blond hair was free of its ponytail tonight. It hung loose, looking soft and silky, attractively framing her pretty face. Slowly his gaze moved over her, appreciating how good her shapely form looked in a soft cream turtleneck sweater and snug-fitting blue jeans.

The makeshift dance floor in front of the jukebox had a few couples swaying to the crooning king. Blackjack watched with gritted teeth as that crew-cutted captain took Sue's hand and led her to the dance floor.

"Uh, Blackjack?" said German.

Hollywood took Sue in his arms, and Blackjack's fingers gripped the beer bottle so tightly that his knuckles began to turn white. "Yeah?"

"You thinkin' about cuttin' in?"

"She's free to make her choices."

"Uh-huh."

"Hey there, boys." Blackjack recognized Peggy's voice and heard her kissing her husband hello.

"Hi, Peg," said Blackjack without moving his gaze one inch from Hollywood and Sue.

"You want a beer, honey?" German asked his wife.

"Okay, but 'Love Me Tender' is playin'. Can we have a dance first, lover-boy?"

"Sounds good," said German, then turned to his friend. "See ya later, buddy," he said, then lowered his voice. "Just don't forget the pilot's creed—Do Something, Even If It's Wrong."

Blackjack nodded. Paralysis was a killer in the sky—and it could be on the ground, as well.

"Don't worry, German," said Blackjack. "If I go down in flames, it won't be without a fight."

"That's the spirit."

SUE SIGHED as she closed her eyes and listened to Elvis's honey-smooth voice pour from the jukebox. She was glad she had accepted Hollywood's invitation to dance. She loved Elvis, and it had been a while since she'd swayed to him in a pilot's arms.

"You're such a sweet dancer," said Hollywood smoothly into her ear. "You want to ditch Curly and take a ride with me?"

She immediately opened her eyes. "Listen, Hollywood, this is just a dance," she warned flatly.

Hollywood flashed his ubiquitous smile. "If you say so."

Sue shook her head. Fighter jocks! Cocky arrogance was their middle name. "Hollywood—"

"Yeah."

"Just shut up and dance."

With a resolute sigh, Sue closed her eyes again. Focusing on the music, she let her cheek rest lightly against his shoulder.

"Say, Hollywood." It was a masculine voice, tight with tension. "Mind if I cut in?"

"Ah, c'mon. The lady's enjoying herself, Blackjack."

"It's *Colonel* McConnell to you . . . *Captain.*"

Sue's eyes opened wide, and she tipped her face up to see Garner's face contort in frustration.

"C'mon, Colonel," complained Garner. "We're off base and out of uniform. You can't *order* me to let you cut in."

"It's true," said the voice behind her, dangerously low. "So I guess I'll just bow out...but then, on Monday, we're back *on* base and *in* uniform, aren't we?"

Hollywood's face suddenly registered the threat. "Well, if you *really* want to dance with the lady, what can I do?" he said with a shrug. "Sorry, Sparks, got my career to think about."

Sue's eyebrows rose in amusement as Hollywood released her and another man's strong arms were at once in their place. When she looked up, she found a slightly taller, slightly more powerfully built pilot now swaying with her.

"Hello, Sue."

"Hello, Blackjack."

His electric blue eyes glittered in triumph like sparkling sapphires beneath his midnight black hair, and the dimples at the edges of his mouth appeared as he flashed her a devilish smile.

"You always get what you want, don't you?" she asked.

"Not always."

He urged her closer, but she stiffened in his arms, unsure of why he had cut in on Hollywood and unwilling to let herself risk getting close to him again.

"What exactly is it you want?" asked Sue. "If you have a question about the new configuration of sensors, I should think it could wait until Monday for us to discuss it."

"To hell with the sensors," said Blackjack, "I just want to dance with you. Now, relax and dance, Captain."

"Oh, that's an order, is it?"

"No," he said softly. "Just a request."

Sue couldn't help but smile at the teasing humor dancing in Blackjack's eyes. Unconsciously her limbs began to relax against the rock-strong body holding her.

This time she didn't resist as he pulled her closer against his soft gray Air Force Academy T-shirt. She let her cheek rest against his shoulder, where the fresh scent of a tangy after-shave tickled her nose.

She felt his long fingers at her lower back, slightly massaging her, and she let her own hand reach up to caress the soft hair at the back of his neck.

"I seem to recall you had a thing for Elvis," remarked Blackjack.

Sue smiled. "And after you found out, I seem to recall *you* insisted we drive all night to Graceland."

"We had to drive. I got caught 'borrowing' us that plane."

"And you talked yourself out of big trouble, too." She laughed. "You had some nerve back then. Always flirting with disaster."

"Naw, I was just young...." He grinned down at her. "Do you still have that clock I bought you?"

"With the King's swinging hips on a pendulum? Yeah, I still have it stored...somewhere." Just like her memories, thought Sue. Memories she hadn't dusted off in quite a while.

"You feel good, Sparks," murmured Blackjack, pulling her closer.

She smiled. "You know, I think that's the first time I've heard you use my nickname."

"I suppose it is. I didn't have much chance to use it back in North Carolina."

"No, I suppose not," said Sue.

Blackjack spun slightly, taking her with him. "Well, I did take off in a matter of hours after you earned that name— and got back at me in the process."

Sue smiled. "I never did get that grease off my skirt after you sank me like a basketball into that oilcan. I had to pitch it."

Blackjack laughed. "Hell, that paintbrush you hurled left a skunk streak down my dress blue suit coat."

"Cleaners?"

"Nope—" Blackjack shook his head "—I pitched it, too. But then, I wasn't going to need dress blues where I was going."

She studied his handsome face as she thought about where he'd gone. Another slow Elvis song came on the jukebox, and they continued swaying.

"How was it for you over there...during the war?" she asked.

"Rough going. But it could have been rougher. Didn't take long for the Iraq Air Force to figure out they were outgunned and outclassed. They stopped flying, and from then on, for our Air Force it was pretty much a battle against ground missiles."

"Will told me you had nonstop missions."

Blackjack nodded. "Mostly we flew patrols, protecting U.S. bombers. A lot of times we were flying twelve to fifteen hours straight. Refueling in the air."

Once again, Sue found herself admiring Blackjack. Not just for his skill, but for his courage, strength and perseverance as a pilot. All of those virtues were in evidence in the air over Flatlands, and she found herself feeling more and more for him each day she watched him fly.

"When we landed after those marathon flights in the Gulf," Blackjack went on, "we were practically paralyzed from sitting in the cockpits. A lot of times the ground crews had to physically lift us out of our seats."

She could barely imagine it. "I'm glad...that you made it."

He smiled down at her. "I'm glad that you're glad."

Sue swallowed. "And thanks. For saving Will," she managed to say, her mouth suddenly dry. "I never got a chance to tell you."

Blackjack's eyebrows rose. Clearly he had never expected to hear her say the words. "He'd have done it for me," he said simply.

She looked up again and met Blackjack's blue eyes. He was gazing down at her with such gentleness, such openness. It touched her. Suddenly Sue wanted to tell him the truth. That there was something she'd never told him in all these years. That there was a reason she herself wasn't sent overseas when Desert Shield became Desert Storm. That she'd been pregnant.

I had your baby. She heard the words in her mind. *You have a son.* But she couldn't bring herself to say it.

In all these years, Blackjack McConnell had never contacted her, she warned herself. And though she hated to admit it, she knew the reason. It was because he had never loved her.

For some fighter jocks, a love commitment was nearly impossible. To a man like Blackjack, whose life was in the air, love was simply an anchor to the ground.

Sue wanted more out of life than to be a man's anchor. And she wanted more for her son.

Another Elvis number came on the jukebox, but as the King began crooning the words to "Are You Lonesome Tonight," she suddenly needed to go.

"Thanks for the dance, Blackjack," she said, breaking away.

"Wait a minute—"

"It's late, and I—"

"Don't go," pleaded Blackjack.

"I have to...."

She caught a glimpse of the confused look on his face, but it didn't slow her. Within sixty seconds, Sue was pulling Jane through Afterburners's squeaky wooden door and out into the dark desert night.

Chapter Six

"Twenty-nine, thirty, thirty-one," murmured Sue a week and a half later as she sat on her bed in red silk shorts and a loose white T-shirt, brushing her blond hair. The nightly ritual had become more of a tension reliever than a grooming practice.

Oh, her work on base was going fine. The tests were getting back on schedule with the Reeva system. But it wasn't the testing that bothered Sue, but the test pilot.

The truth matters she had asserted to Blackjack on the first day she'd come to Flatlands, yet Sue knew she was living a lie—a lie of omission.

What would Blackjack do if he ever found out about Max?

Ever since their dance at Afterburners, the question had constantly nagged her every time she saw him.

"Forty-eight, forty-nine, fifty," she finished. It didn't matter, she told herself, setting down her pink plastic brush; she would never tell him. Max meant way too much to her to ever risk what Blackjack's reaction might be.

A roar sounded in the distance, and Sue knew it was probably one of the fighters having its night-flying system tested. Her quarters were only about a half mile from the airfield, which made for some loud takeoffs and landings, but the place was quite comfortable.

Lieutenant General Simpson was obviously happy to have her here. After her first week on base, he'd issued a reassignment of billeting. Sue was moved from her single room in a dormitorylike housing unit to this spacious three-bedroom, full-kitchen VIP guest house.

She knew Max would love this house if he saw it—it was much bigger than the tiny two-bedroom apartment they had in Maryland.

Her little Max. She could hardly wait to see him again. Her hand automatically reached for the phone receiver. She'd already spoken to him this evening, but suddenly she wanted to talk to him again. Then her eyes glanced at the bedside alarm clock: 9:15 p.m. That meant it was 12:15 a.m. in Maryland, and way past his bedtime...in fact, it was even past her parents' bedtime.

She set down the receiver with a sigh.

Rising from the bed, Sue moved out of the master bedroom and down the stairs. Her bare feet made no noise as they sunk into the plush wall-to-wall carpeting. She was too wound up to sleep, so she walked to the kitchen to brew some herbal tea.

She'd just sat down in the living room with her teacup when she heard a light rapping at the door. Sue sighed. She was barely presentable, but she didn't want to run upstairs for a robe. Instead, she just cracked the door open a bit to see who it was.

Her eyebrows rose at the sight of a brown leather jacket revolving toward her on the porch. She recognized the Desert Shield and Desert Storm patches and the squadron insignia before she even looked at the pilot's face.

It was Blackjack—looking much too good, as usual. His legs were clad in worn, snug-fitting blue jeans, and his white sport shirt was stretched nicely over his powerful chest. Sue eyed his brown leather jacket again and decided it made him look every inch the bad boy that she knew he was.

"Hi, there," he said, his voice low, his blue gaze sweeping across her face with interest. His raven dark hair was slightly damp, and she guessed that he had come right from the base showers.

"Uh...hi."

"Well, are you going to open the door?"

"Ah...sure," said Sue, not knowing what else to do. She pulled the door open wider.

Blackjack paused a minute. His gaze eagerly took more of her in. His vision started low and rose slowly, traveling from the tips of her bare toes to the long, shapely bare legs, to the silky red shorts and braless T-shirt.

She felt her face flush under his obviously heated scrutiny. "What do you want?" she asked, uneasy.

"What do I *want?*" He smiled and rubbed his chin a moment, obviously weighing whether or not to make a teasing pass. Then he answered her straight. "I wanted to show you something."

Sue eyed him with wary curiosity. "What?"

Blackjack turned and stepped off the porch. She noticed a rectangular black case in his right hand.

"Come on," he said, half-turning and motioning her to follow him. "I won't bite..." he said. "Yet," he added with a wink.

Sue threw him a pointed glare as she grabbed her sheepskin coat and jammed her feet into a pair of loafers by the door. What did he *want?* she railed silently. Why was he here?

The mid-March night felt dry and cool as she stepped across the porch and into the yard. A dozen more housing units like hers occupied this small stretch of gravel road, but right now they were dark. She and Blackjack were the only people around.

"What did you want to show me, Blackjack?" she asked, hugging her coat more tightly around her. "I've already seen the road."

"Listen, Rigger, you'll thank me for this," he said.

"For what?"

"For this. Look over there," he said, pointing up.

With crossed arms over her chest, she peered into the clear, dark sky. "What?" she asked. "The stars are gorgeous, but I find it difficult to believe that even your colossal ego would take credit for them."

"Not the stars, Rigger. Come on, really look. And listen."

Sue sighed in frustration but saw *nothing*. She listened. But heard only the low whistle of a night breeze. "Well?"

Those deadly dimples appeared as Blackjack smiled down at her. He unlatched the rectangular black case in his hand and drew out an oddly shaped pair of binoculars. She recognized the equipment. They were night-vision goggles.

Blackjack placed the goggles to his eyes. He gazed in the same direction he'd asked her to look. "Yep, there she is."

Sue's heart beat faster. *Could it be . . . ?*

He presented the goggles to her. In a heartbeat, she snatched them from his hand and put them to her own eyes. *It was!*

The darkness of the night disappeared as Sue looked through the goggles. The night world looked like green-tinted day through this wonderful piece of high-tech military equipment that used the smallest ambient light to turn daylight-suited humans into perfectly comfortable nocturnal creatures.

But she had looked through such goggles before. That wasn't what excited her. "There it is!" she cried. "It's the Horizon, isn't it? Yes, it has to be!"

The Horizon was the top secret stealth plane that the Air Force was supposed to be testing with Reeva at this base. And now Sue could see that the specialized plane was finally off the drawing boards and flying in the night sky.

The sleek black delta-wing aircraft was invisible to the human eye and ear. And Sue knew its design would make it invisible to radar and heat-seeking missiles, as well.

"I can't believe she flies so quietly," murmured Sue, watching the narrow black triangle glide across the stars.

She felt like a kid on Christmas morning. The Horizon rolled into a turn, dipped and began to climb again.

"She's really something, isn't she?" whispered Sue with joyful exhilaration. "She seems to float in the night—as if the sky were an ocean."

"Yep," agreed Blackjack.

Then Sue heard Blackjack's voice again, but this time much lower. He was reciting something softly, almost to himself. "'Out to seas colder than the Hebrides I must go. Where the fleet of stars is anchored and the young Star captains glow.'"

Sue took the goggles away from her face, blinking a moment as her eyes adjusted to the darkness.

"That's beautiful," she said, the words sending an odd shiver through her. "But it sounds so...sad."

He didn't look at her. His profile remained steady, his eyes fixed on the sky. "I can't take credit," he said. "James Flecker wrote that. It's from a poem called 'The Dying Patriot.'"

She swallowed uneasily. "Dying?"

"My father recited it. At my brother's funeral."

"Your *brother*?"

"Whitman McConnell," said Blackjack, shoving his hands into the pockets of his leather jacket. "He was eight years older than me. On the Air Force fast track, like my father. And me, I suppose. He...uh...bought it. In the sky."

Sue was stunned. Will had never mentioned Whit. Certainly Blackjack hadn't. "When?"

"Oh, ancient history. I was just a kid."

Sue took the goggles away from her eyes and looked over at him. He was just staring up at the sky. She wondered why he was telling her this now...or *what* exactly he was trying to tell her.

Unsteadily Sue turned her face back up to the sky. She knew Blackjack would be flying the Horizon soon—she knew he understood the risks in testing the Reeva system with it. She also knew, though she didn't want to, that this beautiful black bird could easily become a black death, a flying coffin.

Is that what he was trying to tell her?

Sue glanced back over at Blackjack again. "You must think about it, then?"

A strange, wry smile came to his lips as he continued to stare into the dark night. "Buying it, you mean? In the sky...like my brother?"

Blackjack's blue gaze finally turned downward to look at her. He studied her face a long moment. "Nope. I don't think about it."

Sue met his steady gaze. *You're lying,* she thought, but couldn't bring herself to say. Instead, she placed the night-vision goggles back onto her eyes. She stared at him through them.

"What are you doing?" asked Blackjack.

I'm trying to see inside you, she thought. *Inside the darkest part of you. What will I really find there, if I look deep enough?*

"Sue?"

She pulled the goggles away. "I'm frightened for you," she blurted.

Blackjack took a deep breath and let it out heavily. He stepped away, turned and ran a hand through his hair. Her words had obviously disturbed him.

"Oh, don't panic, Rodger," she asserted. "I'm not falling in love with you again or anything."

"Don't *worry* about me, Sue," he snapped, obviously irritated.

"Too bad," she snapped right back. "Live with it." *Just please don't die with it,* she added to herself.

A long silence returned between them, and Sue put the goggles back to her eyes. She returned to watching the easy rolls and turns of the Horizon.

"Looks like she's just going through basic maneuvers," she said, trying to change the subject, sound casual.

"Well, she just arrived tonight, and Simpson ordered her taken up immediately," he said, attempting to sound just as casual.

"Who's in her?"

"Hollywood Garner—you know, your favorite dance partner."

Sue laughed, the tension finally fully broken. "Come on, don't tell me you're jealous."

"Maybe. Maybe a little."

Sue smiled, handing the goggles back to him.

"Well," said Blackjack, taking a last look. "Soon enough, the Riggers' Reeva system will be installed in that beauty. Then we'll see what she can do."

"Yes. I guess we'll see," said Sue. She looked up at his chiseled jaw and handsome face as he put the goggles to his blue eyes again. Despite her intense fear of the dangers he faced—or maybe because of it—a warm feeling began to wash over her as she looked at him. Though she tried to dispel it, she couldn't.

"So..." he said, still looking at the Horizon.

"Yes? So...what?" asked Sue.

Blackjack removed the goggles and looked down at her. He smiled a devilish smile, and she saw his blue eyes dancing from the dim glow of the nearby porch light. "So...I told you that you'd owe me some thanks for this."

Sue heard the sexual innuendo in his tone, and she immediately tore her gaze from him. "Sure is cold out here," she said before bolting for the house.

But Blackjack was on her heels as she entered the living room. "Oh no, you don't," he said, pulling the front door closed. "You're not getting out of this that easily."

Sue shrugged out of her coat, kicked off her loafers, then picked up her teacup. "Well, I suppose I could thank you by making you some tea. Mine's cold now anyway."

"That's a start," said Blackjack, shrugging out of his leather jacket. He threw a jeans-clad leg over a stool and leaned his bare forearms on the breakfast bar that separated the living room from the kitchen.

Sue felt his gaze following her every move as she filled the teakettle and fired up the stove. "So what happened to you after the Gulf?" she asked conversationally.

He looked puzzled. "Your brother didn't tell you?"

"About you? No. I mean, I never asked."

"Oh," said Blackjack, looking a bit hurt.

Sue couldn't believe it. "Rodger, don't give me that wounded-puppy-dog look. You never wrote. Or called. Or anything!"

Blackjack looked down at his hands. "No."

"Well, why not?"

"I didn't think..." He paused, rubbing his neck a moment. "I didn't think you'd want to hear from me."

She crossed her arms over her chest. "You're right. I didn't."

"Well, then, I was right, wasn't I?" he challenged.

She couldn't argue. So she uncrossed her arms and asked him again, "So...what happened to you?"

"Well, I'd been made a squadron commander pretty quickly during the war. After the fighting, I was sent to Turkey."

"Reconnaissance?"

Blackjack nodded. "I had my men flying a combination of recon sorties and tactical exercises for about two years. After that, I was stateside again. Then a friend at Red Flag persuaded me to spend six months as a visiting top-gun instructor—that's when Simpson recruited me for Flatlands. I've been here a little over two years now."

Sue nodded. "No wife. Or anything...in all that time?"

Blackjack smiled. "What do you think?"

"I think...once a lady-killer—"

"Sue—"

"—always a lady-killer."

"You know, you might not believe me," he stated, "but you're the one lady who could probably kill me."

A long pause followed as Sue realized that his words could be taken two ways. She looked into his eyes. They were wide open for her. Waiting for her to pursue the meaning of his statement.

Instead, she turned away, reached for the box of tea.

"So why didn't Simpson have you take up the Horizon tonight?" she asked, getting back to business.

"It's just basics tonight—routine," Blackjack said. "He wants me in the F-16 tomorrow morning."

"Tomorrow? That soon?"

"Not so soon, Sue. You know that's the next step for Reeva now that you put us back on track. I still can't believe how much smoother the tests are going now."

Sue smiled and nodded. He was right. Now that the added sensors were in place, his performance was amazing.

"Anyway," continued Blackjack, "tomorrow, with the F-16, I'll be pushing the envelope a bit—testing her stress levels manually before you install the virtual-reality systems."

As she listened to him, Sue chewed her bottom lip in pensive thought. She knew that the F-16 Falcon was more advanced than the F-15E—but it was also a *single* seater. That meant no Jerry Bruckman. Blackjack would be alone, and at a greater risk if anything went wrong.

"What are you thinking about, Sue?" asked Blackjack.

"What?" she asked, unable to get the image of his two angry scars out of her mind. The sudden piercing whistle of the teakettle startled her, further stretching her nerves.

Sue turned and switched off the burner, then reached into the cupboard shelf for two mugs. Her hands shook slightly as she pulled them down and one slipped. The crash brought Blackjack into the kitchen.

"Damn," she said, stepping back to keep her bare feet clear of the porcelain shards.

"Here, let me," he said, ripping a paper towel off a nearby roll and quickly scooping up the pieces.

"Blackjack, you don't have to do that," she began, stepping forward. "I'll just get a broom—"

"You're barefoot," he said, then before she knew it, he had scooped her into his arms.

"Blackjack! What are you—" But Sue wasn't able to finish. She found herself crushed against his powerful chest and transported into the carpeted living room.

"I'm helping," he said, amusement in his eyes. "Or trying to, anyway."

Slowly he let her feet touch the carpeting of the floor, and something suddenly changed in his piercing blue eyes as they took in the close proximity of her braless T-shirt. His gaze darkened as it swept over her flushed face.

"Blackjack," she began in a soft, shaky voice, "maybe you'd better go."

"I didn't come out here to make love to you," he said flatly.

Sue's eyes widened at the bluntness of his words.

His hand came up slowly, his index finger curling under her chin to tip her face more toward his.

"And I didn't come out here for tea, either," he said, his gaze raking her lips.

She searched his face, admiring his strong chin, the raven black windswept hair, one shock falling over his forehead.

"Why did you come, then?" she asked.

"The day you got here—you said the truth matters to you," said Blackjack. "I want to know the truth."

Sue felt her body tense at his words; her head began to dip downward. She did not want to meet his eyes. But she felt his finger firm beneath her chin. He would not let her avoid his penetrating blue gaze.

"What truth?" asked Sue, her voice slightly raspy, her heart beating faster. *Could he really know about Max?*

"The truth of us—how we are together."

Sue's lungs took in a relieved rush of air. *He doesn't know he has a son,* she realized with extreme relief. She broke away from Blackjack. Turning, she started back for the kitchen, but a firm hand on her upper arm made her turn toward him again.

"I want to know," he insisted.

"Fine." Sue licked her dry lips and eyed him warily. "You're a damned good test pilot, McConnell. And I'm a damned good scientist. So far, we work well together."

"That's not what I meant and you know it."

She shook her head, a sudden irritation crawling up her spine. "Have the rules changed, Colonel? Because when I first got here, I recall your advising me to avoid the *cost* of the past."

"This has nothing to do with the past," he said. "I want to put the past behind us. I'm here for you and me in the present. Right now."

"And what about the future?" She couldn't believe she'd asked him. But something inside her needed to hear his answer.

"The future doesn't scare me like it used to," he admitted.

Blackjack's gaze never wavered, but suddenly Sue's did. She didn't expect this. The man she remembered fled from conversations like this one.

"I—I don't know what you want from me—" she said, faltering.

"Don't you?" he whispered. "Then I'll just have to show you." Before she could stop him, he leaned in and brushed her full, soft lips with his own. As usual, the result was highly explosive.

When he lifted his head, Sue's voice was shaking. "I thought you said you didn't come here to make love."

"I didn't," said Blackjack. "When I got in my Range Rover tonight, I was coming here to thank you."

Sue couldn't believe her ears. "Thank me? For what?"

"What do you mean, *for what?* Everyone on the project is grateful for your presence, Sue. Things are moving faster than they ever have—and it means a great deal to everyone involved."

"You mean careers?"

"It's much more than that. Everyone cares about performance. About reaching goals. You're making that possible now."

She was genuinely touched; a small smile of satisfaction touched her lips. "That's nice to hear."

"Like I said. I didn't come here to make love to you. But I find," he said, leaning close again, "that just being near you makes it something I can't stop thinking about."

Sue felt her cheeks growing warm with his words. As he leaned closer, she took in the scent of night air that still clung to his freshly washed skin. Faint traces of citrus after-shave mixed with the earthy aroma of leather from his worn jacket—she inhaled that, too, like an intoxicating wine.

Somewhere deep in her brain, Sue could hear the warning Klaxons sounding. She tried to heed the warning and found herself backing up a step and then another.

Blackjack matched her moves, following her backward motion until she felt the cool, hard inevitability of the wall against her back. From the corner of her right eye, Sue saw the short staircase that led to the second floor.

"It's a quick trip to the bedroom from here, McConnell," she whispered, "and I don't think it's a good idea at all."

He was undaunted by her words. "For once, Rigger, don't think," he murmured, "just feel."

Then his lips were on hers again, but this time it was no gentle brushing. The searing contact sent shock waves through Sue's body. Her arms curled around his neck, holding on for dear life as his tongue hotly penetrated her lips and filled her mouth. He was on fire for her—she could feel it—and he was doing everything in his power to make her respond to him.

Sue wasn't superhuman. She desperately craved the physical release he could give her, and she could resist for only so long. Yet still, she tried. Breaking away, she found herself needing air. Blackjack, too, looked less than steady.

"I do want you," admitted Sue, "but I still say, the bedroom is not a very good idea—"

"Fine, then," said Blackjack. "Who needs a bedroom anyhow?" And with that, he jerked the white sport shirt from his jeans and in one swift move pulled it over his head and flung it to the floor.

Once more she was confronted by the magnificent sight of that sculpted chest, now bared to the waist—the two scars a harsh reminder of the risks of his chosen duty. But they were also a reminder of the kind of guts and discipline it took to attempt such duty, not to mention the skill and strength it took to survive it.

His hands were on her now, pulling her close, touching her body. His breathing was heavy as his right hand moved up her side. He used the backs of his fingers to gently brush the sensitive sides of her full breasts, naked beneath the thin white material of her cotton T-shirt.

"Tell me to stop," he whispered, leaning closer to her ear, letting the long fingers of one hand move to the front of her T-shirt and graze deliberately over her nipple. "And I will."

Sue couldn't say a word. She'd closed her eyes to feel the aching sweetness created within her body. And the next thing she felt were his soft, full lips again, against her own. He deepened the kiss and brought his hands to the edges of her T-shirt.

In another moment, it would be over her head and off her. Then there would be no going back—

That's when Sue got a hold of herself. Though her body was more than willing to go down this road again with Blackjack McConnell, she knew that her emotions were far from ready.

She just wasn't certain of the consequences of getting involved with this man again.

Maybe she was strong enough this time around. And maybe she wasn't. But one thing was certain. This time around, she had to think about the consequences for her son.

Her hands stilled his as he began to lift the edges of her T-shirt. She met his eyes, and he could see her answer there.

"I can't, Blackjack," she whispered.

"You can." His lips found hers again. "You want to."

"Yes. Maybe. But not yet..."

His blue gaze studied Sue a long moment.

He looked as though he were about to argue the point, but then he stopped himself. Instead, he simply nodded slightly. He picked up his shirt and quickly drew it back over his dark head.

Then his fingers gently touched her cheek, and his lips lightly touched her mouth in the sweetest, most caring kiss Sue had ever felt.

"I'll wait," he said, then grabbed his jacket and went out the front door.

Chapter Seven

The next morning, Sue stepped out of the hot shower not sure if she was ready to face Blackjack. Today. Or ever again.

She'd dreamed of him. All night. They were decidedly X-rated dreams. And she knew, deep in her heart, that she wanted more than dreams with him. *Consequences,* she cautioned herself. *Consider the consequences.*

After quickly dressing in her standard Air Force uniform—dark blue skirt, low heels, light blue blouse—she descended the stairs and poured herself a cup of coffee. The sound of an approaching car made Sue glance out the front window with curiosity; not many cars came down this short gravel road.

Taking a sip from her coffee cup, she opened the door and saw a base jeep pulling up next to her own in the driveway. She stepped onto the porch to find two people jumping from the vehicle. And when she saw who they were, she nearly dropped her second cup in less than twenty-four hours.

"Mommy, Mommy!"

"Max!" Sue exclaimed, watching the little boy with bright blue eyes running toward her. Setting down her cup, Sue bent down to take her son in her arms.

"Oh, how I missed you," she said, closing her eyes and hugging the little body close. She smelled the fresh, sweet scent of his raven black hair and kissed his little head.

"Uncle Will brought me all the way from Maryland!"

"Hey, Sue!"

Sue looked up to see her big brother walking toward her, a duffel slung over his left side. She saw that his right arm was in a cast and sling.

"Oh, my God, Will, what happened?"

"Accident," he said, setting down the duffel. "In the middle of the Atlantic. Stupid accident. All my fault."

"Are you—"

"I'm fine, except for this unfortunate inconvenience. I'm technically on medical leave, but I figured I'd try to make myself useful. When I got back to D.C., I was filled in about your little adventure, so I thought I'd bring Max down."

"Is this our new house, Mommy?"

Sue set Max down on the porch. "Just for a little while, honey. Go on in and look around."

Max ran inside as Sue warily studied her brother. "You're going to look after him?"

Will nodded.

"God, Will," said Sue, crossing her arms over her chest. "I'm glad to see him. And you. But—"

"What?"

"You knew that *he* was here."

Will ran a hand through his short, dark blond hair. His sharp green eyes studied his sister a moment, then he averted his gaze. "Yeah. I knew Blackjack was here," he admitted.

An angry flush turned Sue's cheeks bright red.

"Mommy, Mommy, there's a *bunch* of bedrooms here!" came an excited voice from the top of the stairs.

"I know, darling," shouted Sue, "you can pick one of the smaller ones, okay?"

"Okay!"

She turned an anxious gaze on her brother. "Why did you bring him, Will?"

Will sighed. "To visit his mother—why do you think?"

"You know what I think!" Glancing at her watch, she sighed in frustration. "I don't have time for this now."

Sue and her brother had been having the same running argument for many years now. He strongly felt that Max had a right to know his father. Sue felt otherwise. Up to now, Will had respected her wishes.

"Don't worry about it, Sue. Just go ahead to work. We'll talk about it later."

Sue didn't budge. She gave him a no-nonsense glare. "Keep him away from McConnell, Will."

Without a word, Will picked up his duffel and brushed past his little sister. Sue's fists clenched in frustration. "I mean it! Did you hear me?"

"I heard you" was all her brother said before he dropped his bag in the living room and headed up the stairs.

ABOVE THE CLEAR bubble canopy of the F-16 Falcon attack fighter, Blackjack took in the brilliant blue sky of a warm spring day. The 360 degrees of pure visibility gave him a free, exhilarating feeling as he knifed through the air.

It was the first time he had flown a plane with his *hands* and not his mind in almost a week. For the past hour, he'd been moving the F-16 through basic maneuvers—he was not only testing the plane, but himself.

Blackjack checked his instrument readings, then flexed his fingers inside his flight gloves. Using his hands to fly a plane now felt a bit strange, and he knew that was dangerous.

Maybe for the three-day weekend coming up he'd go up to the ranch and take up his vintage biplane—reconnect with the *feel* of piloting an old-fashioned flying machine. Yeah, he could invite Sue along, too. He'd certainly enjoy showing her the remodeled house and . . . well, there were plenty of other pleasurable things he could think of doing with her, as well . . . *very* pleasurable things.

Beneath his oxygen mask, Blackjack's lips turned up in a devilish smile. His mouth could still feel the touch of her lips last night, and his nostrils still smelled her sweet feminine scent. He'd never felt so turned on in his life. But it was more than that, more than just physical—the way it had been years ago.

He blinked in thought as he easily banked the plane at seventy-five degrees, pulling back on the throttle to lift the aircraft. He felt the intense 6 g's of pressure on his body and the tightening of his gravity pants on his legs and waist to keep the blood from dropping to his feet. Sweat poured from his brow as he jinked the plane hard, pushing continuous random changes in altitude and position to simulate evasion of hostile radar.

Blackjack had always lived by one firm rule: never think about the future. That kind of thinking had always served him well—helped him keep his edge. It had kept his mind rock steady as a top-gun combat pilot and now as a top test pilot. But he'd trained his mind to think only of the present for so long, he almost didn't know *how* to think about the future.

These days, though, Sue Rigger was making him feel more alive than he'd ever felt before. He was finally beginning to see the future stretching beyond him like the cloudless blue sky stretching before him now. And, he had to admit, he liked the feeling. He liked it a lot.

Blackjack glanced at the clock in his cockpit. Twelve hundred hours. Exactly noon. Pushing the throttle forward, he began his descent.

"Flatlands Tower," he called over the radio. "This is Blackjack. Landing information, please."

"Roger, Blackjack," returned the control tower. "You are clear for landing runway zero-seven."

"Roger, Tower."

He smiled as he slowed his jet and banked her to line up with the runway. "Mmm-mmm," he murmured, practically licking his lips as he thought of Sue's creamy skin and caramel brown eyes. "Lunchtime."

"WHAT ARE THESE THINGS?" asked Max, sitting on the living room sofa. His small, five-year-old fingers had trouble handling the heavy rectangular black case he'd found there.

The blare of cartoons came from the television in front of the little boy as he curiously opened the case. "They look like binoculars," he mumbled.

"What's that, honey?" Sue asked absently. She'd been home five minutes and was looking for food to prepare lunch. Shutting a nearby empty cupboard, she opened the fridge—it, too, was pathetically bare.

"Hey, Sue," called Will from the stairs. "What are you looking for?"

"Food."

"Forget it. I already took inventory an hour ago. You've got two eggs, half a loaf of bread, a canister of tea bags. Oh, and one dusty box of macaroni and cheese."

"Now I know how Old Mother Hubbard felt," she mumbled.

"What's that?" asked Will, leaning on the breakfast bar counter.

"The macaroni and cheese is suspect—it was here when I moved in. Sorry guys, I've been eating most of my meals at the base mess. Actually it's more of a regular cafeteria than a mess hall. With all the testing going on here, it's open twenty-four hours."

"It's okay, we had breakfast on the plane," said Will. He called to his nephew on the couch, "Right, Max?"

"Yeah, eggs and ham. I got my own tray, too," shouted Max over the noise of the television.

"Should we pick up some groceries at the base PX?" asked Sue.

"Either that or take Max to the cafeteria."

Sue shook her head. The last thing she wanted to worry about was the three of them running into Blackjack. "No, let's just go to the PX. We can show Max the base later, when it empties out a bit more—"

"You mean when there's less risk of seeing McConnell," challenged Will.

"So?" snapped Sue. "What's wrong with that? You know how I feel."

"Yeah. I know. And you know how I feel. Max is getting older now, Sue, and—"

"Not here," she said firmly.

"Max," called Sue, "Uncle Will and I are going out the back door for a minute. We'll be right back."

"Okay," said Max, still engrossed in his cartoon show and the strange-looking binoculars he'd found.

Sue motioned her brother to follow her, and they stepped onto the flat concrete deck just outside the back door.

"It's none of your business, Will," she began, her voice full of barely controlled anger.

"Like hell. He's my godchild and nephew, and Mc-Connell is an old friend."

"I know, Will. But Max is *my* son."

"Sue—" Will stopped himself. He took a deep, calming breath, then let it out. "Don't you think he deserves to know his father?"

Sue moved away from her brother, her dark blue low-heeled shoes stepping off the concrete and onto the soft dirt of the backyard. For a long minute, she gazed toward the horizon. High above them, a black stealth bomber floated across the sky. "Not a father...who can't return his son's love," Sue answered finally.

"How can you say that?" asked Will, his temper obviously rising again. "You don't know that!"

"I know Blackjack McConnell—a different Blackjack than you do. You know a fearless pilot, a buddy who'll stick his neck out for you, a man who's a genius in any machine with wings. That's all well and good for the Air Force. But I see another side of it. He is a man who lives for flying, and *only* his flying. He doesn't want a life on the ground."

Sue paused a moment, her voice growing softer. "The strangest part is, after working with him now day in and day out, I've come to understand it—him. I understand why he lives on the edge."

"Sue, he's just a man—"

"No. He's a fighter pilot and a test pilot—and he's remarkable at both. I admire his abilities. But I also recognize that it's his number-one priority. That's why he never loved me years ago, and why he could never love me today. And if he couldn't love me, he couldn't love Max."

"Sue, other pilots have managed to have families and dangerous careers—"

"Yes, I know, but for whatever his reasons, Blackjack just can't. He's not capable of it, Will, and I'll be damned if I let my son be subjected to the kind of pain he put me through."

Will sat down on a lawn chair near the house. He shook his head. "You're playing God. Why don't you just let Blackjack make that choice for himself. He may choose to want his son."

Sue shook her head. "He made his choice over six years ago when he bedded that redhead the night after I told him I loved him."

Will's gaze dropped at Sue's words. Obviously her brother had nothing to say to the unvarnished truth.

"*That* was his choice," she said softly, "and *this* is mine."

Will's head shot up at those words. "Then you're punishing him."

"What?" That idea had never occurred to Sue before and it caught her off guard. She stared blankly at her brother for a moment, unable to admit that just maybe...there was some truth to what he was charging.

"No...*no*," she denied instead. "I—I already told you...I'm protecting Max—protecting him from a father who can't love him, a father who'll hurt him."

Will released a resigned but unhappy sigh. "All right, Sue. I won't tell the man."

"Thank you," she said, regaining her composure. "The project is almost back on track. In another two weeks, we should have Reeva ready to test inside the Horizon, then Lieutenant General Simpson will have no reason not to honor my request to be sent back to Washington. Until that time, I think it would be best to simply keep Max away from Blackjack McConnell."

"WELL, HELLO THERE," said Blackjack from the screen door of the front porch. Like tiny twin mirrors, the pilot's dark sunglasses reflected the surprised face of a cute little dark-haired boy sitting a few feet away on the living room couch.

The boy studied Blackjack's gray flight suit a few seconds, then smiled. "Hi."

Taking off his sunglasses, Blackjack pulled the screen door open and sauntered through. "You know what those are?'' he asked the boy, pointing to the heavy piece of equipment in his little hands.

"No! They look like binoculars, but when I put them up, they're so *bright,* I can hardly see anything."

Blackjack smiled as he knelt down on one knee near the boy. "That's because they're not binoculars. They're called night-vision goggles. They help soldiers to see at night. In fact," he continued, noticing the little boy's blue eyes widening with fascination, "they make the night look just like day."

"Really?"

"Sure. I'll tell you what. Those are mine, I left them here by accident. But if you take real good care, then you can keep them tonight and try them out."

Max's little head was nodding in excitement. "I'll take care of them. I *promise!*" Then the boy looked Blackjack over a moment. "You're a pilot, aren't you?"

"Yeah, I am," said Blackjack. "I know your daddy is, too. In fact, I know your daddy very well. A friend of mine at the base told me he brought you here today."

"You know my daddy?" asked Max, confused.

"What's your name?"

"Max Rigger."

"Well, now, that seems plain for a junior pilot," said Blackjack, sitting beside the boy on the sofa. He made a show of rubbing his strong, square chin in thought, then he sneaked a peek at the boy. "How do you like 'Mighty Max' for a call sign?"

The boy grinned and nodded. "Mighty Max...I like that. I'm Mighty Max!"

"Or are you Mighty Mouse?" teased Blackjack.

"Mighty *Max,*" he said.

"Okay," said Blackjack "I'm Blackjack, nice to meet ya—" he held out a hand and Max took it "—Mighty

Mouse." And with that, Blackjack launched at the boy in a tickling attack.

"Mighty Max!" shouted Max with ferocious joy, trying to tickle Blackjack right back. In another few seconds, they were rolling on the floor in a fit of laughter.

"DO YOU HEAR SOMETHING?" asked Sue, still in the back-yard with her brother.

"What?"

She pulled open the back screen door and entered the house. What she saw there sent her back a few steps in shock as Will walked by her.

Fits of laughter coming from man and boy echoed through the room. But it wasn't just any man and boy. Sue could not believe she was watching her son, laughing and wrestling with his *father.*

Blackjack glanced up to see Will coming toward him.

"Hey, Blackjack," said Will. "Man, it's good to see you!"

Blackjack and Will were embracing in the next moment, Blackjack careful of her brother's broken arm. Max looked on with curiosity, his face flushed, his cheeks red from the roughhousing.

"What the hell happened to you, Wild Will? Get too fresh with one too many ladies?"

Will smiled, "Naw, I wish it were that exotic. This one was an accident, plain and simple—I never did have sea legs."

Blackjack shook his head. "Man, from now on, stick to the wide blue sky."

Blackjack flashed Sue a dimpled smile. "Hi, honey," he said to her, then turned to Will. "Your sister's been saving our asses out here for the last few weeks."

Will threw his sister a cautious look. "That right?"

"Yeah," continued Blackjack, "and I met your boy here. How'd you all like to come out to my ranch house for the three-day weekend coming up next week? I was thinking of taking my Stearman biplane up—do a few touch-and-goes."

Sue and Will stood in tense silence. "How 'bout it, Sue?" prompted Blackjack. "I bet you never flew a vintage Stearman like this one before."

Sue had no breath, no voice; she was too stunned to react. Max had crept up behind Blackjack's pant leg and was now looking up at the pilot with something akin to smiling awe. *Oh, God,* she thought, *I'm living my worst nightmare.*

She wanted desperately to snatch Max to her and run far away, but she was paralyzed. She simply stood, like a sculpture, imprisoned in this awful scene, unable to move or speak.

"How about it, Max?" asked Blackjack, smiling down at the little boy by his pant leg. "How'd you like to copilot a little plane with me next weekend?"

"Yeah!" said Max, "but remember it's Mighty Max. Hey, Uncle Will," he called, "my new pilot's name is Mighty Max, Blackjack said so! Okay, Mommy?"

The three adults stood there like silent sentinels for long, tense moments. She watched Blackjack's face carefully—watched as Max's words registered the fact that Will was his uncle, not his father. And that Sue was Max's—

"Mommy?" whispered Blackjack. His bright, carefree smile began to slowly melt from his face as clouds seemed to form in his clear blue gaze.

Somehow Sue knewn this storm would come, despite her best efforts to prevent it. But she never thought it would come this soon. She simply was not prepared for it.

Blackjack looked down at the boy again as if measuring the resemblance between them—the raven dark hair, the piercing electric blue eyes, the strong chin. If he looked closely, she knew he'd even see the slight dimples that formed at the edges of his mouth when he smiled.

The big pilot bent down and picked up the little boy. "How old are you, Max?"

"Blackjack—" Sue began, but he shot her a sharp, threatening glare that stopped her in her tracks.

"I'm five. But I'll turn six on May 5, and I want a puppy for my birthday. Right, Uncle Will?"

Will looked at his nephew in his father's arms. "I know, but your mom thinks you should wait a few more birthdays." Then Will's eyes met his old friend's. "I've always respected your mother's wishes, Max," he said pointedly, "even when I haven't agreed with them."

Blackjack's stunned gaze turned to Sue. She saw the truth clear as day in his eyes. *He knows.*

All those years ago, she had been a virgin when she first slept with Blackjack. She'd tried a lame attempt at sexual sophistication, but Blackjack had been too experienced to fool. He'd always known that he'd been her first lover. And with Max's dark hair and blue eyes staring Blackjack in the face like a youthful mirror, Sue knew it would be ludicrous to deny that this was his son. He'd never believe it.

"Blackjack says he knows my daddy!" said Max excitedly. "Mommy, you always said my daddy worked far away from us, but Blackjack says he knows him!"

"Hey, Max," said Will, taking him from Blackjack, "are you hungry?"

"A little."

"Let's you and me go for a little drive to the base cafeteria. You want to see where the pilots eat, don't you?"

"Sure! Come on, Mommy—"

"No, I think Mommy and Blackjack need to talk about a few things. It's just you and me, partner."

"Well . . . okay."

"No, Will," said Blackjack, backing up a step. "You don't have to go. I've got some things to do—"

Sue tried to read what was going through his mind. She knew he was angry—very mad, but his blue gaze remained hooded. She guessed that he was too upset to trust himself alone with her.

With a long last look at Max, Blackjack turned and strode through the front door. In another minute his Range Rover was pealing out of the driveway, a cloud of dust and gravel in his wake as he sped away.

Sue's direct stare met Will's confused gaze. "I told you," she whispered, her voice suddenly gone. "I know a much different Blackjack than you do."

Chapter Eight

Blackjack's foot jammed the gas pedal of his Range Rover, pushing it to the floor. He wasn't scheduled for another flight until very late in the day, and he needed some time to compose himself.

He rolled down the driver's-side window of his Rover and let the dry desert air blow through his hair and roar in his ears. He wanted the shooting spring breeze to clear out his pounding head—but it did no good.

A son. I have a son.

The words ran through his brain again and again in an endless loop of incredulity. The desert cactus, rocks and brush rushed by at ninety-five miles per hour—the flat, empty road stretching ahead of him for miles.

Finally, after close to an hour of high-speed driving, he began to see signs of civilization, a suburb on the very outskirts of Las Vegas.

He slowed the Rover to the speed limit as he twisted around the familiar streets. He turned down each tidy lane, passing the ranch-style wooden houses freshly painted, the front yards well manicured. Every other house seemed to have a kid's bicycle or basketball net in the driveway.

At last, he came to the final turn. He slowed the Rover to a crawl and pulled in to the curb in a cul-de-sac. A half-dozen houses sat in the tiny circle, including the pale peach ranch-style house he knew so well.

He noticed a small group of school kids walking around the circle. Two boys broke from the pack and raced forward, into the pale peach house. In a matter of minutes they'd reappeared in play clothes and were shooting baskets in the long concrete driveway.

Blackjack watched the boys a long time in the vehicle, his mind not thinking, just numb. A trickle of sweat slipped down his neck.

Finally he saw Jerry the German Bruckman's tall, lean form walking out into the front yard to greet the mailman. It didn't take long for Jerry to notice Blackjack's familiar Range Rover parked in the small circle, a few houses down.

German walked toward the vehicle slowly, obviously sensing something was wrong. When he reached the open driver's window, he gave his friend a slight smile. "Hey, Rodger, what's up? If you're the new shuttle service, I'm not due on base for two hours. Or is slumming in the suburbs your new style?"

Blackjack rubbed his chin. His voice wasn't quite there for him to use—even for a good comeback.

"You want to come in?" asked Jerry. "Peg's at the store, but she made some fresh lemonade before she left."

Blackjack was ready to shake his head no, but then he changed his mind. Without a word, he followed Jerry to the front door of his house.

"Hey, look, it's Blackjack," said ten-year-old Ricki Bruckman to his older brother.

"Hey, Blackjack," called twelve-year-old Jerry Jr., "want to shoot some hoops with us?"

Blackjack waved at the kids. But before he could answer, Jerry spoke up.

"We'll be out later, boys," said their father. "Blackjack and I have a few things to talk about first."

The cold lemonade felt good against Blackjack's parched throat. He and Jerry had settled down on the back porch. They were quiet a long time. Jerry knew he'd have to wait until Blackjack found the right words to tell him what was wrong.

Finally Blackjack just blurted it out. "I have a son."

"A *son*." Jerry blinked a minute in surprise. "Ah—"

"He's Sue Rigger's boy," said Blackjack, saving his friend from having to ask any embarrassing questions. "He's almost six."

Jerry nodded his head slowly as he added it all up. Then he took a long drink of lemonade. "Holy cow, Blackjack."

Blackjack's blue eyes scanned the well-manicured lawn of Jerry's backyard. "He's a cute kid."

Again Jerry nodded. "And?"

"And . . . I want to kill her."

"Lord." Jerry sighed. "She never told you?"

"I want to kill her."

"Take another drink, Blackjack. A long one. Because I can tell you from experience, you've got some real thinkin' to do."

Blackjack took his advice and tried to let the chilly fluid cool him off. It didn't work.

"What does she want you to do?" asked Jerry.

"I don't know."

Jerry scratched his head. "Well, she didn't tell you after all these years. Guess she never wanted you to know, huh?"

"Guess not."

"Are you at all *happy* that you have a son?"

Blackjack grunted. Then his mind began to comprehend the idea. "Yeah," he said after a long moment. "When I think about the boy, I am happy."

His gaze wandered over the Bruckmans' backyard. "I guess, for a while lately, I was beginning to think I'd never have kids . . . and now . . ." He noticed a dirty football lying near a freshly turned bed of garden soil, and a slow smile spread across his face. "Yeah, German, I'm happy about it. Very happy."

"Okay," said Jerry. "So, what do you want to do?"

It didn't take long for dark clouds to return to Blackjack's eyes. "I want to kill her."

Jerry released a pronounced sigh. "I can see this is going to be a *long* conversation."

IT WAS LATE AFTERNOON. Sue watched Max sip at his glass of milk. The big chocolate-chip cookie sat untouched on the plate in front of him. His excited blue eyes seemed as wide as silver dollars as they took in his surroundings.

"Mommy, is this really where the pilots eat?"

"Yes, Max," she said. "Look over there. The airmen at that table work on the ground crews to keep the planes in good shape. And over there are three pilots. See, they're wearing their flight suits."

Max nodded, then looked up at his uncle, who was sipping at his foam cup of coffee. "Uncle Will has a suit like that. And so does Blackjack. Where's Blackjack, is this where he eats? Is he coming back to see us?"

Once again Sue felt a terrible stab of guilt. This was about the fifth time in as many hours that Max had asked about Blackjack. "Ah . . ."

"Blackjack's pretty busy, trooper," said Will, coming to his sister's rescue. "We'll see him later."

She was grateful Max only asked about *Blackjack* this time and didn't start up again about wanting to meet his *daddy*. She and Will had agreed, after Blackjack left, not to try to explain anything to Max about Blackjack being his father.

Blackjack's leaving the way he did made it clear to Sue that he wanted *nothing* to do with Max. That was exactly how she thought he would react. No big surprise there.

But the question was, what to do with Max? Right now she decided it would be best not to tell him anything. She'd just try to put the boy off and hope he'd tire of the subject—at least until he was old enough to understand better.

More than anything, Sue wanted what was *safest* for her son. She wanted desperately to protect him from disappointment and pain. Now it was more than clear how much Blackjack could have hurt her boy if she had told Max the truth.

Sue cursed herself. She should *never* have allowed herself to get close to McConnell again. *How could I have screwed things up this badly?*

"Hi, there, Captain," said a bright female voice behind her. Turning, Sue saw her new friend, Second Lieutenant Jane Cortez. Like Sue, she was dressed in her regular Air Force uniform.

"Hey, Curly," said Sue, returning her friend's warm smile and noticing something was different about her.

Her *hair,* Sue realized. Jane's long, brown curly hair was usually up in a tight bun when she was on base. Now it hung down around her shoulders, softly framing her pretty face and luminous gray eyes.

This was the first time Sue had seen Jane's hair loose while in uniform. She wondered what the occasion could be—

"You must be Colonel Will Rigger," said Jane, facing Sue's brother.

Sue watched her brother take in the attractive, intelligent woman in front of him. Ever the gentleman officer, he rose and gallantly extended his left hand—since his right was still in cast and sling. "And you are—"

"Jane Cortez, *First* Lieutenant Jane Cortez," she said, grasping Will's hand in a gentle greeting.

"First?" asked Sue, glancing quickly at Jane's collar. Sure enough, the single gold bar of a second lieutenant's rank was now replaced with a gleaming silver one.

"My promotion came through this morning," she said, practically beaming.

"Congratulations," said Will, his hand still holding hers, his green gaze alive with sparkling energy.

Sue had to bite her lip to keep from laughing out loud. She knew that look in her brother's eyes. And she had a hunch Jane knew it, too. *Good for you, Jane.*

"I'm Max," said the little boy at the table between them. "Mighty Max."

"This is my son," said Sue.

Jane removed her hand from Will's and held it out to the little boy. "Pleased to meet you, Mighty Max. I bet you're a pilot. Are you waiting for your plane to be serviced?"

"I wish! I want to fly an F-15 like my uncle."

"How about like your mom?"

"My mom?"

"Sure," said Jane. "You can watch her go up in about an hour."

Sue's smile disappeared from her face. "What?"

"Simpson's orders, I'm afraid. We're short a backseater, and we have to run a tactical-engagement sequence to stay on schedule with the Reeva testing."

"I know about that dogfight, but I'm supposed to monitor it from the ground."

Jane shook her head slowly. "You're monitoring from the air, as my backseater. Simpson is short pilots tonight."

"What about Jerry Bruckman?"

Jane shook her head. "That's Hollywood's backseater. You remember Captain Garner—your gung-ho dance partner? He's supposed to be bandit number one, and I'm bandit number two, that is, *we* are."

"Wait a minute—" began Sue.

Will laughed. "Come on, Sue, stop trying to get out of it. You know you're qualified to handle both positions on the Eagle. It's just a test."

"It's a dogfight, Will. Against Blackjack McConnell."

AN HOUR AND A HALF LATER, Sue stood uneasily on the tarmac beside Jane Cortez. The silvery gray metal of their F-15E gleamed cleanly in the late-afternoon sun. Short boarding ladders hung from both front and rear cockpits.

An engine roared in the distance as an aircraft came down for a landing, and Sue glanced over at Blackjack's plane. By this time, Blackjack knew he was flying a dogfight against Sue. He had barely looked at her at the preflight briefing. He'd sat in his chair, stiff as a corpse, his jaw locked tightly into place. It was painfully clear he was making every effort not to glance even vaguely in Sue's direction.

Now Blackjack was standing on the tarmac next to his F-16 and speaking with a master sergeant in charge of one of the many ground crews.

Nervously switching her helmet from one arm to the other, Sue glanced back at the tower. On the ground, near the airfield fence, Will and Max stood.

She waved her arm back and forth. The boy waved back immediately, jumping up and down in delight. She saw him chattering to his uncle and pointing at her excitedly. Sue grinned from ear to ear.

Her son was proud of her.

Sue's heart filled with love for her child. It seemed to her there was no better feeling on earth. That little boy was her reason for living, as far as she was concerned.

"Excuse me, Lieutenant, would you mind if I had a private word with the captain?"

"No problem."

She glanced back at the voices, and her broad smile died on her lips. Blackjack's tall, powerful form, closely outlined by his trim gray flight suit, was walking toward her. He stopped stiffly—entirely too close. His blue gaze was especially piercing, and he fixed it on her with barely contained fury when he spoke.

"Are you *qualified* to fly a test as a weapon-system officer, Captain?"

Sue's fists clenched at his words as her initial nervousness melted into a slow-boiling anger. She threw her flight gloves into her padded helmet.

"You know, McConnell, it's not that I *wanted* to fly today—it's just that I couldn't pass up a chance to shoot down your egotistical ass."

"Check your instruments, Rigger," said Blackjack through gritted teeth. "I believe it's *your* ass that's my target today," he said, his finger poking her shoulder. "I mean, did you even graduate from pilot training?"

"You're way out of line, Colonel," she charged, poking him right back.

"*I* am?" he challenged in a dangerously low voice. Leaning down, his face came close to hers.

"You don't even know my history—" began Sue.

"Apparently not," snapped Blackjack, cutting her off. His angry blue gaze broke from hers. His hand gesturing toward Max, waving in the distance. "Especially one significant part. A part that I had a *right* to know about."

"I warn you, Colonel," she said, her voice firm. "Don't make this personal."

"There's no way in hell to get around this being personal, Captain. And I warn *you*, we're not through yet."

"That's where you're wrong," returned Sue. "We're through, all right."

Blackjack brought up his fist. She could see he wanted to punch the belly of the plane. By the furious look in his eyes, she'd bet he actually could have put a dent in the fuselage.

But he didn't. With supreme control, he managed to keep a lid on his rage as he released a shaky breath.

"Fine," he said in a low tone, again through a tight jaw. "If that's the way you want it. But chew on this, *Captain*— I'm not through with my *son*. Not by a long shot."

Sue nearly dropped her helmet at his words. She stood, dumbfounded as he turned on his heel and strode to his F-16.

Not through with his son?

What did he mean? She had been absolutely certain that Blackjack wanted *nothing* to do with Max. The idea that he wanted any kind of relationship with her son sent her head spinning.

He's bluffing, Sue decided as she watched him moving across the tarmac. She studied his broad back as his hand grasped the rail of his plane's boarding ladder and he hoisted himself up and over the edge of the F-16's body.

He *couldn't* want to be part of Max's life, she thought. He must have said those words in anger, she assured herself, or to get back at her somehow. Well, damn him to hell for it!

"What was that all about?" asked Jane, returning to Sue's side.

"Nothing, just some history catching up with me," she managed to reply, still recovering from the tense encounter.

"Uh-huh," said Jane, pulling herself onto the short hanging ladder and climbing into her pilot's cockpit. "Nice set of buns on that history of yours."

"Never mind, Curly," said Sue, climbing into her back-seat position. "Let's just get up there and fry those buns for dinner."

"You got it, Sparks."

FROM BEHIND the tall glass windows of the operations lab, Will Rigger stood silently watching the three jet planes on the radar. Remote video cameras on the wings projected pictures on screens nearby.

"Which one's Mommy?" whispered Max, sitting in a padded swivel chair in front of the radar.

Will had told his nephew to remain quiet, and the boy was behaving very well. This was Max's first question since they had watched the planes lining up for takeoff fifteen minutes ago.

"That one," said Will, pointing out a blue triangle on the green radar screen. The aircraft was zigzagging at a low altitude above the desert.

Lieutenant General Simpson walked over to Will. "Looks like they're trying the oldest trick in the book on the guy."

Will laughed. "I know. I feel sorry for my sister. I've seen Blackjack outmaneuver that strategy dozens of times."

For the mock encounter, Blackjack was to fly some miles away from the base and then return. At a random point, Hollywood and Curly were to engage him in a dogfight and try to "down" him with mock missiles.

"What's the oldest trick?" asked Max, his voice still in a whisper.

The lieutenant general smiled at Max. Hunkering down to the boy's level, the older man pointed to the screen. "Your mom and her pilot are flying low, waiting for Blackjack. When he flies by, she'll lure him to chase her. Blackjack will be so busy chasing your mom that he won't notice the second plane, which is way high up here. That second plane will fly down, get behind Blackjack and shoot him out of the sky."

Will yawned slightly and reached for his coffee cup on a nearby table. "Only, the thing is, Max, Blackjack *knows* that strategy so well, he'll simply *pretend* he's chasing your mom. When the second plane shows up, he'll be ready for it. His F-16 is *the* most maneuverable operational aircraft in the world. It can easily get away with enough time to shoot down both Eagles."

Simpson looked up at Will, then back down at Max. "Do you want me to explain it again, son?"

Max shook his head. "Nope. I get it. The Falcon's a better plane. It's got a fly-by-wire system. Right, Uncle Will?"

Will smiled down, knowing by now that his nephew had inherited the Rigger genius genes. "Right, trooper."

"Mom's a goner."

Will took another sip of coffee. "Yep." Will figured that when it came to Blackjack, his sister always would be a goner, even if she hated to admit it.

The radio crackled, and Will listened in on the conversation between the pilots and backseaters in their cockpits.

"Hollywood, any sign of Blackjack yet?" asked the voice of Jane Cortez.

"Negative, Curly," said Captain Garner. "Nothing yet."

"Roger, Hollywood," answered Jane. "We're sitting tight."

"Don't you mean sitting ducks?" joked Jerry Bruckman's voice over the crackle of the radio.

"Funny, German," returned Jane. "Just don't say dead ducks." All four members of both crews laughed.

Will laughed, too. He could see that Jane Curly Cortez was flying well. He noticed her dive, then execute a climbing roll and knew she was pulling enough g's to cause discomfort.

"Jane Cortez," he murmured low, liking the feel of the words on his tongue.

"What about her?" asked Simpson beside Will.

Will blinked, realizing he'd said her name out loud. "She's a good tactical pilot, isn't she?"

Simpson nodded. "Very good—for her age. She's young but she's got good instincts and a good background for flight testing, which is why she's here."

Will nodded slowly. "Married?" he asked carefully, trying to sound casual.

Simpson eyed Will, not missing a thing. "She's available, Colonel. *And* she seems to be enamored with your...theories."

Will's eyebrows rose. "Really?"

"But I have an ulterior motive for telling you."

"That so?"

"With your talent, I wouldn't mind at all seeing you request a change of scenery. Join your sister out here permanently."

Will nodded his head. "That's flattering. Thanks." He took another sip of coffee. "Is Jane Cortez part of the bargain?"

Simpson smiled. "Not technically. But I'm sure she wouldn't object to your inquiry."

"That so?"

"Like I said, she's a good pilot. And I'd say she's got you in her sights."

"Well, well..." Will couldn't hide his pleased smile—so he didn't even try.

Chapter Nine

Within ten minutes after takeoff, Blackjack's gleaming F-16 was firing its afterburners and ready for the hunt. He immediately began searching the sky for Sue Rigger.

"Where are you?" he murmured beneath his oxygen mask.

Blackjack checked his instruments, then dropped five thousand feet. That's when he spotted the jet. It was circling below in the distance. She was low, maybe ten thousand feet.

"*There* you are."

A slow smile spidered across his face, and he felt that familiar shot of adrenaline. Then another feeling began to surge through his veins.

He thought of Sue and how she'd lied to him...for years. Because of her, he'd lost *years* with his son.

Blackjack was known for the emotionless precision of his flying. His cool control. But right this moment, emotions were roiling inside him, clouding his vision.

He dived and rolled his plane, positioning his F-16 straight for Sue's tail. Suddenly he needed to spend his aggression. When he'd gotten low enough, he identified the craft for certain. It was Sue Rigger with Curly Cortez, all right.

"Tallyho, girls. It's time to play."

"HEY, CURLY, guess who's coming to dinner?" remarked Sue from the backseater's position. She saw Blackjack's F-16 on the radar, heading right for them. Turning in her seat, Sue searched the sky to make a visual sighting.

"Tallyho," Sue called to her pilot. "Bandit at six o'clock, right on our tail."

"Roger, Sparks," said Jane. "Hollywood, do you see him?"

"Roger, Curly," said Hollywood Garner in the second plane, high above them. "Give him a good chase, girls."

"Roger, Hollywood," said Jane, "Just cut the 'girls' crap."

Jane was careful to reel Blackjack in. She waited until his range was close enough, then she banked the plane sharply, pulling enough g's on the turn to cause both her and Sue to gasp for breath.

"Where is he, Sparks?" came Jane's voice.

Sue searched the sky. "Six o'clock, he's still on our tail. Keep him coming," said Sue, seeing that Blackjack was far from phased by the sudden maneuver. His skills were as sharp as ever.

"We've got tone!" exclaimed Sue, suddenly hearing Blackjack's radar lock on to their position. In another few seconds, if he held them in it, that would mean his missile would have downed them.

But Jane was ready to shake him. She took the plane into a quick vertical climb. In another second, they were inverted. It felt like a looping roller coaster ride culminating with a terrifying plunge straight toward the brown desert.

Sue was breathing hard from the force of the turn, her oxygen mask pressing down on her face. She fought the gravity as sweat began pouring from her brow. Turning in her seat, Sue found Blackjack coming on strong.

"We shook off the hit, but he's on our tail again," cautioned Sue through labored breaths.

"Damn, he's good," said Jane, diving again. Their plane was rocketing low across the desert now, paralleling a dry riverbed etched into the cracked earth below. Blackjack was diving right behind them, trying to get them in his sights for another shot.

"Hey, Hollywood, *anytime,*" said Jane, waiting for Garner to descend and ambush Blackjack.

A high-pitched tone began to sound in the cockpit as Blackjack once again locked Sue's F-15 into his weapon's sights.

"Curly, use the sun," shouted Sue to her pilot. "Come right and then go for the moon. Now!"

Curly listened. She sharply turned the plane straight into the bright light of the setting sun, then she went vertical and rolled quickly, again shaking off the mock missile hit.

By now, though, Sue saw that Hollywood was in range.

"Sit tight, girls," came Hollywood's voice on the radio. "Cavalry's here."

"I can't believe this," came Jerry Bruckman's voice over the static of the radio.

Sue couldn't believe it, either. Hollywood was in range, but Blackjack was *still* coming after her and Jane. He was ignoring his radar, not paying any attention to the obvious second plane that had come down for combat!

Had Blackjack actually been drawn into this simple-minded trap? Had he really allowed himself to be fooled by the oldest trick in the book?

"He's target fixated," said Sue over the radio.

"Good God, it's actually working," said Jane.

Blackjack had become so focused on downing Sue that he'd forgotten everything else—even another threat—right behind him. It was such a basic error, Sue still couldn't believe it.

"I've got him locked in," said Jerry Bruckman from the second plane.

"Okay, girls," said Garner. "On three, bank left and get the hell out so we can fire. One, two, three, go!"

"Firing," said Jerry Bruckman.

Sue listened intently until she finally heard Jerry's voice calmly state, "We got him. I can't believe it, but we got him."

"Wahoo!" shouted Garner. "He's dead! Blackjack's dead!"

Sue exhaled with relief that the dogfight was over. But the words *Blackjack's dead* echoed sickly in her ears.

Frantically her gaze searched the sky for his F-16. Behind her mask, Sue took in a deep breath of pure oxygen when she saw that he was alive and well beneath the aircraft's clear bubble canopy.

Then, in the next moment, his jet engine's afterburners fired angrily and he was knifing forward, beyond the two F-15s. At top speed, he'd be back at the base in a matter of minutes.

Closing her eyes, Sue took another deep breath as something in her gut began to twist.

"Let's go home, girls," came Hollywood's voice in her ears. His insistence on calling them "girls" continued to grate.

"Hey, Sparks," said Jane.

"What is it, Curly?" asked Sue.

"Hold on."

Suddenly Jane took the plane into a sharp vertical climb. She banked to position them right behind Hollywood and German. "Sparks, got them targeted?" asked Jane.

"Give me a second." Sue smiled as she used her radar to get them in the mock missile sights.

"Hey, what the hell are you girls doing!" shouted Garner.

"Sparks, how's it look?" asked Jane.

"Go for it, Curly," called Sue, knowing they could be reprimanded for screwing around but suddenly not giving a damn.

Jane pressed the button that produced a high-pitched tone in the cockpit of the other Eagle.

"Uh . . . you're dead, *boys*," said Sue.

"That's not funny," said Garner, though Jerry Bruckman was laughing his ass off.

"Just a little reminder never to underestimate us *girls*," taunted Jane. "Roger, Hollywood?"

"Hey, eat my afterburner," said the cocky captain, then he fired his engines and banked his F-15 for the base.

THOUGH HE'D FULLY STOPPED the F-16, and an airman had hooked a ladder to the canopy rails, Blackjack sat for a full three minutes in his cockpit without moving a muscle.

He pulled off his helmet and gloves, then ran a hand through his dark hair, thoroughly damp with sweat.

"Stupid," he muttered to himself. He closed his blue eyes and knocked the back of his head three times against the top of his cushioned seat. "Stupid, stupid, stupid," he chanted. Then, with a sigh, Blackjack rubbed his eyes. "Face it, Rodger, this just isn't your day."

"Hey, Blackjack!"

His eyes opened at the sound of his old friend's voice. He looked to his left to see Wild Will Rigger smiling and striding across the tarmac toward his plane. Little Max was tagging along, right behind him.

Blackjack watched the little dark-haired, blue-eyed boy moving toward him, and his mind seemed to stop. His heart, however, began to beat faster.

This is my son.

Rising slowly from his cockpit, Blackjack hoisted himself over the side of the plane and stepped down the rungs of the ladder. No sooner had his heavy boots touched the ground than little Max's big blue eyes were peering up at him.

You look like me, thought Blackjack, feeling dazed by the idea.

"We were watching from up there!" announced Max, pointing toward the op lab just below the tower.

"Is that right? And what did you think?"

"You got creamed!" exclaimed Max.

Blackjack's eyebrows rose as he shot a wry look toward Will.

"Target fixation?" remarked Will, his amusement clearly showing in his eyes.

"Yeah, I know," he said, lifting a cautionary finger toward his friend. "Let's just say I had a little...emotional problem today."

"Mom suckered you in good, didn't she!" declared Max.

Blackjack peered down at the little boy again. Then he hunkered low. "Yeah, she did," he said to Max. Then he looked back up at Will. "I guess I asked for it."

"Can I fly your plane?" asked Max.

"Oh, so you think you can do a better job than me, huh?" teased Blackjack.

"Sure!" announced Max.

Blackjack glanced up at Will. "Looks like he's got the first qualification for being a fighter pilot."

Will smiled. "You mean complete and total arrogance about one's own abilities?"

"Sure." Blackjack laughed. He looked back at the boy. "Well, Mighty Max, you're a little too young to fly her. But you can sit in her cockpit. How about it? You want to try her on for size?"

Max's eyes widened in awe, then he looked to his uncle. "Can I, Uncle Will?"

Will nodded. "Sure, trooper," he said, his smiling green eyes meeting Blackjack's. "I think it's in your blood."

"Okay, then," said Blackjack with a wide grin. "Elevator up!" And with that, he hoisted the boy under one arm and climbed the ladder.

"Wow!" exclaimed Max as Blackjack plopped him down in the padded seat of the F-16. With the engines disengaged and the safety pins plugged into the ejection seat, Blackjack knew it was safe for the boy to sit inside the plane. Even so, he cautioned him not to touch anything.

"You want to try my helmet?" asked Blackjack.

"Sure!" said Max, and in the next second it was obvious the world just went from day to night for the boy.

"Hmm. Looks like lights out, kiddo. Guess my helmet's a little big for you," he teased.

Max pushed back the large crash helmet so he could see out of it. "It's just fine!" he insisted. "Now, what do I do first to fly this thing?"

SUE CLIMBED DOWN from the back seat of the F-15 Eagle and patted Jane Cortez on the back. "Nice goin', Curly."

"Thanks. I still can't believe we helped shoot down the infamous Blackjack McConnell," said Jane as she pulled off her helmet and walked toward a ground-crew sergeant.

Sue walked by the two, knowing Jane would be tied up briefing the sergeant for a few minutes. Heading toward the base of the tower, she pulled off her helmet. Her hair, pinned tightly to her head, was damp with sweat, and the spring desert breeze felt good against her face and neck.

As her gaze passed over the dozen or so planes lined up on the tarmac, she noticed a couple of bodies by an F-16. What she saw next made her steps speed up double time.

Her brother was standing on the ground while Blackjack was balancing himself on the plane's hanging ladder. Sue didn't miss the tiny head, barely visible in the cockpit of the jet.

"Max," she whispered in horror as her quick steps turned into an out-and-out run.

"Will!" she shouted as she neared the F-16. "Where's Max?"

Will's green eyes widened in surprise at the sound of his sister's voice. But the answer came from the ladder above him.

"He's here. With me." Blackjack said the words with distinct certainty, a clear challenge in his tone.

"Please bring him down, Colonel," said Sue as evenly as she could manage. "It's much too dangerous to have him in that cockpit."

Blackjack's jaw worked a moment as he looked down at her. "It's not too dangerous, Captain, I've seen to that. But I won't argue with you." He turned toward Max, and his cold tone immediately warmed as he playfully addressed the boy. "C'mon, Mighty Max. It's time to land and file your flight report."

Sue could hear the disappointed "Awww" sounding from the cockpit above. Her heart was beating fast and hard as she watched her baby being lifted from the jet, a crash helmet on his head.

"Hi, honey," called Sue as Blackjack hoisted him by his middle and carried him like a football under his arm as he descended the ladder.

"Mommy!" shouted Max. "Did you see me in the Falcon! I was in the Falcon!"

"Yes, honey," she said, shooting a furious look at Blackjack as she held her hands out for her child. She wasn't relieved until his warm, little body was back in her arms.

"I saw you fly, too, Mommy. I watched how you guys creamed Blackjack, but he said he asked for it anyway," chattered Max as Sue lowered him onto the tarmac. "I'm hungry—can we get something to eat now?"

"Sure," said Sue, leaning down and lifting the big helmet from her son's small head. She hadn't missed Max's words— Blackjack had actually said he *asked* for it today. That was practically saying he knew he'd acted like a jerk. But did that mean he was sorry?

Sue's brown gaze lifted to Blackjack's face, but he wouldn't meet her eyes. "You'll want this back, Colonel," she said, straightening up.

Blackjack finally looked at her, but his expression and his emotions were carefully hooded. His hand reached out and took the helmet from her. It brushed hers, and she was all too aware of the brief contact.

"Uh . . . Mighty Max," said Blackjack, hunkering down to the boy, his helmet in his hands, "you want to do me a favor and carry this back to the op lab? Uncle Will will go with you. You have to be careful with it, though."

"Sure!" exclaimed Max, clearly awed by a chance to do something important for a pilot. The boy took the big helmet carefully into his tiny hands. "You coming, Mommy?" asked Max.

"I'll be there in a minute, honey," said Sue.

"Okay," said Max. "Hey, Blackjack, don't forget about next weekend! You said I could go up with you in your old biplane. Right?"

"Don't worry, Mighty Max, we're still on."

Sue's gaze shot to Will at this exchange, but her brother averted his eyes, refusing to get involved.

"C'mon, Max," said Will. "Let's get that helmet back to the op lab for Blackjack."

Sue watched as they left. No sooner had the two begun heading across the tarmac than Will was calling out to a pilot a few yards ahead of him: Jane Cortez.

Within moments, the three of them—Will, Jane and Max—were heading back toward the tower. They looked good together, Sue thought. Her brother and Curly Cortez.

"We have to talk," said Sue, turning toward Blackjack.

Blackjack's blue eyes were all too fierce as they suddenly turned on her. She got the uneasy feeling that she was back in her F-15E, once again being targeted by a deadly ace.

"Do we?" fired Blackjack. "But aren't we, as you put it, *through?* Pretty ironic, since we barely got started again."

"We're through. Done and over, Blackjack. That's what it is I need to make clear. I don't want you in Max's life—"

"Too late," he snapped, leaning dangerously close to her. "I'm in. And I'm staying in."

Sue shook her head. "Forget next weekend, Colonel," she said. "It's not going to happen. You made your choice over six years ago and I made mine."

"That's a load of bull," returned Blackjack. "You gave me no *choice* at all. You kept the truth from me all these years. I still can't believe it!"

"Believe what? *You're* the one who walked away from me, Rodger. You have a selective memory on this one."

"The past is past," said Blackjack, shaking his head in fury. "I went to war—"

"You left me *before* you left for the Gulf. You made it abundantly clear that you did not want long-term attachments. You did not want love. You did not want me."

He took in a deep breath. His head was bent, his eyes on the tarmac. "If you want to punish me for the past, Captain, be my guest. But don't—" his voice grew dangerously low "—*don't* punish your son."

"My son needs love and attention. He doesn't need a man who doesn't want long-term attachments."

Blackjack's gaze came up to meet Sue's. The ferocious blue intensity was back in his eyes. "I can see you're not hearing me. But you better hear this—it's *not* six years ago now. I'm *in* the boy's life. Get it through your head."

Then abruptly he turned to go. Sue watched silently as the man strode away, anxiously putting space between them.

"NINETY-EIGHT, ninety-nine, one hundred," counted Sue a week later as she tugged at her plastic pink brush.

With Max soundly sleeping in the bedroom down the hall, Sue had changed into her thin nightgown and was now sitting on her bed, trying to relieve her stress. It wasn't working.

For the past week, Blackjack's on-the-job performance had been exceptional. With the Reeva system installed in the Falcon, the tests were working like a dream. The next step—the Horizon testing—was scheduled for next week. Sue couldn't believe it, but now they were actually *ahead* of schedule.

Laughter drifted up from the floor below her, and Sue smiled. Will was in the living room downstairs, still entertaining their dinner guest, Jane Cortez. Sue had enjoyed Jane's company that evening. And, as for her brother, well, he'd practically been inseparable from Jane since the day he watched her fly.

Quite the opposite was true of Sue and Blackjack. The man had been avoiding her like the plague.

Tomorrow was Friday, Sue reminded herself, and according to Will, Blackjack was coming here to pick up Max for the long weekend. Also according to Will, Blackjack meant to do this come hell, high water or Sue flinging herself in front of Max.

For over a week now, she had been trying to talk to Blackjack—tell him that she did not want him involved in Max's life. But the stubborn, square-jawed pilot simply ignored her, continually shutting out her words.

"Let's not discuss personal issues on Air Force time, Captain," was all she ever got out of him.

It was enough to make her grind her teeth.

Sue closed her eyes. She couldn't let Max watch his mother go for his father's throat tomorrow. She *had* to put a stop to this, she decided. Tonight.

Rising from the bed, she threw down her pink brush and reached for the dresser drawer. In less than a minute, she had pulled on her jeans, tucking the skirt of her thin white nightgown into them. Not bothering with socks, she slipped on a pair of tennis shoes and jammed her arms through a white cotton cardigan. Then she stopped.

"But where is he tonight?" she murmured, realizing Blackjack might not even be on base.

Sue quickly grabbed the keys to her base jeep and headed straight for the stairs. To hell with it. Wherever he was, she'd find him.

". . . and that's when I decided to scratch the whole thing and begin again," Will was saying to Jane in the living room. "You see, unless a solution is elegant, it is not the *best* solution."

"You're thinking like a physicist. But how do you reconcile the theoretical with the practical. I mean, the real world is a different place than the research lab. What if you're under a time constraint for a solution?" argued Jane.

Sue noticed the two were very cozy, sitting close together on the couch. A jazzy sax number was softly playing on the small living room stereo, and Jane was refilling the wineglasses on the coffee table. Will's good hand was resting comfortably on Jane's crossed knee.

Sue cleared her throat as she descended the stairs and headed for the front door. "Excuse me, you two," she called out, "but I'm going out for a little while."

"Where are you going?" asked Will, glancing toward her. Sue noticed he hadn't even bothered to remove his hand from Jane's leg. And Jane didn't seem to mind one bit.

"Just out," said Sue in a clipped, none-of-your-business tone. "Don't worry," she added, trying to soften her words.

"I'm not," said Will, in fact looking far from worried or even surprised. He'd probably already guessed where she was going—and why.

"Max is sound asleep," said Sue. "But if he wakes up, just give him a glass of milk and—"

"I know," said Will with a wry smile. "Are you forgetting I gave that kid milk when he still took it from a bottle?"

"So sue me," she said, pulling open the door. "I'm a *mother.*"

"Uh-huh. Hey, sis!" he called before she closed the door behind her.

"What?"

Will turned to Jane. "Was Blackjack going with Hollywood's group to Afterburners tonight?" he asked her.

Jane shook her head. "No. Colonel McConnell said he was working out tonight."

Will checked his watch and looked back toward Sue. "Try the Bachelor Officers' Quarters," called Will. "You're likely to find him there."

Knowing it would be utterly useless to pretend she *wasn't* trying to track down Blackjack, Sue simply nodded her head. "I'll see you soon," she called before heading for the BOQ.

Will turned back toward Jane. "I hope not *too* soon. They've got a lot to talk about." Then he gave her a devilish smile as he leaned perceptibly closer. "And so do we."

Chapter Ten

"Eighty-two, eighty-three, eighty-four," counted Blackjack, finishing off a double set of push-ups in his room.

After six miles of laps around the airfield, a pick-up basketball game and some lifting at the base weight room, Blackjack thought his stress levels would have been back to normal. But after walking back to his weeknight crash room at the BOQ, he found he still needed to work off some energy, angry frustration . . . as well as sexual.

Even after the push-ups, Blackjack felt far from relieved.

Rising from the carpeted floor, he stripped off his gray academy T-shirt and used it to wipe the sweat from his face and the newly pumped muscles of his chest. He went to the small bathroom's stand-up shower and turned on both nozzles.

Hot water began to steam up the room as he stripped off his shorts and stepped into the pelting spray. Lathering his chest, he closed his eyes and tried to will away the incessant vision of Sue Rigger's face and body. It didn't work.

He grabbed a bottle of shampoo. As if he could soap the images from his brain, he thoroughly scrubbed his hair, then let the hot spray beat down on him.

Reeva's voice—Sue's voice—was still with him, inside his head. But he well knew the woman herself, and what she could do to him, was no computer simulation. Tipping his face to the rinsing spray, Blackjack finished with his shower. He turned off the water, stepped onto the bathroom rug and grabbed a thick white towel.

He needed to forget how much he wanted her, he told himself as he rubbed his damp head. He tried to remind himself that she had lied to him, rejected him and now wanted to shut him out of his own son's life. Yet still he burned. And he was angry as hell at himself—for still wanting her, despite the fact that she didn't want him.

In another week or so, perhaps he would no longer feel such a strong need for her. Then maybe he could coolly sit down with her to discuss how to handle raising their son.

As he finished toweling off, Blackjack heard three sharp knocks at the door. He wasn't surprised. Major Bronski down the hall had invited Blackjack out for a late drink at the base's Officers' Club.

Blackjack wasn't in the mood to go out after all. He figured he needed a good night's sleep. Tomorrow he'd have to face a lioness mother who was sure to be fighting mad when he tried picking up her cub for a weekend.

Knotting the towel around his waist, he walked barefoot across his bedroom floor, not ready for what would greet him beyond the wooden door. Pulling it open, he had to blink to make sure he wasn't hallucinating.

Sure enough, he wasn't. His eyes opened to find that same recurring image still blighting his vision. It was Sue. And she looked as beautiful as ever in tight blue jeans and an open cardigan sweater that revealed a glimpse of something sheer and sexy beneath. Her face, however, looked as angry as any lioness he'd seen in *National Geographic*.

Blackjack knew he was far from ready to face her. His mind began to race for a solution. Maybe there was one, he advised himself. *Just scare the hell out of her.*

SUE WAS DOING HER BEST to maintain her control, but standing there facing a half-naked Blackjack McConnell made it far from easy.

The man had obviously just stepped out of the shower. His midnight black hair was damp, and beads of water were still clinging to the dark mat of hair on his naked chest. His arm muscles were bulging as if he'd been working out all night, and the white towel, knotted low around his lean hips, revealed the ripples of a washboard stomach.

Sue tried to regain her quickly waning composure. She realized that he had also been caught off guard. It took a few moments for him to focus his piercing blue stare.

"What are you doing here?" he finally asked, his voice none too friendly.

"I…ah…" Sue licked her lips a moment and tried to keep her gaze from straying to that magnificent broad chest. "I came to talk to you," she managed to say.

Blackjack's eyes flashed blue fire. "Forget it. We already talked enough—"

"Wait one damned minute," she broke in. Thank goodness her anger was now quickly rising. It helped her to remember why she had come. "I may have *tried* to talk to you," she snapped, "but you have refused to hear one word I've said—"

"I heard you loud and clear," he said. "And I don't give a—" Blackjack stopped suddenly as two young men walked down the hallway. Obviously the sight of an attractive blonde arguing with a colonel wearing nothing but a towel was a rare curiosity to the lieutenants.

Suddenly Sue felt a steel grip on her forearm. In the next second, she was lurched forward into Blackjack's room and the door was shut firmly behind her; the click of a dead bolt sounded in her ears.

"Listen to me now, Sue Rigger," he said in a low voice, his face dangerously close to her own. "You're playing with fire."

"Playing?" challenged Sue, her back flat against the cool wood of the bedroom door. "That's my point exactly. This isn't a game. Max is my son, and I don't want him used—"

"Be careful—" threatened Blackjack, pressing closer.

Sue swallowed nervously. For the first time, she noticed there was a danger in his sharp blue eyes—anger and something else, a kind of heat. Sexual heat, she realized. *Oh, God,* she thought. *I shouldn't have come here.*

"I just want you to understand, to—to accept how I feel, as Max's mother," she went on, her fingers groping behind her for a reassuring grip on the doorknob.

"That's not what you were going to say," returned Blackjack. "You were going to say something about not wanting him *used.*"

Sue's brown stare became focused, and she took a deep, fortifying breath. "You want the truth?" she asked defiantly.

"If you can manage it."

Anger flared inside her, and her fingers forgot all about their death grip on the doorknob. "Oh, I can manage it fine, Colonel. The truth is, I don't want *you* using my son—"

A sharp burst of cynical laughter came from Blackjack's throat. "You don't want *me* using Max? Is that right?" he asked.

"That's right."

"And what about *you?* Is it okay for *you* to use him?"

"What—"

"You're using him, Rigger. To get back at me."

"That's the lowest thing you've ever said—"

"Oh, really? You think there's not a *speck* of truth in that, huh?"

Sue swallowed, measuring the man so close to her. "I need you to understand. I'm thinking of Max's welfare. I don't want him hurt or confused."

"Neither do I."

"Then, please, don't interfere. Leave us alone. Pretend that you never learned about him."

Blackjack just shook his head. "Sue...can't you put yourself in my place? Even for a second? He's my flesh and blood. I can't turn my back on my own son...can't you see that? I at least deserve a chance with him."

He paused a moment, his voice growing calmer. "And what's even more important...is that Max deserves a chance...to get to know his own father."

Sue felt frustrated and unsteady. This wasn't going the way she'd hoped. She thought she would be able to persuade him to forget Max. But instead, he was persuading her to rethink her own argument. "I don't know."

"There...you see," he said. The words sounded accusing but the voice was not; it was surprisingly soft, almost...tender. "Maybe you don't know, Sue. Not everything."

Blackjack studied her a long moment, then it seemed that an idea occurred to him. Slowly his powerful left arm rose, his hand leaning heavily against the door, partially trapping her.

She shifted uneasily, tried to step away, but Blackjack moved his half-naked body even closer, his other arm coming up to entrap her completely.

"What are you doing?" she whispered.

"Testing a theory," he challenged.

"Come on, Blackjack, step back—"

"Why?"

"Because..." Sue's breathing became labored as her senses were caught up in his nearness. She noticed his fresh, clean skin and the precarious angle of the towel; all of a sudden she was very aware of the silky sheerness of her nightgown against her naked breasts.

Closing her wide brown eyes a moment, she tried to steel herself against her own body's reactions to this man standing so close to her.

"Last week, on the tarmac, you said we were 'through, done...over,'" said Blackjack, his voice low. "But if that's true, then why does being so close to me bother you so much?"

"It doesn't," Sue lied.

His eyebrows rose. "Then why are you breathing so hard? And why is your face flushed?" he whispered, the backs of his fingers moving to lightly brush her cheek. "And why do you shiver when I touch you?"

"I don't know, Blackjack, maybe you just see what you want to see."

"Maybe...but then so do *you*."

"What do you mean?"

"I mean you've brought up the past a lot to me, Sue. I'm beginning to think it's all you can see."

"That's not—"

"It is true. You refuse to consider that maybe I've changed in the last six years. That maybe I'm ready to do what it takes to be a father, a *good* father, to a boy like Max—"

"*Maybe* isn't good enough."

"*Maybe* you don't want to see that I'm willing to give this my best shot. I'm willing to try. And *maybe* you don't want to admit that you and I...we're not over."

For a long moment, Sue considered his words. She didn't move away when his hands found the back of her neck, his thumbs feeling all too familiar in their gentle massaging of her chronically tense muscles there.

Her wide brown eyes met his intense blue stare, and she wondered, down deep in her heart, if he was right. There was evidence, she knew, that he had changed over the years. She herself certainly had.

But something had never changed in all these years. The chemistry between them.

You're crazy, a voice inside her declared. But deep down Sue wondered if *maybe* she wasn't quite finished with taking chances in her life.

Blackjack seemed to sense the struggle within the woman so close to him, and he seemed prepared to sway her with more than words. His fingers moved to brush back the silk of her blond hair. Then his hand dropped between them to finger the lacy edge of her nightgown. His knuckles brushed lightly over the tender skin at her cleavage, and another shiver of excitement slipped over her skin.

His every movement was deliberate and slow—achingly slow. His steady gaze never left her face, as if he wanted to read every change in her expression with his every move.

"And maybe," he whispered, his lips nearly brushing hers, "if I haven't yet scared you away, then you and I should try to find a way to... connect."

Then his mouth came for hers, his lips soft as they moved against her own.

Sue's arms began to raise unconsciously, her body all too aware of the broad, naked chest only inches from the thin silk of her sheer nightgown, the strong hand pulling her closer. And all she could think for a moment was how dangerous it was for her that she needed this kiss—this connection—because she needed it far too much.

Suddenly a loud rapping sounded on the door behind Sue's ear. It startled them both, and they broke apart as a male voice called out, "Hey, Rodger, are you coming to the O.C.?"

Someone was inviting him to the Officers' Club, she realized, her head still reeling from the kiss.

"Ah...no, thanks, Tom," shouted Blackjack through the door, his voice slightly breathless, his blue gaze studying Sue. "I'm...ah...calling it a night."

"Roger, Rodger," joked the voice. "See you later." Then came the receding sound of footsteps down the hall.

Sue was still slightly stunned as she stepped quickly away from him; her legs felt weak and she wanted to sit down. Unfortunately the only chair in the room was holding a pile of technical manuals. And the only other place to sit was the bed—*not* a good idea in her present, thoroughly aroused state.

"Retreating, Captain?" asked Blackjack, his hands on his hips. He moved his powerful body toward her, forcing her to take a step farther into the bedroom. "Why?" he challenged as he took another step.

"I...don't know," Sue murmured as she backed away from him. Suddenly she felt something at her knees—the edge of the double bed. *Dammit.*

Blackjack was closing in. His hands reached for her sweater, and he pulled it quickly down her arms, then threw it on the bed.

Beneath her sheer nightgown, the rise and fall of her full breasts were even more revealed to him. By the hungry look in his blue eyes, she knew he hadn't missed the clear outline of her naked breasts visibly pressing against the thin white silk.

"I want to see you," he said, his voice slightly gravelly. Slowly his hands went to the lacy straps of her nightgown and began to pull them from her shoulders, but Sue stopped him. She revolved away, her hands flying to hold up the falling bodice of her nightgown.

"No, Blackjack. This is not why I came here," she whispered, struggling to regain her logical senses as she fixed the straps back onto her shoulders.

"Does that matter?" he whispered. "You're here now."

The loud sound of a jet engine came from the nearby airfield. Sue waited until its roar died down.

"Everything matters," she said gently, turning back toward him. She took his face in her hands. "Now more than ever." Then she softly kissed him, and, with a great effort, she stepped away from the pilot.

Grabbing her sweater off the bed, Sue headed for the door. "I'll see you in the morning" was all she could manage to say before leaving him behind.

Chapter Eleven

Waking up alone in an empty bed didn't cheer Blackjack.

He slammed around his quarters for an hour, showering, shaving, then dressing in faded jeans and a dark blue flannel shirt that set off the electric blue of his eyes.

Many of the base personnel had been granted a three-day weekend, and Blackjack was one of them. He swore to make the most of it with his son, regardless of the boy's unpredictable mother. He'd tried to make his feelings about Max clear last night, but he still wasn't sure how Sue felt. He couldn't guess what she'd do when he showed up on her doorstep this morning.

The uncertainty put him in a generally foul mood.

Cursing silently, he picked up his duffel, grabbed his leather jacket and stalked down the hall of the BOQ.

His emotions continued to simmer as he loaded his Range Rover. But as he devoured coffee and eggs at the base cafeteria, he felt his temper subsiding somewhat. Though calm had descended as he pulled up to the Riggers' temporary base housing, he decided to stay frosty toward Sue for his own good.

Unconsciously he held his breath before knocking on the screen door. He figured his chances were maybe fifty-fifty that Sue would actually *let* him take Max for the weekend.

Though he'd convinced Will he'd stop at nothing to take Max away, Blackjack knew it had been a bluff. There was no way he would risk tearing the child's heart apart by starting a screaming match with his mother. If Sue stopped him today, he'd just have to find another way to be a part of his son's life.

His light rapping was answered almost immediately by a small black-haired, blue-eyed replica of himself.

"Blackjack's here!" the little boy shouted up the staircase behind him. "Come on in," he said, pushing the screen door out.

"How's it goin', Mighty Max?"

"Great! I'm all packed and everything."

As Blackjack stepped inside the door, he looked beyond the boy for evidence. Sure enough, a small brown suitcase sat by the stairs, a tiny red backpack beside it. Blackjack sighed in relief.

"Mom's coming, too!" exclaimed Max.

"Is she?" he asked, the tension immediately stiffening Blackjack's body as a more significant question pricked him: *why* was she coming? Simply to keep a watchful eye on Max? Or to give her and Blackjack a chance?

"Hey, there," called a female voice behind him.

He turned to see a woman standing on the front porch. Behind the screen door, Jane Cortez pushed some of her loose brown curls behind an ear as she smiled a hello.

"Hi, there, Curly," said Blackjack, turning to open the screen door. "What's up?"

"Don't you mean *who's* up? I hope Will is," she said, eyeing her watch as she brushed past Blackjack. "We were supposed to be on the road by now, but last night ran a little late."

"Late night?" queried Blackjack, a curious dark eyebrow rising. "Well, well, is my old buddy making some moves?"

"Max! Hello, there," said Jane, pointedly ignoring Blackjack's prying question.

"Hi," said the boy with a flirtatious grin. "Are you coming with me, too?"

"Nope," called a masculine voice from the stairs. "Sorry, Max, but I saw her first. And we're heading south." Will nodded a hello to Blackjack as he descended the staircase.

"Hey, Will. Going to Vegas for the long weekend?"

"No," said Will, setting his large duffel beside Max's bags. "I thought something a little quieter would be...better."

Jane spoke up. "I know this beautiful spot on Lake Mead. And believe it or not, Will has *never* seen the canyon."

"For shame, old buddy," said Blackjack.

"What canyon?" asked little Max.

Blackjack hunkered down to Max, not missing the fleeting kiss between Will and Jane. It was the kind of sweet kiss given in front of company, the kind that came with significant eye contact. Instinctively he knew another kiss would come in private, one that would burn everything around them to ashes.

Just like Sue and me were once. Blackjack sighed, wondering what the odds really were on things ever being that good between them again.

"The *Grand* Canyon," said Blackjack, answering Max's question. "You haven't heard about one of the world's great wonders?"

"Oh, the *Grand* Canyon," said the little boy. "Of course I know about *that*. It's a whole *mile* deep, you know."

"I do," said Blackjack, tousling the boy's hair. "But thanks just the same—good pilots always like to check their info."

"I haven't really *seen* it or anything," cautioned Max. "'Cept in a book."

"Well, I'm sure I can remedy that one of these weekends. My biplane can make that trip in a few hours. And there's nothing like seeing the Grand Canyon from the sky, right, Jane?"

"You bet," said Jane.

"We'll see about that, Max!" called a voice from the stairs.

"Aw, Mom!"

Blackjack looked up to find Sue adding her own suitcase to the pile at the foot of the stairs. He found himself holding his breath with the sight of her. His heart was beating faster, and a slight cold sweat broke out at the back of his neck.

She looked wonderful. Brown boots peeked out from beneath those long, slender legs clad in tight blue jeans. A simple yellow T-shirt set off the light golden of her shining hair, softly framing the delicate features of her pretty face.

He slowly rose to his full height and reminded himself to remain frosty until he knew the score. "Good morning, Sue," he said without a smile, his voice low and steady.

"Good morning, Rodger."

Blackjack's eyebrows rose at her use of his real name. Was it a message? If it was, he wasn't sure what it meant. An awkward silence descended for a few moments.

"Well," said Will, breaking the silence, "I'd say we're burning daylight, but it's pretty obvious we're all late getting on the road." He shouldered his duffel with his good arm.

In another ten minutes, Will and Jane were waving good-bye and speeding toward the security gate and the long desert road that would lead them off the secret Flatlands Base.

"I guess we better hit the road, too." At Blackjack's words, an excited Max grabbed his backpack and ran for the Range Rover.

Sue nodded as she turned for her bag. "I hope it's okay that I'm coming," she said carefully.

Blackjack didn't look at her. He simply placed his sunglasses on his nose. "Sure," he said coolly, "we've got room."

Then, without glancing at her, he grabbed Max's bag, took Sue's from her hand and headed out the door.

Warily she followed, locking the door behind her.

BLACKJACK HAD never enjoyed a meal at a fast-food restaurant so much in his life.

For about sixty minutes after they'd left the base's gated perimeter, the three of them had been driving along the quiet emptiness of a long desert highway. Blackjack and Sue hadn't spoken much.

Max's chattering had kept them occupied for a while. Then the road's monotony and the warm spring air had lulled the boy into a light nap, and silence had become a more comfortable alternative for the couple than the few awkward attempts at conversation. Nothing, it seemed, was going to bridge the frosty tension between them.

Finally Blackjack mentioned stopping for a break and Max awakened. No sooner had the Range Rover pulled into the small town of Tonopah, population about 3,600, than Max spotted a favorite hamburger joint across from the ten-year-old Station House hotel-casino.

"Strange that the golden arches is the first thing you see in an old silver boomtown," remarked Blackjack.

Sue laughed despite her wary silence all morning. She explained that her concerns over Max's nutrition made fast food a rarity for the boy. "So of course he's desperate to get it."

"Well, Max, it's your lucky day," said Blackjack, parking the car in the busy lot.

An odd feeling came over him as he pulled open the glass door for Sue and Max, then joked with them both as they placed their lunch orders. It was a feeling he couldn't quite identify.

Sue and Max grabbed a booth near a window, and Blackjack brought over their tray of food. Barely touching his own lunch, he instead became caught up with the mother and son sitting across from him. Max bit into his cheeseburger, then dipped a french fry into a messy puddle of ketchup.

"Mmm. This is *good!*"

Sue bit her own burger. "I just wish it were good for you."

"Aw, you always say that, Mom," said Max, still chewing.

"Don't talk with your mouth full," scolded Sue.

"Hey, Max," said Blackjack with a wink, "just remember, what's good for your body isn't always what's best for your soul."

"Bazooka Joe?" asked Sue, a teasing look in her eye.

"And what if it is?"

Surprisingly Sue didn't argue with him. She just smiled and took a satisfying sip of her vanilla shake.

An odd feeling again surged through him, and he tried to put his finger on it. He was aware of the families sitting around him, parents feeding chattering kids of all ages. That's when it hit him: *This is what it feels like to be a father. To be a husband.*

Right here, right in front of him, was the chance for Blackjack to finally have his own family. It was a powerful realization for him—and far from an unpleasant one.

A smile touched his lips.

It stayed on his face as he raced Max to the front door of the Rover. And it remained well after he turned the car out of the parking lot and back onto U.S. 95.

FROM THEN ON, they were acting like a family. Old songs, driving games and stupid jokes did much to occupy the two adults and child sitting between them on the front seat.

All three admired the colorful beauty of the Monte Cristo Range. The treeless slopes of the mountains were made from layers of volcanic ash and lava. Pastel purples, browns, yellows and fiery pinks glistened gloriously in the bright midday sun.

As they drove, Blackjack entertained Sue and Max with stories of old Nevada—from the dangers of the pony express to the tales of old gold- and silver-mining towns.

Blackjack couldn't recall when he'd felt this happy. For a fleeting moment, he saw himself at Max's age, roughhousing with his older brother, Whitman, in the back of their parents' station wagon. James Whitman McConnell, Jr., was always pushing the limits with their strict father, and a young Rodger learned quickly from it.

Rodger pushed the limits, too, but he'd figured out how to pull back just in time—and use his charm to circumvent punishment. His hardheaded brother had never learned the art of such strategy, and he suffered many a lickin' for it.

As the memories came back to Blackjack, so did that same cold emptiness in his gut. He still had Whit's worn Air Force cap. His brother had slapped it onto his young head before leaving for duty for the last time. Whit had pushed the limits much too far once too often—and he hadn't made it back.

"Are we almost there?" whispered Sue.

Max had dozed off again, his small dark head cuddling up to his mother's side. Blackjack glanced at them and felt his insides warm considerably—thoughts of his brother faded. He smiled, adjusting his sunglasses. "Just about there now."

They'd already made a stop for groceries at Walker Lake—a glistening oasis of deep blue. It was quite a change after miles of dusty beige basins and gray rock ranges. After their stop, their drive took them past alfalfa farms and into the lush green of irrigated grasslands.

They turned off the main road for about twenty minutes until they reached a gate marked Flying M Ranch. After venturing through, they drove a quarter mile down a long gravel drive and soon came within sight of two structures.

"Over there's the ranch house," said Blackjack, pointing.

"What's that other building?"

He smiled. "The barn—but I turned it into a sort of workshop and hangar."

Sue's eyebrow rose. "Your biplane?"

Blackjack nodded with pride. "Wait till you see her."

She bit her lip, saying nothing, and he guessed she was already worrying about Max's safety. Obviously, giving Max a taste of challenge and adventure was going to be a battle for Blackjack. But it was one he meant to win.

BALANCING A SACK of groceries and a small white box, Sue used her foot to slam shut the Rover's door. She took in a deep breath of fresh, clean air. The irrigation and green of this area lent a moisture to the atmosphere—quite a change from the dryness of the Flatlands's desert surroundings.

She watched little Max skipping beside Blackjack, trying to help him carry the rest of the grocery sacks up to the ranch house. "They look so much alike," she whispered, liking the vision of this father and son together more than ever before.

With a great deal of faith, she had purchased what was inside the little white box in her hand. If things went well, she didn't doubt she'd be wearing what was inside for the man now striding into the big ranch house. Now more than ever, Sue needed things to go well.

"Come on, Mom!" shouted Max

Sue followed the two up to the large, two-story ranch house. She admired the wide wraparound porch, the dark red of the wood frame and the gray-stoned chimneys at either end of the building.

"Blackjack," she said, stepping onto the polished wood floor of the tall entryway. "It's gorgeous, but how could you possibly—"

"Take care of it? Or afford it?"

Sue nodded. "Are you kidding? Both questions are in order, I'd say. Nobody's gotten rich off a career in the service—"

Her neck craned to the right, curiously gawking at the large living room, dominated by a gray-stoned fireplace and a brightly colored Native American area rug.

"I'll get to that later," said Blackjack. "For now, how about we settle you two in."

Sue followed Blackjack up the stairs, admiring the desert colors in the house's design scheme. Brownish reds, deep mauves and fiery pinks, along with lots of exposed stone, carved woods and well-placed skylights, made the place feel warm and welcoming. He dropped her bag in a large, cozy room at one end of the hall.

The cream walls were a perfect backdrop to a gorgeous landscape painting showing off the purples and reds of a spectacular desert sunset. Ivory curtains hung at the large window, a bentwood rocker sat in the corner and a double bed covered with a thick goose-down quilt looked comfortably inviting to her tired body. But first she wanted to see where Max was settling in.

She followed man and boy into the room beside hers. It was about the same size, but it held carved wooden bunk beds—to Max's squealing delight. Sky blue walls, blond wood shutters and colorful patch quilts gave the room a cheery feel, and Sue noticed one wall was covered with framed posters of airplanes. Clouds were painted on the ceiling, and model planes were lined up in a side case that also held school trophies.

"My bother and I once shared this room," said Blackjack, watching Max dive for the lower bunk, then scramble up the ladder for the higher one.

Sue's mind caught a moment on the words *my brother*. She looked around the room and felt a sad emptiness, despite the cheerful decor. She remembered the emotion in his voice a few weeks back when he'd mentioned Whitman McConnell. And she wondered how the young Rodger had coped with his loss; she pictured a little boy, looking much like her Max, sitting alone in his room and feeling sad and confused and missing his brother.

"This is great!" exclaimed Max.

Sue's gaze came back to the present. She focused on her excited son, perched on the top mattress of the bunk beds, and she immediately began worrying about the height.

"Can I sleep up here?" asked Max.

"Sure," answered Blackjack, overlapping Sue's "No way!"

A pause came after Blackjack and Sue spoke together. A terrible, long silence. Each eyed the other with a stubborn sense of righteous authority.

"Well, can I or not?" asked Max.

"It'll be fine," said Blackjack, his voice trying to cajole her.

"I don't know," said Sue, though she really did. The top bunk was *much* too high.

"Come on," said Blackjack, grabbing Sue's hand.

"What," she blurted as she felt herself being guided into the hallway. "Where are we going?"

"To talk," he stated evenly before calling back into the bedroom. "Max, just take a load off a few minutes. There are airplane model sets in the closet—why don't you pick out one for us to work on."

"Oh, boy!"

Sue found herself being guided down the stairs and through the ground-floor hallway. When they reached the large, sunny—and spotless—kitchen of the house, he released her, sauntered over to the refrigerator and pulled it open.

"Iced tea or cold water?"

"Tea is fine," she snapped, her agitation showing as she crossed her arms over her chest.

Blackjack eyed her pointedly as he slowly unbuttoned the cuffs of his dark blue flannel shirt and rolled the sleeves to his elbows. She became even more annoyed when she found herself admiring the masculine strength of those forearms and the attractive deep blue of his eyes, now crackling with anger like a cold blue lake reflecting sparks of jagged lightning.

She watched in silence as he reached up to the cupboard, bringing down two tall glasses and filling them both with tea.

"Sit down."

Sue let her brown eyes glare at him a long moment, just so he knew she didn't like being ordered around. Then she uncrossed her arms and sat at the large butcher-block-style table.

"I think we should establish some ground rules for this weekend ahead of us," Blackjack began.

Sue took a long drink. She supposed he was right, yet it galled her to give up any ground when it came to Max.

"Rodger—" she began, then hesitated, trying to cool her flaring temper. "You have to understand. I'm Max's mother. I'm responsible for him, and you have to respect my wishes when it comes to his safety."

Blackjack seemed to be ready for her words. "Sue, this talk between us is long overdue, and it's not going to be our last, you can be sure. But for now, let's take a small step, okay?"

"I don't know what you mean."

"Yes, you do. You're Max's mother, but I'm his father. And though I haven't been there for him before..." He paused a moment as if trying to control his emotions. "I'm around *now*. And I want you to start getting used to the idea of my being in his life. That's going to mean understanding something basic—that Max has a part of me inside him, just as he has a part of you."

Sue swallowed some more iced tea. Her hand was shaking slightly when she lowered the glass. "I know," she said, her voice barely there.

"So," he said, his tone a bit softer, "let me help you with him. Let me bring out the part of me that's inside of him. It's the only way to be fair—not to me, but to Max."

She had never thought of it quite that way before. Now that she did, something within her seemed to move aside a step. She didn't trust her voice, so she simply met his gaze with her own, then nodded her agreement.

Blackjack visibly relaxed at her nod. "Thanks."

Sue was surprised he'd thanked her. But she was also more than surprised—even stunned—at the depth of thought Rodger McConnell had obviously put toward his son.

It wasn't what she'd expected. "You're welcome," she whispered.

"Top bunk?" he asked.

"Okay," said Sue, worry still evident in her voice.

"I'll put up a safety board—how about that?"

A relieved sigh escaped her lips. She smiled up at Blackjack. He returned the smile, and she noticed his hard blue stare had softened considerably as he gazed at her. The changes meant more to Sue than she cared to admit.

WITHIN THE NEXT half hour, Sue helped Blackjack put away the groceries, then went to her room to unpack. When she heard Max and Blackjack talking in the next room, she walked to her son's door.

"Here it is," said Max, presenting Blackjack with an airplane-model box. "I picked one out like you said."

She noticed Max had barely unpacked his own bag.

"Hmm. An F-16 Falcon, huh?" asked Blackjack with a smile—it was the same type of plane that Max had seen Blackjack fly. "You sure don't mess around, do you? You go right for the best."

Just like his father, thought Sue.

"Can we put it together now?" asked Max.

"Yes," said Blackjack, "we can. Go on downstairs."

Max took off so fast, he nearly knocked Sue over as he rushed by. "Oh, hi, Mom—"

She watched his little body flying toward the stairs. "Max! Slow down! Be careful on those stairs."

She was so intent on watching her son, she nearly jumped through the ceiling when she felt a warm, strong hand curling around her waist.

"Say, *Mom*," teased Blackjack, his body close to her own, "do you want to help us glue our model together—or should we call you when it's ready for a good coat of paint?"

Blackjack's blue eyes were shining with mirth, his dimples creasing the edges of his smiling mouth.

"Sorry, Colonel, you two are on your own. After that dusty ride, I'm taking a long, hot bath."

"Mmm...good idea," he whispered in a low voice at her ear. "Need help?"

"I'll let you know."

"Blackjack! Are you comin'?" came the little voice from the bottom of the stairs.

"Uh...duty calls," said Blackjack, stepping away from her. Then he turned to brush her lips, promising, "We'll finish this *later*."

An excited heat coursed through Sue's body at his words.

"On my way, Mighty Max, superpilot!" Blackjack shouted as he flew down the stairs.

Sue's eyebrows rose as she watched the father take the steps exactly the same as his son. Then she turned toward her bedroom.

As she stripped off her dusty clothes, she eyed the white box on the bed. At their last stop along Walker Lake, Sue had ducked into a little gift shop while Blackjack and Max were filling the Rover with gasoline. She'd bought a sinfully silky garment along with some expensive bath oil.

She grabbed the small bottle of oil from the box, then wrapped her thick terry-cloth robe around her naked body

and padded down the hall. In the large second-floor bathroom, she filled the big claw-footed tub and gently poured
in some of the fragrant oil.

Dropping her robe, she sighed with a pleasure she seldom took time for as she sunk into the hot bath. The rose-
scented water smelled wonderful, and her skin luxuriated in
the moisture-rich indulgence.

"Maybe it's time to indulge yourself a little," she whispered to herself, thinking of the silky lingerie and Blackjack's promise of taking things up between them *later.*

And maybe, another, more wary voice cautioned, *you'd
better just wait and see.*

Chapter Twelve

As early evening came around, the three sat down to a wonderful steak dinner. Sue couldn't praise father and son enough for their hard work on the fully built plastic model of an F-16.

After the meal, the three cleared and cleaned dishes as a family, then stretched out in the large living room. The sun had already descended, bringing with it the cool of evening.

"Hey, does this thing work?" asked Max, staring curiously up the chimney of the large gray-stoned fireplace.

Sue smiled at Blackjack. "A fire might be nice at that."

In no time, with Max's help, Blackjack had red-orange flames crackling cozily around two fresh logs, and Sue had cut them each a slice of a locally baked blueberry pie.

"Blackjack, tell us more stories," urged Max as he finished his pie, then settled down on the rug by the hearth. "About your family."

At dinner, he had begun telling Sue and Max about the tradition in his family—from his father's and two uncles' World War II service as Army Air Corps and naval pilots to his older cousin Janice, who'd just gotten word from NASA that she'd made the cut for the space-shuttle program.

"Well, I could tell you about Granddaddy McConnell," offered Blackjack as he reached for the serving thermos on the side table and refilled Sue's and his cups with hot coffee.

Max nodded enthusiastically. "Was he a pilot, too?"

"Yes. He was a barnstormer. Back in Pennsylvania."

"Does that mean he crashed into barns?"

"Uh...that wasn't the plan, Mighty Max, although with those old Jennys, you never knew—"

Sue laughed. "They were stunt pilots, Max, and they usually flew in rural districts—around farms. And farms have barns."

"One of their tricks was to fly right through the barn—in one door and out the other," explained Blackjack. "That's how they got their name."

"Really?"

"Do you want to see a picture?" asked Blackjack.

"Sure," said mother and son together.

"Well, crew, follow me."

Sue trailed Blackjack and Max into a combination den and library at the back of the house.

A large desk dominated the far end of the room, and a leather couch and chair sat in the center. Hardcover books were packed into built-in shelves that covered an entire wall. And when Blackjack stepped into the darkened room and flicked on a stand-up lamp, she nearly gasped. Every other inch of wall space was covered with framed photographs.

"These are—"

"Planes!" shouted Max.

"Oh, but not just any planes. Almost all of these are planes the members of my family flew. See, here," he said, picking up Max and lifting him behind his head and onto his shoulders, "this is my cousin Conlan in front of his F-18 Hornet—see, he's stationed on an aircraft carrier. And this is my father, James, with his World War II squadron. See the P-51 Mustangs lined up behind them?''

"Is that what he flew?" asked Max.

"Sure is."

"England?" asked Sue, examining the over-fifty-year-old black-and-white photo.

"Yes," answered Blackjack.

Her gaze wandered to the next photo, and her eyebrows rose. It was a close-up of a valiant-looking James McConnell in front of his Army Air Corps plane. His dimples were flashing as he smiled, his aviator's jacket was zipped up and his white scarf was tied gallantly around his neck, its ends fluttering in the breeze.

Sue could see how much Blackjack resembled his own father—and she knew at once what Max would look like in fifteen or so years. It sent a strange feeling through her.

She looked closer at the plane's nose. "The...*Clansman,*" she read, noting the distinctive picture painted on the nose.

Blackjack nodded. "That's what he named his Mustang. The nose art is a Scottish sword called a claymore."

Max leaned forward on Blackjack's shoulders. "Why did he have a sword painted on his plane?"

"Is it because of the McConnell name—your Scottish ancestry?" Sue guessed.

"Partly," said Blackjack. "But my father used to say it reminded him of the truth about piloting a fighter aircraft."

"The truth?" asked Sue.

"It's like always balancing on the edge of a sword, between disaster and triumph." Blackjack reached out to run a finger along the blade in the picture. "And these days that difference can come in a split second." He glanced at Sue.

"I always think of that sword when I climb into a cockpit."

She nodded, understanding. "He passed on recently?"

"Three years ago now," said Blackjack. "But he gave me a lot of good advice in his lifetime—he was an ace in his day."

"Easily," said Sue, counting the sixteen crosses painted on the Mustang that marked the number of enemy planes James McConnell had shot down.

"And in my father's case, he lived to tell about it," said Blackjack. "A lot of men didn't. But it's a good thing he did, Max, or else I wouldn't be here—and neither would you, son."

She gasped at Blackjack's words.

"What do you mean?" Max asked Blackjack. "I wouldn't be here?"

"Max," Sue quickly jumped in, "Blackjack just meant that the soldiers who fought helped keep everyone back home safe."

"Oh," said her son, looking confused.

Sue caught Blackjack's penetrating glare. She knew what he wanted. He wanted to explain the truth to Max—that *he* was Max's father, and that James McConnell had been his grandfather. But Sue felt it was too soon for the boy. Now wasn't the time.

She silently shook her head, her own glare thankfully getting the message across. Blackjack held his tongue, but she could see his jaw working in agitation.

"What about your granddaddy?" queried Max. "Is he here?"

"Ah…let's see," said Blackjack, moving down the wall. "Look up here. See the photo of the biplane—that means there are two sets of wings, one on top of the other—"

"I know that!" said Max.

"Good. Now, do you see this young man on the right? That's Granddaddy McConnell. And do you see that other fellow with the big, stinky cigar in his mouth—"

"Yes."

"That's the man I'm named after. Cal Braigh Rodgers. He was my granddaddy's good friend—and brother-in-law since Granddaddy married Cal's sister. Cal Rodgers was the first man ever to fly across the United States."

"Geez. Ever, ever?"

"Yep. Ever, ever."

Sue was again beside him. "When was this taken?"

"In 1911, somewhere around Pittsburgh," said Blackjack. "That's where granddaddy used to barnstorm."

He pointed to another picture. This one showed a daring barnstormer stunt. One man was flying an old Curtis JN-4 Jenny biplane about fifteen feet off the ground while another man hung upside down, his knees curled around the landing gear. The hanging man was reaching out to grab the hat off the head of a man standing on the ground.

"Looks like they were real daredevils," commented Sue.

"Yep." Blackjack threw her a pointed look. "Runs in the family."

"What's this say?" asked Max, his little finger pointing to the writing across a photo of Cal Rodgers in front of his biplane.

"Says To Mighty Mac, My Friend In Flight, and it's signed by Cal."

"Mighty Mac?" asked Max.

"That's what they called granddaddy," said Blackjack.

"That's just like *my* name, Mighty Max!" the boy exclaimed in delight.

"Sure is...." Blackjack's blue gaze met Sue's surprised brown eyes, and a terrible pause followed.

Sue knew what he wanted. But she wouldn't give in. She wasn't ready to tell Max. She tore her gaze away, trying to find a distraction.

"What about this photo?" she asked, pointing at random, then regretting her choice the moment she saw Blackjack's face.

He looked at the photo a long moment; pain was immediately evident in his features, and he didn't speak right away. Eventually, with a subdued voice, he said, "That's my brother, Whitman, in front of his Thud. Ah, Max, that's an older type of jet bomber called a Thunderchief. He flew it during Vietnam."

And died in combat, Sue knew, but Blackjack said nothing of this.

For the first time, she noticed the dust in the room—on the photo frames and the side tables. It was far from the spotless state of the rest of the house, and she realized on a heavy wave of sadness what this room really was: a shrine.

"What about you, Blackjack?" asked Max in the midst of the dark silence.

"Me?"

"Uncle Will says he flew with you. He showed me a picture of you guys in front of his plane."

Blackjack smiled weakly. "Well, then, you've seen me already. You don't need to see me again."

"Yes," said Sue in a firm, clear voice. "He does."

Blackjack's startled gaze met Sue's eyes. But she tore away and quickly searched the photos herself.

"Here he is, Max," she said, pointing at a color photo near the door. "He's standing in front of his F-15E from Seymour Johnson Air Force Base. Look, Max, you can see the SJ on the tail. Looks like this was taken during Desert Storm."

"Did you win any medals?" asked Max, still riding Blackjack's shoulders.

"Ah, yeah... Listen, I think that's enough reminiscing for one night. Why don't we—"

"Max," interrupted Sue, "Blackjack won the Bronze Star for bravery."

"Sue—"

"Can it, Colonel," she said matter-of-factly. "Now, Max, Uncle Will knows this story well, and if you ask him, he'll tell you all about it again. During Desert Storm, your uncle was shot down, and Blackjack saved his life."

Max's little blue eyes widened with awe. "Wow! What happened?"

"Tell him," said Sue.

Reluctantly Blackjack recounted how he'd been low on fuel and out of missiles. With little to defend himself, he remained, circling above the downed pilots until the extraction helicopter could get there and rescue them.

"I used the plane's machine gun," explained Blackjack, "to hold off the enemy infantrymen on the ground and an enemy plane until your uncle and his wizzo could be airlifted out."

"Wow, that's neat."

"It was also very dangerous," she said, her brown eyes searching his face. "And we're very proud of him."

Without meeting Sue's eyes, Blackjack nodded his head slightly, then turned from the wall. "Okay, Max," he said, lifting the boy from his shoulders and placing him back on the floor, "I think you've heard enough war stories for one night."

Max stood on the floor, his neck craning to look up at the tall, blue-eyed pilot. "Blackjack," said the little voice as a small hand tugged on the pilot's pant leg.

Blackjack crouched down to the five-year-old's level.

"If it's so dangerous, like Mom says...then why—" The boy hesitated, pulled at the front of his T-shirt, then wrapped the bottom edge around his small hand.

"Then why do the pilots fly?" came Sue's voice, finishing her son's question. Max nodded.

Blackjack rubbed his jaw a moment. He looked up at Sue, then back toward Max. "You know, I recall asking my granddaddy that when I was a kid—"

"What did he say?"

"He didn't say anything. It was my grandmother who answered the question. She showed me a quotation from someone she admired. I have it framed somewhere in here."

Blackjack rose from his stooped position and walked over to the large, heavy wooden desk. Sue noticed a model of the *Kitty Hawk* hanging above the desk and an antique photo of Orville and Wilbur Wright hanging on the wall near it. Blackjack walked to the photo of the Wright brothers and reached for a framed quotation hanging right next to it. He handed the frame down to Max.

Max scratched his head, looking at the framed quotation, then began to read aloud. "'You gain...strength... co-coo-rage...and con-fi—'" He stopped. "I can read," he announced proudly. "But this is...kinda hard," he admitted.

Sue immediately crouched by her son to help.

"'You gain strength, courage, and confidence by every experience in which you really stop to look fear in the face.... You must do the thing you think you cannot do,'" read Sue, noting the words were attributed to Eleanor Roosevelt.

She looked up. Blackjack's hooded blue gaze was fixed on her.

"Grandma always knew what was in granddaddy's heart," he said, his voice not quite there. "She…understood him."

"She loved him," concluded Sue.

Blackjack nodded his head.

She rose, carefully handing the framed quotation back to Blackjack. When their fingers touched briefly, she felt him holding the contact a moment longer than necessary.

Then, suddenly Max pulled at his pant leg again. "Are we done in here now?"

Blackjack smiled. "Yep. Let's go check to see if the fire needs another log."

"Okay!" said Max, racing out.

Blackjack walked to the door, then turned back a moment before leaving the room. No words were said. He simply held Sue's gaze a long moment before turning again and striding away.

She moved to follow Blackjack but paused at the door with a new realization. This room was more than a shrine. Much more. This room held a *legacy*. And whether she liked the idea or not, Max was a part of that legacy.

Flicking off the lights, she glanced back one more time at the darkened photos. She decided that she did like the idea very much.

"GOOD NIGHT, HONEY." Sue kissed Max on the forehead and pulled the covers up around him. He was cozy and happy as a clam in his top bunk. Sue had to pull a chair over to stand on, just to kiss her son good-night.

"'Night, Mom," said the boy, then just before she stepped down, he called her back. "Mom?"

"Yes, honey?"

"Blackjack's really nice, isn't he?"

"Yes, honey. Now, get some sleep."

"Do you think so, too—that he's nice?"

"Yes, sweetheart. I think so, too."

"Good."

Sue switched on the small plane-shaped night-light as she left, then flicked off the lamp. She moved to leave the room, but stopped at the half-open door, turning to look again at her son. She couldn't help scrutinizing—for the tenth time—the height of the top bunk from the floor. She started slightly at the touch of a hand on her shoulder.

"He'll be fine," a low voice whispered behind her.

Sue bit her lip. "Mother's prerogative to worry."

She felt warm, callused fingers massaging her tense shoulder muscles. "Father's prerogative to distract the mother."

Sue smiled, shaking her head as she closed the door to Max's room. "You got that right, Blackjack. You've always been a distraction for me."

She revolved to find him smiling down at her, his dimples flashing, his blue gaze smoldering as he studied her face with heated interest.

"Sue, maybe it's time that we were more than distractions for each other. And it's time for Max to know the truth."

The words caught her off guard. She found herself breaking away from Blackjack. "Ah...I'd better clean those pie plates."

Sue descended the stairs and entered the living room. Blackjack remained in close pursuit. He helped her pick up the plates and coffee cups, then followed her out to the kitchen. When he saw her reach for the kitchen faucet, he leaned toward her and stilled her hands.

"Leave them. We need to talk—"

"No, we—"

"Yes, we do."

Sue's heart was beating fast as she felt him take her hand in his, interlacing their fingers. He led her back to the living room, then released her. Bending toward the fire, he stirred the ashes, then threw another piece of wood on the dying flames. Sue settled down on the thick pillows of the large couch and studied the man in front of her.

The blue flannel shirt didn't hide the breadth of his shoulders, and she found herself admiring the trim waist and hard thighs encased in worn jeans. Sue could feel her body responding to the man so near. She could feel herself wanting him again, and tonight she did not feel the need to fight it.

He rose and turned toward her, one hand leaning against the mantel. "First off, I owe you an apology."

Sue's eyebrows rose. "Apology?"

"I should never have questioned your flying abilities before the air-to-air tactics last week. I was wrong, and I'm sorry."

"No harm done. You were angry—I understood."

Blackjack nodded. "I also want to thank you—for telling my son about me in there."

"He deserves to know—" began Sue.

But Blackjack cut her off. "What he deserves to know is *everything*."

"Yes," agreed Sue. "You're right." She let a long silence fill the room, then she tried to explain her conflicting feelings. "I don't know if Will ever mentioned this," she began, "but he and I were adopted."

Blackjack's surprised gaze shot up to meet Sue's eyes. He shook his head; he hadn't known.

"I love my adoptive parents," she said quickly, "very much. And so does Max. But what you showed me in there...the family history...it was...overwhelming for me. I hadn't considered it before—for Max, I mean."

Blackjack sat down next to Sue and let his arm rest along the back of the couch, behind her head. The warmth of his nearness seemed to surround her like the hot bath water she'd enjoyed earlier in the day.

"Sue," began Blackjack carefully, his voice low and gentle, "I want to tell Max that I'm his father."

"But is right now the time? I know he likes you, that's very clear. And very good. It's just that—" She was becoming distracted by the touch of his fingers as he began to caress the back of her neck.

"It's just that—what?" he asked, his heated blue gaze reminding her of the flames now leaping up around the fresh piece of wood he'd just thrown on the fire.

"It's just that...he's so young, and I guess that...I'm afraid for him."

Blackjack leaned close, his lips near her ear. "Don't be afraid, Sue. I won't let Max be hurt. I love my son. Do you understand? I love him."

She closed her eyes at the sound of his words; her heart nearly stopped. *Thank God,* she thought. She never thought Blackjack McConnell was capable of saying those words, and she knew, for Max's sake, how important it was that he did.

Sue turned to face him, her brown eyes dancing. She smiled with pure joy and long-suffering relief. "It's decided, then. Tomorrow. We'll both tell him tomorrow."

His lips were on hers in a millisecond, and her arms were around him a moment later. She reveled in the feel of his strong body holding her close, as her own limbs seemed to melt at the touch of his hands.

The kiss was long and heartfelt. His lips played hungrily upon hers, his tongue quickly skimming across them. Beneath her closed eyelids, Sue pictured last night's sight of

Blackjack's strong bare chest. She wanted to see him again like that. Tonight.

"I do want you, Blackjack," she whispered against his lips.

"Mmm," he murmured. "Now, what kind of host would I be, not to give my guest anything she wants?"

"Anything?" she teased. She felt his fingers tangling in her soft blond hair. Slowly he pulled her head back to expose the creamy smooth skin of her neck. Then his lips traced a hot path along her jaw, and when he got to her mouth, his hand pulled a little bit more. She didn't resist. Her head was tipped even farther back, her lips parting.

"Anything...and everything," he whispered as his mouth came down on hers again, his tongue dipping in, then out of her mouth in a suggestive promise of things to come.

Sue was mesmerized. Her head was spinning so much, she barely realized he had stood and was now pulling her to her feet. Her legs were weak as she followed him up the staircase and down the hall. As she passed her bedroom door, that little white box beckoned....

"Blackjack, I want to get out of these clothes."

Blackjack's dimples showed his amusement. "Yes, and that's what I want, too."

"No, I mean—" She caught the teasing in his eyes. "Oh, forget it. Just go on to your room—I'll be there in a minute."

Flicking on her bedroom light, Sue closed the door and pulled off her clothes. The rich red silk of the lingerie felt wonderful in her hands. She slipped it over her head and eyed herself in the dresser mirror.

Her eyebrows rose with surprise at how good she looked in it. The thin straps held up a bodice that dipped low, revealing a tantalizing glimpse of cleavage. The silk clung closely to her curving form, and the skirt ended high, showing off her long, bare legs to their advantage.

"Well, well . . . not half-bad for a boring egghead scientist," she murmured. After wrapping her bulky terry-cloth robe around her, she padded in her bare feet down the long hallway.

Sue's logical mind knew there were no guarantees against future heartbreak with Rodger, but there was one thing both her mind and heart were sure of. Rodger McConnell would be a good father to Max. He loved and wanted his son. Of that, she now was certain.

And that was enough.

Taking a deep, calming breath into her lungs, Sue rapped lightly on the master bedroom door.

Tonight Sparks Rigger was finally persuaded to take another gamble on a pilot named Blackjack.

Chapter Thirteen

Blackjack got busy at the upstairs fireplace as soon as he entered the master bedroom. By the time he heard the light rapping on the door, the kindling was dancing with red-orange flames and he was just stripping out of his blue flannel shirt.

He couldn't believe that Sue actually *knocked*, and he decided to tease her for it. Tossing his shirt aside, he opened the door and looked down at the woman in the bulky bathrobe.

A slow smile spread across his face as she tried to step by him. But he wasn't about to budge.

"What's the pass phrase?" he teased, his muscular forearms crossing over his bare chest in a show of power and strength.

"Hot, steamy sex."

Blackjack shook his head. "Nope."

Sue's brown eyes narrowed. "You know, Pentagon Intelligence warned us about guys like you—always changing the pass phrase."

"Just try again."

She smiled as she made a show of thinking hard. "Well, how about 'Anything and everything.'"

"Bingo."

Blackjack stepped back. With satisfaction, he watched Sue step forward and take in the large master bedroom. After he had inherited the place from his late father, he'd pumped a lot of money into remodeling. The master bedroom had been a major project.

At one end of the plushly carpeted room, the gray-stoned fireplace was crackling cozily with the newly lit fire. As with the rest of the house, the bedroom reflected desert colors. Floor-to-ceiling drapes framed two sliding doors that led to a second-floor balcony. An overstuffed armchair sat in the corner with a few books on the table beside it—not technical manuals but books of poetry and philosophy.

In the center of the room was a king-size bed, nestled in a four-poster frame of carved pine. The dressers and nightstands were built from the same wood.

"Rodger," she said on a breath, "it's gorgeous."

"Thanks." He moved to take her into his arms, enjoying the fresh, sweet scent of roses on her soft skin. "So are you. And you really didn't have to change into such a sexy terrycloth bathrobe just for me," he teased.

"Bandit," she said on a smile. "You'll eat those words." Then she stepped away from him, one hand indignantly on her hip, the other pointing toward the bed.

Blackjack moved backward and sat on the bed as ordered. A broad smile was now plastered on his square-jawed handsome face as he leisurely crossed his arms over his bare chest.

It seemed to him that Sue was working hard to keep a straight face as she slowly untied the robe's belt. And when she let the thick terry cloth drop away, he felt the broad smile drop from his face as a jolt of pure desire hit him.

The incredible vision revealed before him put a hot, flaring need into his loins. As his piercing blue gaze raked the silky red curves, he decided Sue had done more than change her clothes. She had turned into a seductive temptress, with hungry needs of her own clearly burning in her steady brown gaze.

"My God, Sue—"

"You like?"

It took a few moments for Blackjack to find his voice, but he did, needing it only to convey two firm words.

"Come here."

Slowly, with her hands on her hips, she walked toward him. He felt himself growing hard at the sight of that lovely face and form stepping closer and closer. When she reached the bed, he stood. His worn jeans were riding low on his hips, and he watched her gaze taking in the broad muscles of his bare chest and washboard stomach.

Her slender hand reached up, and he felt intense heat where her fingers touched. Then, suddenly he froze.

Every muscle in his body tensed as he realized that Sue's gaze was fixed on his scars.

His *scars*. Again. *Dammit*.

He hated this intrusion. Hated the reminder of his chosen career.

With other women, it had never mattered. Now, with Sue, it mattered. A great deal.

He gritted his teeth, trying yet again to block out the conflicts and the pain that came with the truth. He could block it out tonight, as he'd done before, and just try to pretend that he didn't risk his life every day.

He'd pretend that he could promise to be around for his son and for Sue. Pretend that he could keep that promise.

You're fooling yourself, Rodger.

Maybe. But that was something he'd ponder in the morning. Tonight it didn't matter. Because he'd become a master at living in the moment. And this moment, he wanted Sue Rigger in his bed.

His hand moved to cover Sue's. With gentle firmness, he took her hand from the scar on his chest and brought it low, to the button of his jeans.

Her brown gaze remained steady on his as she unbuttoned them, then brought the zipper down. In a few seconds, he was naked and clearly aroused as he pulled her onto the large feather mattress, a wonderfully luxurious bed, softer than a cloud.

He lay back, pulling her on top of him. Then he reached his hand up to the back of her head and urged her closer.

"Sweet Sue," he murmured, his lips lightly brushing hers, a hand cupping her full breast.

"Yes, Blackjack..."

He closed his blue eyes. That voice. Her voice. He could almost feel the rushing air of the sky around him, the free feeling of coasting on the wind and through the clouds.

"Take me with you," she whispered.

His hand moved beneath the hem of her red silk lingerie and traveled up between her thighs. He sighed when he found her naked and wet, thoroughly ready for him. He used his fingers to make her even more ready. She moaned, her eyes closed in ecstasy at his touch. Soon he was moaning, too, as he felt her own soft hand reaching down to caress him.

"I want to see you," he murmured, brushing at the thin straps of the silky red lingerie. Slowly the soft, creamy skin of her full breasts was revealed to his hungry eyes. "Beautiful."

He moved his mouth to taste one and then the other. Again Sue moaned, whispering, "Yes," as he lathed and teased each pink bud with his tongue and teeth.

Then, when he felt her moving her body impatiently against him, he carefully pulled her close and rolled her over. Her back was now against the soft feather bed, and he was positioned above her. It took every ounce of his control to hold back as he settled between her legs, gazing at the beautiful, sensuous creature below him.

The wanting in her eyes was nearly his undoing. *She wants me,* he realized. *She really does want me.*

"Say my name," he murmured, poised to join with her.

"Blackja—"

"No."

Sue hesitated a moment, staring into his intense blue eyes, then she smiled in understanding.

"Rodger," she whispered, and in the next moment she was crying out with joy as his strength and power thrust forward to claim her.

"Oh, yes, Rodger, yes," mewled Sue softly, feeling at last the connection she so desperately craved.

A smile formed on Blackjack's lips as he watched her enjoying him. Then he began to move and his own eyes closed, his own voice moaned in pure ecstasy. "There's nothing as sweet," he whispered hotly into her ear, "as being inside of you, Sue Rigger."

"Yes, Rodger," she said on a breath, thoroughly enjoying every sensuous stroke of his lovemaking. "Don't stop...Rodger...."

"Nothing," he whispered.

Dozens of sensations overtook him as he began to move faster inside her. Prickles of heat raced over his skin as he felt himself spiraling higher and higher, taking her into the clouds and beyond, into the very stratosphere, where every movement left them both gasping for oxygen.

Then finally she was calling his name, and the tension inside him was strained to its breaking point. Suddenly he, too, felt that spectacular shattering inside of him and he joined Sue in a slow, calming glide back down to Earth.

"Rodger," said Sue, still breathing hard after a few quiet minutes. "That was wonderful...."

"That was just a test flight," he whispered hotly into the pink shell of her ear.

"Then take me up with you again...."

"I promise." Blackjack closed his eyes. Tonight that was one promise he *could* make her—and keep.

SUE AWOKE ABRUPTLY. The rumbling sound of a fifty-year-old biplane motor served as her alarm clock.

Rubbing her sleepy eyes, she threw on her robe and made her way down the hall. Max was gone from his room, his door wide open. Quickly she washed up, ran a comb through her hair, then threw on jeans, sneakers and a white cotton blouse.

Tucking the shirttail into her jeans, she made her way down the stairs and out the house's front door. She saw Blackjack's biplane in front of the barn. He'd obviously taxied the Stearman out of its "hangar" and into the open yard.

The small vintage biplane really was a beauty—its top and bottom wings were painted a shining red, its fuselage sported a white racing stripe and its silver propeller gleamed in the midmorning sunshine.

Sue smiled even wider when she caught sight of the man who'd kept it in such pristine condition. Dressed in jeans and a gray work shirt, its long sleeves rolled to the elbows, Blackjack was crouched beside their son and pointing at the rear cockpit—the pilot's seat. Max was nodding his head excitedly.

She walked down the path toward them. "Hello, there!"

"Mom!" shouted Max excitedly. "Look at Blackjack's biplane!"

"I see." Sue watched Blackjack slowly rising to his full height. His blue gaze was covered with dark sunglasses, but his wide smile conveyed his pleasure at seeing her.

"Good morning," he said, striding up to meet her. Immediately he leaned in for a warm kiss. "I was going to wake you," he whispered, "but you looked like such an angel sleeping. I hated to disturb you."

"So you let the biplane motor do your dirty work."

His eyebrows rose. "Captain, if you haven't yet learned to sleep through the sound of a taxiing plane, then I haven't got much hope for you in this man's air force," teased Blackjack.

"Can it, Colonel. I'm off duty. Got any coffee in that kitchen?"

"It's ready to brew."

After a few cups of coffee and a stack of pancakes, Blackjack, Sue and Max walked back out to admire the biplane. Max had already dashed up the stairs to find his sunglasses that were "just like Blackjack's."

As the three strolled toward the plane, Blackjack pointed out the long runway he'd constructed. "Sod?" she asked. "Why didn't you use something more stable, like concrete or asphalt?"

He shook his head. "Sod has give and absorbency, that's what you want on this baby when you're landing her. You want those two big rubber wheels to *stick* to the runway, not bounce on it. If she bounces, she'll likely catch the wind and go back up into the air. You'll feel it when we land her."

"We?" asked Sue. "Oh, no—"

"Oh, yes. You're taking a ride, all right, and Max is, too. Right now, in fact."

"Yeah!" came Max's response as he joined them, his sunglasses now perched on his small face.

In no time, Sue found herself railroaded into strapping on a helmet and settling in with her son into the front cockpit of the bright red Stearman.

"Oh, I almost forgot." Blackjack reached into his jeans pocket and brought out a handful of small pink rectangles. He unwrapped one and placed it in his mouth.

"Here you go, Max," he said with a smile.

Max carefully took a piece of bubble gum, unwrapped it and placed it into his mouth.

"Don't forget to look at your Bazooka Joe comic," instructed Blackjack. Max nodded reverently.

He offered Sue a piece, too, and she accepted, biting into the sweet pink bubble gum as Blackjack took up the pilot's seat in the rear.

As they taxied out, then lifted off, Sue became more and more worried about Max. "Are you scared, honey?" she asked him again and again.

"No!" was the continual response. "Mom, this is fun! Aren't you having fun?"

Sue finally had to admit that she was. In fact, she was amazed at how much she enjoyed the ride. The open cockpit was a big change from the closed canopy of a supersonic jet. Of course, the Stearman's speed was practically a crawl at only seventy miles per hour—compared with upward of one thousand miles per hour—but in the biplane, Sue could actually feel the wind on her cheeks as it rushed by. She could smell the fresh air and feel the joyful effort of the wings, lifting and banking the aircraft.

"Wonderful, isn't it?" said Blackjack over his headset.

She was smiling, her arms around her little boy. "Yes!"

"Makes you really feel like you're part of the sky."

"Yes!"

They flew for about an hour, over the green grasslands, up to Pyramid Lake, where a single stone sentinel seemed to guard the oasis of turquoise nestled in a sandy valley. They circled the lake and its strange and beautiful stone rising from the fresh water, then they headed for home.

"You're flying naked in this thing, aren't you, Blackjack?" asked Sue, realizing the biplane was not equipped with technical instruments and indicators.

"This is the way the barnstormers flew," he said, "by map and compass, following landmarks."

"Would it cost so much to install it?" teased Sue.

"Hey, babe, Charles Lindbergh flew from New York to Paris with nothing but a compass, chart and watch. If he could fly that way, so can the namesake of Cal Braigh Rodgers."

"Mmm, competitive to the end, aren't you?"

They laughed and Max seemed as happy as ever as he chomped on his bubble gum.

"Hey, Max," called Blackjack over the intercom.

"Yeah."

"I read my Bazooka Joe comic. Want to know what it said?"

"Sure."

"Joe dreamed he was the pilot of a supersonic transport. And when the stewards were ready to serve breakfast, they asked Joe to help them flip the pancakes. 'No problem,' said Joe. And you know what he did?"

"No."

"Hold on!"

Before Sue could stop him, she was watching the world turn upside down as Blackjack looped the plane 360 degrees. Sue panicked a moment when she heard Max squealing and realized he might not be able to take the pressure of the loop.

When they came out of it, she was ready to set Blackjack straight. But she held her tongue. Max wasn't squealing in fright, she realized. He was squealing in delight.

"Wow, that was great, Blackjack! Let's do it again!"

"Okay," said Blackjack, "one more time."

Sue couldn't believe it when her son again whooped with glee. Maybe Blackjack had been right, she decided. Max *was* a McConnell.

After they landed, Sue climbed down and thanked Blackjack for the ride. Max did, too. Grinning happily, the boy pulled off his helmet, then announced that he was so excited he had to pee.

Blackjack laughed as he watched Max race for the house, then he turned to Sue. "Well, Max had a good time. How about you?"

"I don't have to follow Max to the bathroom. But I did have a good time. And—" she turned to look at Blackjack "—I understand now. I understand why you're so proud of her."

Blackjack watched Sue as she pulled off her helmet. He removed his sunglasses, and his blue gaze seemed to smolder as it took in the glint of sunlight on her shining blond hair, now lifting a bit on the stiff breeze. Sue felt her heart racing as he stepped closer.

"It was important to me that you understood," he said. "I don't even know why."

Once again Sue was drawn in. Without thought, she let her body move closer, her lips find his. Her arms lifted as effortlessly as a bird's wings on the wind, encircling his neck as she felt him pulling her closer to deepen the kiss.

"You taste good," she said when their lips parted. "Like bubble gum."

Blackjack laughed, and she stepped away, turning back to look at his beloved biplane again. "You think you can teach me to fly her?" she asked.

He smiled broadly. "You bet, Captain," he asserted. "Of course, it won't be as thrilling as breaking in that sexy-voiced virtual-reality system of yours."

Sue's eyebrows rose. "You think this boring, monotonous voice of mine is *sexy?*"

Blackjack's arm slipped around her waist, and he pulled her possessively against his strong, broad chest. "Sue," he murmured at her ear, "why do you think I asked you to say my real name last night?"

Sue's heart nearly stopped at his words as her mind replayed her own voice. *Rodger... Yes, Rodger, yes. Don't stop, Rodger.*

"Oh, my God..." she said, realizing that to Blackjack's ears, it would have sounded identical to her recorded instructions on the Reeva system. She turned her head to search his face. "Do you mean to tell me that you—you—"

A devilish smile crossed his lips. "It felt just like flying—only much more—"

"Hey, there!" a voice shouted from behind them.

Startled by the strange voice, Sue turned to see three people riding up on horseback—an auburn-haired lanky man and a plump but attractive woman with a dark blond ponytail. Both looked to be in their forties. Riding behind them was a girl.

Blackjack turned to see who was coming. He gave them a hearty wave, then he faced Sue again. "Looks like my neighbors are coming for a visit. We'll take this up later," he said with a suggestive smile.

She nodded, but was secretly relieved at the interruption. It would give her some time to think through what he'd said and why it unnerved her.

The three visitors dismounted. Blackjack shook the man's hand and gave the woman and girl a hug. He introduced the couple to Sue as Deke and Deb Butler. The twelve-year-old girl with a slightly freckled face and a single strawberry blond braid was their youngest child, Dorey.

After some pleasantries, Blackjack explained to Sue that the Butlers were the main reason he was able to hold onto the ranch.

"When we drove in yesterday, Sue was asking how I managed to keep this place up to well," said Blackjack.

"We have a nice little arrangement," explained Deb, her hazel eyes conveying an uncommon warmth.

Sue learned that the Butlers had about twelve thousand acres adjoining the Flying M Ranch. Blackjack's land measured about seven thousand acres. By combining the ranches, the Butlers were able to graze a much larger herd of cattle than they could otherwise. Apparently this was an inherited arrangement—their fathers had made the neighborly deal years ago.

Blackjack turned to Sue. "My mother's family actually left this ranch to her," he explained, "and my dad wasn't about to go into cattle ranching, so he made a deal with the Butlers to rent the land. And since Dad was stationed a few hours' drive away at Nellis Air Force Base, he made it our family home. Granddaddy McConnell lived here with us, too, till he passed away."

Deb jumped in. "After Rodger inherited the place, he dropped the price of the rent in exchange for some help keeping his house and land up."

"Made sense," said Blackjack, gesturing to the wooden barn. "After all, what am I supposed to do with livestock when all I've got on this place is an airplane hangar?"

The whole group laughed.

"So, are you takin' her up today?" asked Deke.

"He already did!" came a little voice from behind them. Max had made his way back from the bathroom.

"Who's this?" asked Deb, smiling down at the little boy.

"This is Max," said Blackjack with pride.

"My son," added Sue. Blackjack eyed her, and she read his thoughts. She knew he was waiting for the moment when she would finally say *our son*.

"Hello, Max," said Deb Butler, stepping up to the little boy. She smiled warmly, then hunkered low and held out her hand. "We've been friends of Rodger's since he was your age," she said to Max. "You can call me Aunt Deb if you like."

Max took her hand. "Okay."

"We live nearby," she continued, "and you're welcome to come ride our ponies anytime."

Max's blue eyes widened about a foot. "Ponies?"

Sue chatted happily with the Butlers after that. She smiled as she watched twelve-year-old Dorey Butler show Max how to pet her horse's nose.

The only problem was Blackjack. He wasn't talking much, and she sensed an impatience within him whenever he looked at her.

Clearly something was bothering him.

"Sue?"

Deb and Deke were leading the horses to the other side of Blackjack's barn hangar and Max was following behind them. When she heard her name, Sue turned to find Blackjack's penetrating gaze on her.

"Yes?"

"When are we going to tell him?" he asked.

So that was the problem. "Soon—"

"Today," he insisted, cutting her off. "I want him to know that I'm his father. Today."

Sue swallowed. What could she do? She was still worried about Max's reaction. But she'd agreed last night that they'd tell him today.

"At dinner?" he asked.

Sue bit her lower lip to keep from arguing. She simply nodded her agreement.

WITHIN AN HOUR, Blackjack was giving Deke a flying lesson in the Stearman. Sue, Deb and the kids watched as the men climbed into the biplane, started down the sod runway and lifted off into the air.

"Sue," called Deb, "why don't we take the children up to the shade of the porch?"

Sue agreed and soon all of them were settled in on porch chairs, watching the Stearman biplane perform standard practice touch-and-goes—continuous landings and take-offs.

As Sue watched the bright red plane gliding through the air, her thoughts returned to Blackjack's earlier revelation about their lovemaking . . . and her voice.

Say my name.

Blackjack had wanted her to call him *Rodger.* Just like Reeva. But why?

When he was hooked into Reeva, the system was tuned in to his every thought, his every breath, linking him into the very essence of flight. . . .

Are you ready to turn now, Rodger? . . . Very good, Rodger. . . .

"But Reeva is me," she whispered to herself. "Or . . . at least my voice."

Could it be that Blackjack has somehow been *seduced* by Reeva? she wondered. And now, could he be connecting Sue with his love, his *passion*, for Reeva, for flying?

Could that be why he had become so attracted to Sue after all these years? The idea made her heart all the more wary.

It seemed too strange to be true, she thought to herself. But if it *were* true, then it would mean she'd been right all along about Blackjack: that flying was his one true love. And likely his *only* love.

"Sue," called Deb Butler, startling her from her intense thoughts. "Shall we get some lemonade for the kids?"

Sue nodded. The two women walked into the house's large, sunny kitchen, and Deb went to the cupboard for glasses.

"Rodger's been giving Deke lessons in flying, and Deke's been trying to teach Rodger the finer points of riding a cattle horse," began Deb as she brought down the glasses. "Rodger always says he wants to learn how to help out on a ranch roundup one of these days."

"How's his backside holding out?"

"Not too well," said Deb. "He's been finding excuses to miss his lessons for about six weeks straight."

Sue smiled as she poured the lemonade into the glasses. "Well, you can bet he doesn't have that reluctance where saddling a jet engine is concerned."

"Don't I know it," said Deb. "He's been like that since he was a kid, finding any excuse to get his dad to take him to the base to watch the fighter planes."

Sue smiled at the thought of Blackjack as a little boy, with his plane models and dreams of riding the sky.

"You're the first woman he's brought here," remarked Deb bluntly.

Sue was dumbfounded for a moment. "Well," she finally said as she put the lemonade pitcher back into the fridge, then opened the freezer to retrieve the ice tray, "we've been working closely together on a special project."

"Mmm" was Deb's response. "And...that's all there is to it?"

She stopped at Deb's question and deliberately turned to study the woman's face—what she saw there was not idle curiosity but a sincere, caring expression.

"He's like family to you, isn't he?" asked Sue.

Deb nodded. "Deke and I have known Rodger a long time. We care about him very much. We worry about him, more likely."

"Max is Rodger's son," Sue said, surprised at her own bluntness.

Deb shook her head abruptly. "Sue, you don't have to tell me—"

"It's okay," she said. "I want you to know." Deb pulled out a chair and sat down at the butcher-block table as Sue continued. "And I'm sure Rodger would want you to know. We met when he was stationed in North Carolina. He was sent to the Persian Gulf, and when he came back—well, we weren't together anymore, and I haven't seen him until just recently. For a number of reasons, I chose—"

Sue paused a moment. This was more difficult to discuss than she'd anticipated. "I...chose not to tell Rodger... about Max."

Deb took a long drink of lemonade as she considered Sue's words. "You thought he would reject your son. That he didn't want anything to do with being a father, didn't you?"

Sue's brown eyes widened. "How did you know?" she asked, pulling out a chair and sitting down to face Deb.

"Most of his life, Rodger's never acted like he wanted marriage or a family. But after he was assigned out here a few years ago, and then his father died, we were hoping he had a change of heart about settling down. Not long ago, we even tried some matchmaking."

Sue's eyes widened. "You're kidding?"

"Nope. We thought we were so sneaky. We arranged all these 'chance' meetings with eligible young women around here—"

"Oh, no," Sue said, laughing out loud. "What happened? Disasters, right?"

"Pretty much. Oh, he was nice and polite enough—even took a few out on dates. But these were the type of women lookin' to snag a guy right away—I mean, that was the point as far as we were concerned. Rodger didn't go for it at all. After about a dozen setups, he finally came over one day and very casually asked us to stop with the 'chance' meetings."

"I'm not surprised at that," said Sue. "I learned the hard way that Rodger's only true love is the sky." The thought made Sue's insides churn. She hated to admit it to herself, but if she knew anything about Roger, it was this plain truth.

"Oh, he loves the sky, all right," said Deb. "But his *only* love? I'm not convinced of that. Not anymore."

"Well," admitted Sue. "I'm convinced of it."

"You mean you two aren't talking about marriage?" she asked.

Sue shook her head. "You said it yourself—he's not the marrying kind. I learned that the hard way, and I've learned how to accept it. Now I'm learning to accept that he's Max's father. I want Max and Blackjack to have a good relationship, even if it is long-distance."

"Long-distance? But earlier Rodger said you were stationed at Flatlands with him."

"It's temporary. I'll be requesting reassignment back to Washington, D.C. Probably in another week."

Deb nodded her head, but said nothing.

Sue rose in the ensuing silence and went to the ice tray in the sink. She emptied the ice into a bowl.

"You know," said Deb slowly, "there's something funny about a man who claims he doesn't want to settle down yet never seems to get around to selling a big house like this."

"What do you mean?" asked Sue, dropping cubes into glasses.

"Ever since James McConnell passed away three years ago, Rodger keeps saying he wants to sell the Flying M. But he hasn't. Instead, he puts more money into it. Even remodeled the house."

Sue's brown eyes were fixed on Deb's face. "I don't follow... I mean, can't he find a buyer for the place?"

Deb smiled as she shook her head. "Oh, he's had plenty of offers from the time he first mentioned selling—including a good standing offer from Deke and me."

"I still don't understand," asserted Sue.

"Don't you?"

Sue waited for Deb to continue, but she didn't. She just smiled warmly, picked up the two full glasses of lemonade for the kids and walked toward the kitchen door. Then she turned and gave Sue something to chew on for the rest of the day.

"Rodger McConnell may *say* he doesn't want to settle down—but he's sure been acting like a man who's holding out hope."

"Hope of what?"

"Of finding a woman who'll show him that a soul can soar just fine without being anywhere near a plane. And, honey, by the expression on his face when he looks at you, I'd bet real money he's found her."

Chapter Fourteen

An hour later, the Butlers took Sue, Max and Blackjack for a visit to their ranch. Max was thrilled to see horses and cows on a working ranch, and Dorey even gave the little boy a ride on one of the ponies.

As the sun began to set, Blackjack politely declined a dinner invitation from the Butlers. He was eager to experience again the cozy feeling of having Sue and Max helping him fix dinner in his own kitchen.

Tonight's menu featured his granddaddy's recipe for pan-fried chicken—a mildly spicy dish Blackjack had learned how to cook as a boy. All through the meal, Max's excited conversation focused on the biplane ride and the ranch animals.

"Mom, did you see the dog?" he asked for the tenth time.

"Yes, Max," answered Sue with a patient voice.

"It's a German shepherd. Aunt Deb said German shepherds are a good breed. They're really loyal and smart."

"Max," cautioned Sue.

"You wanted a puppy for your birthday, didn't you?" asked Blackjack.

Max looked at Blackjack. Then at his mother. Then back to Blackjack. "Mom says I can't have a dog 'cause our apartment's too small."

Blackjack looked at Sue; she would not return his gaze. "But that was back East," he tried. "Out here, there's plenty of room—"

"Blackjack," interrupted Sue with a careful tone. "Max and I have a home. Back East."

Despite their soft delivery, her words galled Blackjack. This wasn't the direction he thought they'd been heading in this weekend.

"What are you talking about?" he asked a little too sharply. "You know Lieutenant General Simpson wants you out here permanently." *And I do, too,* he added silently, unable to actually say the words.

"This assignment is temporary, Blackjack. Max knows we'll be going back to Maryland. Don't you, Max?"

Max suddenly found an intense interest in his plate, his fork artistically swirling together his peas and mashed potatoes.

"Max?" prompted Sue.

"Yeah," said the boy reluctantly. "I know."

Blackjack's stomach began to churn at this exchange. He didn't know exactly what he wanted to hear from Sue's lovely lips, but he knew for certain it wasn't that she'd be leaving this time zone in the near future.

He'd take this up later with her. Right now, Blackjack was finding it all the more imperative that they address another issue.

"Sue," he said carefully.

"Yes?" She looked up casually, but when she saw the look in his eyes, her own gaze became hooded with concern.

"It's time now," he stated flatly.

"Blackjack—"

"Please."

Sue swallowed uneasily, but then nodded. "Max..."

Max looked at his mother. "Yeah."

"I have something to tell you—"

"*We*," broke in Blackjack. "*We* have something to tell you."

"Yeah!" exclaimed Max, suddenly excited. "Are you getting married?"

Blackjack watched Sue's face drop about a thousand feet.

"No!" she exclaimed, a little too forcefully as far as Blackjack was concerned. "I mean, that's not what I wanted—what *we* wanted—to tell you."

"Oh," said Max, clearly disappointed.

"Max," tried Blackjack. "Do you remember how we looked at those family pictures last night?"

Max nodded. "Sure."

"Well," continued Blackjack, "how would you feel about knowing that you're a part of that family, too?"

"What do you mean?" asked Max, confused.

"Max," said Sue softly, "what Blackjack means is that you..." She stopped a moment. "Do you remember what I told you when you came home from your nursery school one day and asked me about your father?"

Max nodded. "You said he lived far away from us. That someday I would meet him."

"Well, we're far away from home now," said Sue carefully. "And you've already met him. You just didn't know it."

Max's eyes widened.

"Blackjack is your father," said Sue softly.

"He is?" asked Max, a look of incredulous awe covering his tiny face.

"Max," Sue said carefully, "Blackjack and I...we... couldn't be together when you were born. But he's here for you now."

Max nodded his head. Then he gazed down at his plate in thought. "Blackjack?" asked the little boy, his eyes finally looking up, meeting the identical sky blue color as his own.

Blackjack heard the note of worry in his son's voice, and his brow immediately wrinkled in concern. Automatically he bent his head slightly closer, offering quiet encouragement.

"Is it—" began the boy, then stopped. His gaze suddenly broke from Blackjack's and dropped down to study his plate once again. "Is it *really* true? Are you *really* my father?"

Blackjack glanced toward Sue. Her brow was also furrowed with worry; her gaze remained on her son, who was obviously struggling to understand and accept this.

"Yes, Max," answered Blackjack gently. "It's *really* true. I'm your father."

Max looked up into Blackjack's face. He blinked a few moments, then looked at his mother.

"It's okay, Max. You know I love you, honey."

At one time, Blackjack used to think that saying the words would be too hard. But he'd been wrong about that. They came floating out now with the ease of a glider coasting on a good stiff wind. "Max...I love you, too, son. And I'll always be here for you. Always. I promise."

He watched the boy's face, the young eyes widening. Then Max bit his bottom lip in thought and dropped his gaze down again. "Does that mean—" The boy hesitated a moment. "Can I...I mean, is it okay if I call you Dad?"

A sigh of relief came from Sue and Blackjack simultaneously.

"Sure," said Blackjack softly. "I'd really like that."

Max's smile came fast and bright. He looked at Blackjack and then at his mother. "It's okay, Mom, isn't it?"

Sue nodded, perhaps not trusting her voice. Blackjack noticed her eyes were shining. "Sure, it is."

The rest of the evening was as comfortably domestic as the previous. Blackjack helped Max complete a second airplane model by the living room fire. He wasn't surprised when his son picked out a Stearman biplane as the second project.

"Let's paint her red," said Max, "like yours."

"Sure," said Blackjack.

"Tomorrow," interrupted Sue.

"Aw, Mom!"

"No, Max," said Sue. "It's time for bed."

"Dad, can't I stay up a little longer?"

Blackjack looked at the late hour and then at Sue. He guessed his heart was in his eyes at hearing Max call him *Dad.* But he knew that spoiling his kid rotten was far from being a good idea.

"No, son," Blackjack heard himself saying. "You heard your mother." *Good Lord, I sound like Ward Cleaver,* thought Blackjack. *Am I doing this right?*

"Aw, come on! I want to stay up."

Sue said nothing to Max. She simply smiled up at Blackjack. "Okay, Dad," she mouthed. "You're on."

Blackjack blinked in thought a moment, wondering how to handle this. Then it hit him. He had over thirty good years of lessons in fatherhood to fall back on. All he had to do was ask himself: what would James McConnell do at a time like this?

"Okay, airman," cried Blackjack. "You're toast!"

"But I want to—"

"Don't argue with a superior officer! Now march your butt upstairs—"

"But—"

"Double time!"

In twenty minutes, Blackjack had gotten Max into his pajamas and made sure he'd washed his face and brushed his teeth. Then he tucked his son into the top bunk and kissed him on the forehead.

"Good night, son," whispered Blackjack as he turned to go.

"Hey, Dad?" asked Max.

Blackjack turned back. He searched his son's knitted brow, taking in the shape of the little boy's face. Max's expression made him look a little like Blackjack's brother, Whit. The thought gave him mixed feelings—he tried to push the darker memories away and just think about the good things. He wasn't entirely successful.

"Can we—" began Max. "I mean, you're my dad and all, so...Mom and me. Can't we live *here* now, instead of back East? 'Cause you *are* my dad, right?"

"I'm your dad, Max," said Blackjack. "I'll always be your dad. You can count on that, no matter what."

"But can we—"

"Your mom and me. We have to work things out," said Blackjack. "Just remember that we both love you. Okay, son?"

"Yeah...okay," said Max on a big yawn. "Good night, Dad."

"'Night, son." Blackjack flicked off the lamp. The dim illumination of the plastic, plane-shaped night-light cast odd shadows on the walls of the boy's bedroom.

"It's just that..." came a little voice from the top bunk. "It's just that I like it here. With you. A lot."

In the dim light, the edges of Blackjack's lips turned up. "I'm glad. I like your being here, too. Much more than a lot."

Yeah, thought Blackjack as he stepped through the door, this fatherhood thing had its uncertain moments, but mostly, it sure was nice.

SUE WATCHED Blackjack tiptoeing out of Max's dark bedroom.

"Nice job, Dad," she whispered, smiling when she heard his sigh of relief. He turned for one more look at his son, then shut the bedroom door.

Blackjack stood there, looking down at Sue a long moment before speaking. "He was a lot to handle alone, wasn't he?"

Sue nodded her head. "It was okay. I had my parents helping. And Will."

"And if you stay out here, you'll have me." His blue gaze was unwavering as he reached out to finger an errant blond curl.

"Blackjack—" she started to say, her voice less than steady as her body registered his nearness. "You—you don't have to worry. Now that I see how good you are for him, I won't stand between you two. You can be sure that I'll agree to fair visitation—"

"Visitation!"

"Shh, keep your voice down—"

Blackjack ran a hand through his hair as he cursed silently. Lowering his voice to an agitated whisper, he spoke again. "Do you mean to tell me that you want to bounce this kid back and forth through the air—like he's a ball in some kind of transcontinental tennis match?"

"Blackjack, calm down—"

"No way. We need to continue this conversation, but in an entirely new direction," commanded Blackjack, taking Sue's hand and pulling her toward his bedroom. "We need to talk about what there is between us. About what we want."

Sue didn't resist his pull on her. She knew too well what it was they wanted from each other in any room with a bed in it. No matter the disagreement, no matter the argument, their attraction was like fire to jet fuel, and there was no denying it. Even now she was remembering the heat of his lovemaking last night, the pleasure of his hands on her body.

When she entered the master bedroom, she started for the armchair by the fireplace. But after he closed and locked the door, he caught her elbow and turned her into his arms. Sue studied his handsome square jaw and deep blue eyes, the shock of black hair covering his forehead.

"My God," she whispered. "You're handsome."

"And you're beautiful."

Sue felt Blackjack's hand at her waist, urging her closer to him. His other was at her jaw, caressing the soft skin, then dipping lower to stroke the hollow of her neck. His blue eyes were so intense with wanting, she barely noticed he'd slipped the first button of her white cotton blouse from its buttonhole.

"So," he said, his voice dangerously low. "Admit it to me. What is it you *really* want?"

"I...want..." She felt her blood racing through her veins again. His nearness alone was making her breath quicken.

"I..." she tried to continue as a second button came undone.

"Yes?" he prompted. A third button was relieved of its function. And then a fourth.

"I want you to..."

"Yes? You want me, too," he said, purposely misstating her words. And then his lips were there. On her bared skin.

At her neck and lower. His hands were pulling off her clothes, and then her hands were stripping off his.

It didn't take long before they were on his large, four-poster bed, a tangle of naked limbs in the chilly room. Warmed by the heat of their internal fires, they kissed and caressed, touched and nuzzled.

Sue luxuriated in the feel of his powerful body pressing close beside her. She touched him and he moaned with pleasure until finally, needing more, he moved over her, lifting himself above her.

"Open for me." His deep voice was at her ear, thick with desire as he nipped at her neck.

He lifted his head, and Sue felt herself drawn up and into the blue of his eyes. It was just like the wide-open sky she'd felt a part of just this morning—full of joy and beauty, danger and excitement.

Oh, my God, she realized on a sharp intake of breath, *I feel like I'm a part of him.*

She knew at once it wasn't just the physical. With them, the physical had always been a given. What Sue realized now—this instant—was that her feelings went far beyond her body. She cursed silently as she realized that the thing she had tried so hard to steel herself against had happened: she had become a part of Rodger Blackjack McConnell—body, mind and soul.

"Sue...open...for...me," he whispered the command again, the words coming between nibbling kisses at her lips and throat.

She hesitated, still reeling from her realization. She didn't want this. Didn't want the knowledge that she'd fallen so hard and so far for him again.

Was there a way to pull back? she wondered. Was there a way to keep herself from getting hurt again?

"What's wrong?" he asked, his lips brushing across hers.

"I—I... don't know if I—" she said, faltering, "—if we should—"

But her words were swallowed in a blistering assault. His mouth covered hers in a swift possession, as if he couldn't bear to hear what she was about to say.

His lips were soft and warm, his tongue plunging into her mouth with hungry need. His hands were playing along her body, his palm at her full, naked breast, kneading and caressing, commanding that she let every doubt and worry melt away in the heat of his seduction.

There were no words this time. No asking. Blackjack seemed well beyond taking the time for that now. His knee nudged at her legs, urging them to yield to him. Under the sensual assault from his lips and hands, she did not hesitate. She parted for him and he swiftly joined them, both of them sighing as he made the connection they so desperately needed.

Sue's eyes closed as her mind finally released all of its dark forecasts. In their place came a joyful storm of sensual emotion.

How she loved the feeling of having him inside her, of holding him here. Yes... this was how she wanted him. Always. Close to her—in a place where she could always, *always* keep him safe.

"You feel so good, Rodger," she whispered, knowing her voice—Reeva's voice—would again work its magic on his nervous system. She watched him close his eyes with the feelings of pleasure he was experiencing until they'd both reached the pinnacle and were crying out in release.

After a long, exquisite moment of stillness, he opened his lids to meet her eyes.

"Rodger," she said softly, "it is *me* you're making love to, isn't it?"

Blackjack's eyebrows rose slowly. "It is *you* in this bed with me, isn't it?"

"No, I—I mean, yes, it's me, but I mean . . . Reeva. I was thinking earlier that you—you and Reeva."

"Reeva is a computer program, Sue. *You* are a flesh-and-blood woman—and such very sweet flesh it is," he murmured, his lips tasting the skin of her neck.

"But, what about what you said—"

"That your voice makes me feel as though I'm flying?" he asked. "That's true. It's pretty amazing. But it's not the reason I want to make love to you—"

Blackjack lifted his head to look into Sue's face again.

"God almighty," said Blackjack. "You don't believe me."

"I just think that maybe Reeva has seduced you—I mean, instead of me."

Blackjack's blue gaze seemed to burn into her wide brown eyes with determined purpose. "If you think that, then you'd better think again. And feel. Then you'll know the truth."

He began to stir inside her. Slowly. So very slowly. The feeling was almost excruciating in the pure pleasure it brought to every fiber of her body. Sue's blood was racing now, and beads of sweat began to form on her skin as she felt that familiar sweet tension coiling inside of her.

"Faster, Rodger," she whispered, but he ignored the command. Instead, he remained steady in his slow movements, building a torturous tension within her.

Sue writhed beneath him, her body trying to urge him faster, but his hands flew to capture hers. He kept her firmly beneath him, stroking her again and again with an expert and ruthless thoroughness, clearly determined to possess her on his own terms.

"Rodger—faster . . ."

"No, sweet Sue," he murmured hotly in her ear. "You see, Reeva's voice doesn't control me. *I* control me." His lips brushed against her lobe and then her neck as he plunged deeper and deeper into her, his rhythm steady, relentless. "And I want this woman in bed with me now—not just her voice."

Sue felt her shallow breaths coming quicker. Her eyes remained locked on to his as he continued his torturously slow movements inside her.

"It's *you* I want, Sue Rigger. *You.*"

And then, finally he began, ever so slightly, to increase the pace of his movements.

Sue felt as though she were on a runway, her jet taxiing down the long strip of concrete, the instruments set for takeoff. She felt herself moving with the plane, with this pilot, faster and faster, the world becoming a blur as the roar of the engines, the pounding of her heart, sounded in her ears, louder and louder, faster and faster....

"Let go, Sue," urged the voice at her ear. And she did. As he pulled quickly out, then plunged roughly back inside, deeper than she'd ever felt him penetrate, something within her snapped.

Sweet hot tension at the core of her shattered into a million brilliant sensations. For long moments, she was shaking violently and clutching at his muscular back, gasping desperately to fill her lungs with sweet, calming oxygen. Then finally she began to float downward, a blissful glider on the most tranquil of winds. A slow descent back to the ground.

But no sooner had she recovered than Sue found Blackjack inside her again on another exquisite night flight. They hadn't even come close to the zenith, and he clearly meant to take her up higher and higher, again and again.

MANY HOURS LATER, as they held each other, sated, Sue's submerged logical senses finally began to surface. Half-awake, she realized how completely she'd been swept away by her blue-eyed flyboy.

With his mouth and hands, he'd melted all her doubts and concerns. She felt the passion within him. It was a passion for her, she was sure, not for some computer simulation, and she was glad for the knowledge of it.

She snuggled closer to the warmth of his strong, muscular chest. The room had grown chillier again. At one point earlier, Blackjack had lit a fire in the bedroom's fireplace. The flames were growing smaller now, the embers glowing a faint red in the white ashes.

I like it here, she thought to herself, rising enough off the feather mattress to reach for the soft quilt at the bottom of the four-poster bed. She drew it over them both and saw that Rodger had drifted off to sleep. She took advantage of his unconscious state to admire him—his strong, square jaw, dusted now with a shadow of stubble; his soft, full lips; his broad, naked chest, sharply defined with hard muscle.

No, she thought, *I love it here.*

She reached a hand out to smooth a shock of his raven dark hair from his brow. *I never did plan to fall in love with you again,* she thought, half wondering if she had ever fallen *out* of love with the man.

Maybe she hadn't. But she was still afraid. Nervous to face the possibility that Blackjack didn't know his own mind.

He'd opened himself up to her this weekend. Opened in a way that made Sue feel desired, needed. He'd said that he wanted her. But he hadn't said anything about love. Or marriage.

But what if he did? she asked herself. Is that what *she* wanted?

Sue could no longer fool herself with safe rationalizations. She knew what she wanted. Knew it in the depths of her soul. She wanted a life out here with Rodger and Max— and maybe even more McConnell children, brothers and sisters for Max to play with.

If Rodger McConnell wanted the same things, then maybe . . . just maybe, there was a way to make it work—

The sudden ringing of the phone startled Sue, interrupting her thoughts. Blackjack jerked instantly awake at the first piercing bell, and by the end of the second, he'd sat up and grabbed at the nightstand.

She watched with concern as he mostly listened, asking a few questions. It sounded like the base calling, and Sue knew from the look on Blackjack's face that the news wasn't good.

After he hung up, she waited for him to say something, but nothing came out of his mouth. He simply sat there, in the dark, staring off into space. Sue waited a good ten seconds, then couldn't stand it anymore.

"Rodger, what is it?"

"German. Uh . . . Jerry Bruckman."

Sue waited for more. But when he didn't go on, she prompted, "Is he . . . is he—"

"He's fine."

Blackjack ran a hand through his dark hair a moment, then he snapped the quilt from his body and swung his legs over the edge of the bed. He sat like that, his back facing her, for a long, silent few minutes. Finally Sue tried again.

"Rodger . . . what happened?"

"Prototype failure."

Sue let silence fill the seconds until he was ready to go on.

"That was Lieutenant General Simpson calling," said Blackjack, finally continuing, his voice a distant monotone. "He wanted me to know before I reported in. German went up on a night-flying test for one of the Mason-Remington prototypes. There was a system failure, and they had to abort. He ejected. He's in the hospital with some burns and bruises."

Sue sighed in relief. "Thank God. Do you want me to wake Max? We can drive back now if you want to see Jerry."

"No," said Blackjack. "Simpson assured me he's fine. We'll head back first thing in the morning, though."

"Okay."

Sue watched as Rodger rose from the bed, walked to the closet and grabbed a pair of black sweatpants. He stepped quickly into them, then walked toward the bedroom door.

"Rodger, where are you going?" she asked, not liking the tense stiffness she saw in his movements.

His hand stilled on the doorknob.

"German's backseater," said Blackjack. "He didn't make it."

The words were a vacuum, rushing in and taking every last bit of wind from her lungs. "No..." murmured Sue. "Oh, no."

"It was Captain Landson."

"I—I don't think I knew him."

"I did. I flew with him a few times. He was a good man. Young. Twenty-eight."

Sue swallowed; her throat was suddenly dry. She heard the distance in Blackjack's voice and she realized that ever since the call, he had not looked at her.

"Rodger—"

"He had a family," interrupted Blackjack. "Wife and son."

Sue could say nothing as she watched Blackjack unbolt the door and walk through it. An unsettling chill seemed to envelop her from the inside out.

"The boy was Max's age," came Blackjack's voice just before he closed the door behind him.

A knife's point seemed to pierce Sue's heart, and her limbs went numb. She no longer had to ask him where he was going. She knew he was headed for the room. The room that held the pictures and the faces. The room that was a legacy... and a shrine.

Sue pulled the quilt closer around her, but the chill would not go away. It penetrated her bones, her muscles; it emanated from the depths of her heart. Closing her eyes, she felt her lips moving in a silent prayer for Landson and his family. A second came for Jerry Bruckman... a third for Rodger.

Maybe another woman would have chased after the man who'd left the room. But Sue knew pilots—after all, she was one herself. She knew how useless it would be to try to change what could not be changed. To try to keep him from pulling away.

She stared into the hearth of the fireplace. The flames that had warmed her earlier were nowhere to be seen, and the remaining red embers were slowly flickering on their last breath. All along Sue had feared this—that the change in Rodger would come over him again, just like before. The likelihood of it had always been at the back of her mind.

Sue's eyelids were growing heavier in the dim, cold room. She was tired. So tired. Before she drifted off into a restless sleep, a chill sadness swallowed her, and she knew that the fire had now gone completely out.

THE MEMORIES CAME BACK to him now as they sometimes did. The fact that he'd gotten the call in this house... well, it was inevitable that he'd be reminded.

Blackjack sat alone in the dark, staring out the window at the night sky. The black was lightening perceptibly, a sign of near-dawn; he could still see the stars.

In the room, he sensed more than saw the faces surrounding him. The pictures of the living...and the dead.

Captain Landson was with his brother now.

James Whitman McConnell, Jr.

Blackjack could see the name etched on his gravestone. He remembered how he'd felt when he first read it.

Years ago, the young pilot's sudden death had devastated his family for a long time. Whit had been the eldest, the first born, the bearer of his family's hopes for the future. Whit had been his father's favorite, and Rodger himself had idolized his older brother from the time he could crawl.

He'd never forgotten the look on Sally's face when she'd come to their house after the funeral. Whit's young bride had always been cheerful, warm and loving to Rodger. He'd loved Sally like a sister of his own, and he was somehow hoping she would make things better, that she'd help him find some answers.

But she hadn't. Rodger would never forget the drawn look—the pale, almost chalk white skin, the limp corn silk of her hair, the empty green eyes, the distant voice.

There hadn't been much left of Whit's remains. They'd been placed in a closed coffin. The photos had become Rodger's only source of comfort. He'd sit for hours in this room, just staring at Whit's face in those photos. This was where he'd been sitting when his mother told him that Sally had died. She'd taken too many sleeping pills, his mother had said. One week after the funeral.

"She'd have been better off not loving him," murmured Blackjack as he stared out into the dawning sky.

He sat there, thinking about Landson and his family, thinking about Sally and Whit, thinking about Max. And about his own dangerous career. And finally he thought about Sue and what he felt for her. What he knew in his heart that he'd always felt for her. He wanted quick, easy answers, but none seemed forthcoming.

So he continued to sit and stare at the lightening sky, until every last star disappeared.

Chapter Fifteen

The next few days held no big surprises for Sue. Everything went pretty much the way she figured it would: a visit with Jerry in the hospital; a memorial service for Captain Landson; then back to the reason she'd been ordered here in the first place—testing Reeva.

As she expected, ever since that near-dawn phone call, Blackjack had changed toward her. Oh, he'd been polite enough. Highly civil, in fact. But there was no more intimacy. He could barely even look her in the face.

It was as if he had promised her something and then realized he simply wasn't capable of keeping that promise.

Sue didn't blame him. She knew he hadn't promised her a thing. But though her mind understood the palpable distance he'd put between them, her heart could not help but feel hurt by it.

Yet things felt different than they had when he had pulled away from her over six years ago. *She* was different. This time around, there was no need for curses or recriminations. There was no anger bubbling up through her veins. This time there'd be no vow of vengeance because Blackjack McConnell did not, or could not, love her.

This time she had some years of experience to fall back on, and she knew how to accept loss, how to accept the things she could not change. And there was something else different this time around. This time she had Max.

Now that the project was almost over, she would soon be far away from Blackjack. With two thousand miles of geographic distance between them, she might better be able to cope with his emotional distance.

Her one other source of consolation was his attitude toward his son. Sue was relieved to discover that when it came to Max, Blackjack went out of his way to remain warm, open and giving. She was deeply grateful that he'd been able to keep the promise he *did* make toward loving Max. And she knew now that he really would be a good father, no matter what.

With a sigh, Sue rubbed her eyes. It was Wednesday morning, and she was feeling very tired from another night of restless sleep. She had to get her mind back on track.

"Welcome back to reality," she mumbled as she finished off the dregs of her second cup of morning coffee, hoping it would help her wake up.

"What's that?" Will entered the kitchen and grabbed a cup from the cupboard.

"Oh, nothing. Good morning." Sue was happy to see her big brother. She had barely had time to say hello to him since he and Jane Cortez had come back early Monday morning.

Will had given Jane a kiss goodbye that should have set the house on fire, let alone the porch the couple had been standing on. After glimpsing that kiss from the living room, Sue didn't have to ask. It was obvious her brother enjoyed his long weekend.

"You up for today?" asked Will.

"Yes. No. I don't know. What do you think?" asked Sue.

Lieutenant General Simpson had warned everyone working on the Reeva-Horizon project that today they would have a few VIP visitors. Everyone was edgy, and no one could get inside information on who the visitors would be. Theoretically "visitors" could be anyone from top brass to political contacts for appropriations.

Sue felt her brother's hand on her shoulder. "Well, I think you're ready."

She gave her brother a long look; the confidence in his eyes was almost contagious. "Thanks."

"You're welcome," he said. "What are brothers for, anyway?" Reaching for the coffeepot, Will continued, "You know, I've never seen Max happier. He's upstairs working on another model plane."

Sue let a wan smile touch her lips. "He'll be busy for a while. Rodger pretty much gave Max his entire stash."

"So, then...the weekend went well?" asked Will with obvious curiosity as he poured his cup of coffee.

"Sure," said Sue, trying to avoid looking into his face. "You said it yourself, Max has never been happier."

"And what about you?"

"Me? What's the mystery, I'm the same as ever. Who needs a man like McConnell anyway?" Her voice nearly broke. "I better get going." She turned to go but stilled when she felt her brother's hand on her shoulder.

"Sue. Don't condemn a man for being who he is—"

"I don't," said Sue quietly. "You see, I do understand who he is. All too well. I just wish—" She stopped. There was that word again, a word she never used, except when it came to that damned flyboy.

"What?"

Sue turned and tilted her head a bit to look into her brother's handsome face, his features twisted with concern.

"I was stupid," she revealed. "Stupid to let myself see how good it could have been. Stupid to *wish* for anything with him."

"Suzie..." Will's hand brushed at his sister's hair, the way he had when she was ten and he was going off to college. "Don't stop wishing for things—"

She let out a derisive laugh. "How can *you,* Mr. Applied Science, advise me of such a ridiculous thing?"

A slow smile dawned across her brother's face. "Dr. Rigger, do you mean to tell me you haven't yet learned that wishing—and dreaming—are the root of all experimentation?"

"But..." Sue blinked a moment, ready to argue. But she couldn't. It was elegantly simple. And profoundly true. From the star-gazing of Galileo, to the soaring dreams of Orville and Wilbur, to the visionary theories of Stephen Hawking and beyond. Her brother was right... and yet...

"Don't stop wishing, Sue. Life has a funny way of throwing us curves. But I agree with Einstein."

Sue raised an eyebrow. "Old Albert had something to say about love?"

"Not love in particular. He just said that he didn't believe God played dice with the world."

A sharp laugh escaped her lips. "God might not. But what about Blackjack?"

"He's too smart a gambler to throw away the best odds he'll ever get on happiness."

"You're wrong, Will. I lost him before. And I've lost him again."

"That's *your* theory."

"That's a fact."

IT WAS TIME.

Blackjack stepped into his flight suit in the base locker room, ready to take on the biggest challenge yet on this project.

The Horizon had been retrofitted with sensors. Under Sue Rigger's direction, a research team and ground crew had gone over every inch of the sleek black delta-wing stealth craft, inspecting every aspect of the Reeva application, testing as much as they could before the pilot climbed into the cockpit.

He was that pilot, and now it was time to fly the bird.

At dawn, he'd taken a five-mile run near the flight line. The morning had been brilliant and clear, the pale blue desert sky looking vast and inviting. He had tried to purge himself of distracting thoughts and images—Sue's pert nose and soft lips, her long legs and full, perfect breasts.

Yet in his mind, her wide, intelligent brown eyes had relentlessly stared up at him, silently asking *why?*

Why was he doing this to her? *Why* was he pulling away? *Why* was he throwing away their chance to be together, to be happy? The strange part was that she had never actually voiced such questions—not even a one.

She'd just allowed him to pull away, as if that was what she wanted, too—as if, like him, she had begun to think that it was best for both of them.

Suddenly other images had begun to crowd his vision as he'd run, looking across the tarmac. The face of Captain Landson's widow and of his bereaved young son at the memorial service. Their faces had blurred into others. Suffering families he'd seen over the years, the ones left behind, the ones who always reminded him, never let him forget the terrible, devastating pain that sometimes came with loving a pilot.

He had run until the blood had rushed through his veins, until the sound of rumbling supersonic takeoffs had deafened his ears to the sounds of the past, until the bright, searing sunshine had blinded his vision from ancient images.

It had helped. The hard run.

He'd come away from it with a firm decision.

It didn't matter anymore if it was the right one. It was the *only* one he could live with.

Now, in the Flatlands locker room, Blackjack zipped up his gray flight suit and stepped into his heavy lace boots. His head felt clearer now, and he knew he was ready for the task at hand. Years of training, of combat experience, of test flights, did not go to waste on this seasoned pilot.

Colonel McConnell slammed his locker door.

His mind was sharp, free of distractions and ready to focus on the test flight.

"OH, LORD," whispered Sue just under her breath as she stepped into the operations lab.

She was about to hold a preflight briefing with her staff. But there were more bodies milling around in here than just her staff. Many more. White lab coats, top-brass uniforms and tailored business suits practically filled the large op lab. All in all, this was going to be quite an audience.

"Hang in, sis. You can do this," murmured Will in her ear with a reassuring touch to her shoulder.

"It's *your* system design," she whispered. "*You* should be doing this."

"Nope," said Will, shaking his head. "And it's not a matter of charity, Captain. I designed it. But *you're* implementing it. Testing demands a whole different set of abilities than research. I never had much talent—or interest—in it. *You,* however, are damned good at it."

Sue's eyebrows rose. "But I thought...I thought you would be replacing me here—"

Will smiled. "Get it straight, Sue. Simpson wants me to head his new research lab—and he just may get me. But he wants you as a technical director for testing. Of that, you can be sure—"

"Here you are," interrupted Russell Simpson, striding toward Will and Sue. The black-eyed commanding officer

with the salt-and-pepper crew cut looked trim and powerful in his full uniform, the campaign ribbons affixed
proudly. Three silver stars of a lieutenant general's rank
gleamed on his shoulders.

"Sir," said Sue, "who's giving the party?"

"We are," said Simpson with a smile. "I warned you
we'd have visitors. Come meet the vice president."

"Oh, my Lord..."

Sue did her best to smile and sound intelligent. After
shaking the vice president's hand, she met a few senators
and congressmen, about seven high-ranking Pentagon of-
ficials and a number of civilians and Air Force officers doing aerospace research at various other bases and labs.

"Why?" she managed to ask Simpson after taking him
aside. "Why are they all here?"

"Rigger, get some savvy, will you. Now that you're being promoted to major—"

"What?"

He smiled widely. "Your promotion came through this
morning—but we'll talk about that later. As I was saying,
now that you're going to be a major, you better get with the
program. We've got to thank these folks for our funding."

"But, sir," persisted Sue, "the Horizon is just a prototype—things can still go wrong."

Simpson shook his head. "Rigger, don't you get it? The
program is already a success. The F-15 and F-16 data had
these guys doing back flips as it is! Nobody thought Reeva
would ever get this far so fast. These suits'll wet their pants
when they see even the simplest maneuvers performed on the
Horizon with Reeva. You know it's years ahead of anything else being done."

"But—"

"This is just a show to celebrate the program's future
funding. It's set, Rigger. We're set for years to come. You
should be proud of what you've accomplished—"

"Me? It wasn't me. It's Rodger McConnell, sir, he—"

"You don't have to sing his praises," said Simpson. "He's being promoted, as well. But as I said, we'll get into that later. Right now, we've got to get this show on the road."

"But, sir—"

There was no going back, no stopping this train, no matter how much Sue wanted to. She looked up to call her staff together for the preflight briefing.

That's when she saw him, across the room, shaking hands and laughing with a young brigadier general from Edwards Air Force Base.

Suddenly she was brought back years. Rodger was a higher rank now, his face more rugged, each line a testament to another day of living on the edge, of waiting under the bright sun on the flight line, waiting his turn to outgamble death. But his raven dark hair was still the perfect backdrop to his blue sky eyes, and his powerful physique still looked wonderful—no, beyond wonderful—in a flight suit.

Those bright blue eyes looked up just then, meeting her gaze from across the room. And for the briefest of moments, everything else—the milling bodies, the polite conversation, the hum of machinery—fell completely away.

He broke off from the officer he'd been talking with. Slowly he walked across the room, his gaze holding steady with hers. He stopped in front of her, looking down into her long-lashed brown eyes.

"Hi," he said simply.

"Hi," she managed to whisper, her voice barely there.

"Want some gum?" he asked.

Sue released a pent-up breath. "What?"

He dug into a breast pocket and came out with two small, paper-covered rectangles. Slowly he unwrapped one and popped it into his mouth.

She wanted to say something to him, but she didn't know what. She felt lost and confused. Still trying to wish, to hope, as Will had advised her. Still trying to believe—

"Take it," he said, holding out the gum.

She did, barely looking at it.

"It's all I've got to give you," he said cryptically.

The words hurt, but she knew it was true.

They stood silently, with him looking down at her, and again Sue felt as if it were years ago and he was bending over her on the hot tarmac at Seymour Johnson Air Force Base. She recalled that moment after their final kiss, before he'd gone off to war.

That same look was still there in those blue, blue eyes, she realized. That same look.

Back then, Sue had not understood. She had been too young, too naive. Now, however, the truth of that look was beginning to penetrate—

"I've got to go," he said, beginning to turn. "Don't forget to read the wrapper."

"Wait!" Sue cried, not even sure why she'd called to him.

She had to get a hold of herself. She'd been worried about him before, but this time she felt something more than simple worry. She had a bad feeling inside. A bad feeling, and she wanted to tell him something before he left—something important.

"Good luck." The words came haltingly from her lips. No! That wasn't what she wanted to say!

Sue cursed herself as she saw him turn again with a nod of his head, a small smile on his lips. And then it was too late.

He was gone.

"AND AS YOU ALL KNOW from the studies," explained Sue to the audience of twenty or so bodies, "a female voice has been shown to command attention better than a male voice. So Reeva, of course, is equipped with a female voice."

"Hers," interrupted Lieutenant General Simpson.

"Well, yes. It is mine," said Sue, glancing at Simpson and trying her best to smile. She knew Simpson was trying to loosen her up, but it wasn't so easy briefing a room full of VIPs when the man you loved was about to step into a hurtling piece of machinery that might just kill him.

"And as we also know, pilots are predominantly artists," continued Sue. "Flying planes is a function of the right side of the brain—the creative, artistic side. The left side is administrative—checking data, establishing priorities. Reeva takes this into account when interfacing with the pilot's mind—"

"Excuse me, Captain," said one of the technical sergeants, "the Horizon is cleared for takeoff."

"Thank you," she told the sergeant. "We're ready to begin."

The Horizon taxied down the runway, then picked up speed and leapt into the air. Sue took in a deep breath and released it, her fingers clenched into tight fists.

"Just stay in your left brain, Susan," she advised herself.

After about ten minutes of letting Blackjack gain some altitude, Sue moved forward and depressed a button. "This is Op Lab. How's everything out there, Blackjack? Normal?"

"A-OK, Op Lab, everything's normal-normal."

"Roger, Blackjack."

She turned to Miller, on the medical-research team. "How are his vital signs?"

"They're very good, Captain."

Sue swallowed, saying another silent prayer and recalling the words Blackjack lived by. *You must do the thing you think you cannot do.*

She depressed the mike button. "Blackjack, are you feeling lucky?"

A laugh sounded across the intercom. "Op Lab, have you finally gotten a sense of humor?"

Behind her, she could hear the VIPs chuckling.

"Roger that, Blackjack. It's time to play. Engage Reeva at your discretion."

"Roger, Op Lab. You know I'm a sucker for a female voice."

More laughter sounded behind her, and a small chuckle left her throat, as well.

But the jovial feeling was soon gone from her. A terrible tension overtook her limbs as she watched the computer screen and listened to the sound of Blackjack interfacing with Reeva.

"Relax," purred the computer in Sue's own recorded voice. "Pull me closer."

Soon he was once again in sync with Reeva, and the plane was responding to his thoughts. He climbed and turned, putting the Horizon through its standard paces.

Sue finally relaxed when she felt today's test was under control. She allowed herself to turn and observe the VIPs. Some were smiling broadly, others were staring forward, mouths agape.

Simpson had been right. They were astounded and impressed, every last one of them. She looked over at her brother. "You know they'll have about a thousand questions after this is over," she whispered in warning.

Will shrugged. "They can read my paper. It's being published next month."

"But you'll handle them now, won't you?"

He smiled. "Sure. Anything for my kid sister."

"It's Major Kid Sister to you."

Sue laughed, then stopped when she heard something she didn't expect over the intercom.

"... an inverted roll. Are you ready to roll, Rodger?"

"Yes, Reeva, I'm ready."

She turned quickly, her gaze flying over the computer screen. "He's gone into sequence two," said Sue.

"Yeah," said the technical sergeant, "he's pushing the envelope on the program, like he did last week in the F-16."

"But this is a prototype," said Sue quietly. "We don't have enough data on its performance."

Will was listening beside her. He gently touched her arm. "Sue, it's his job to go as far as he can."

"He's got no backseater in that thing."

"He didn't in the F-16, either," said Will. "Calm down,' he whispered into her ear.

She tried, but it was difficult. She couldn't stop thinking about how much she loved Blackjack. "Oh God, Will."

"What?"

"This is so hard."

"I know."

Sue took a deep breath. She needed to get a hold of herself. Remembering the bubble gum Blackjack had given to her, she looked down, opening her tightly closed fist.

She recalled the look in his blue eyes. *It's all I've got to give you.*

Slowly she opened the wrapper and placed the soft pink gum into her mouth, biting down on the sweetness. She nearly tossed the wrapper into her pocket, when she remembered his rule of always reading the Bazooka Joe comic—that should distract her for a few more seconds, help her calm down. But this wasn't a comic, she thought as she looked down. It was a plain white scrap of paper with something written on it.

"Climbing," said Reeva in the distant background. "Sixty thousand feet ... sixty-five thousand feet ..."

"Captain Rigger," said the technical sergeant, "Blackjack may be in trouble here."

Sue's head shot up. "What's the status."

"The subject attempted a 180-degree roll, successfully executed, then he suddenly went into a pure vertical climb from sixty thousand feet. He's climbing too high, too fast."

"Miller, what's happening with his brain?" she asked the medical officer.

"Tunnel vision. It's the g's."

She knew what gravity could do to a pilot. It was the toughest biological barrier. The vision failed . . . first came dots, then loss of color, then tunnel vision, then blackout and finally unconsciousness. It all stemmed from lack of oxygen to the brain.

Sue depressed the mike button. "Blackjack, Op Lab. We advise you to level off, get out of that climb . . . Blackjack, please respond. . . ."

There was no response.

"Blackjack, please respond. . . ."

But there was nothing, only the op-lab sergeant continuing his counting. " . . . eighty-eight thousand feet . . . ninety thousand feet . . ."

"Disengage the program," commanded Sue.

"Remotely? I've never tried that before," said the technical sergeant.

"Will?"

Before she'd even said his name, Will was moving in to the computer, using his one good hand to punch at the keyboard.

"It's not the program that's the problem," said Will quickly. "It's the aircraft. The Horizon isn't responding to Reeva's commands, which means Blackjack won't be able to fly her manually, either. There must have been a catastrophic failure of the primary and secondary relays to the control surfaces."

"He's passing one hundred thousand feet," came the sergeant's voice.

A few seconds later Simpson stepped forward. In a deadly calm voice, he advised them, "The air's thin up there, even for the Horizon. Watch for engine failure—"

"Engine one in flameout," the technical sergeant's voice practically overlapped Simpson's. "Engine two—"

He'll die, thought Sue.

"He has to eject," she interrupted. "Miller, pilot's status?"

"He's in blackout," said the medical assistant. "He's close to losing—no, he's out. He's lost consciousness."

"Can we get to him through Reeva?" Sue asked Will.

"That's an idea. I—I don't know." Will punched in access codes and brought up the Reeva program. "Looks like Blackjack disengaged her from the cockpit before his blackout. Let me see what I can do from here to bring her back online."

Sue could barely breathe as she watched the small triangle on the radar screen finish its ascending and hang for a terrible second, then begin its deadly fall.

Wake up, Blackjack. You have to eject, she commanded, wishing her thoughts could reach the pilot.

She realized it was now up to her own voice to save his life. Ironic, she thought, cursing silently, since right now she felt completely helpless. She looked down at her hands in frustration, trying desperately to think of something that would help her to keep believing, help her to hold out hope—

Sue saw that scrap of bubble-gum wrapping still lying in her palm. Her eyes automatically read it. It didn't take long. There were only three words scrawled across it: "I love you."

BEFORE THE DARKNESS had come for him, Blackjack had been fighting gravity.

Breathing hard, he could feel the tight, heavy pressure of skin against bone, the push of the oxygen mask against his face. Sweat was pouring from his brow, straight down into his eyes. His gravity pants were squeezing his legs and waist, trying their best to keep the blood inside him from pooling at his feet.

"Come on, baby, come on," he murmured, fighting the pain and pushing the performance on both the Reeva system and the Horizon, not to mention on himself.

When his vision registered dots, he hung in, but when he lost color and began to see the world through a diminishing tunnel of light, he knew he didn't have long.

"Medical warning. Rodger, your field of vision is becoming limited," stated Reeva. "You are in danger of g-force blackout."

Blackjack used his mind with Reeva, trying to level off the Horizon. But something was wrong. They were still in vertical climb. The desert sky was falling quickly away as his body was slammed back in his seat by the tremendous thrust.

"Aircraft not responding," stated Reeva. "Restate command."

"Damn," cursed Blackjack.

"That is not a command. Restate command."

He bit out a silent curse this time and spoke again. "Reeva, level off," he said loudly, hoping the verbal command would put the program on track. But the Horizon continued rocketing higher and higher, into the indigo twilight above the atmosphere.

"Reeva," he barked, "state status."

"Vertical climb," came the calm female voice. "Ninety-one thousand feet . . ."

"Level off!" he repeated. *Damn female, listen to me!*

"Warning. Aircraft is not responding. Medical warning. Rodger, your field of vision is now limited. Warning. Level off."

"Damn!" cried Rodger once again. "Reeva, disengage."

Rodger's hands went to the controls. Manually he tried to get the Horizon to respond, but it was no use. The failure wasn't Reeva's; it was this aircraft's relays.

He was still climbing, past the sky's light and into the darkness waiting silently beyond it. It was quiet up here, so quiet, and he could see stars appearing as he glanced at his instruments and saw altitude reaching one hundred thousand feet.

"No!" he cried, hoping weightlessness would drive off the demon. But it was no use. Rodger was going into blackout, and there was nothing he could do about it.

The darkness was closing in...pulling him down...he was sinking further and further...suddenly an image floated before him...from deep in his memories.

It was Sue.

Her face. Innocent and lovely...all those years ago...when he'd first fallen in love with her...

Just before he lost consciousness, an imperceptible smile touched the edge of his lips. He hoped that damn stubborn female had listened to him for once...and read the wrapper....

EVERY SINGLE BODY in the op lab was frozen as still as a corpse. Not a sound could be heard beyond the hum of machinery and the furious clicking of one keyboard.

"It's done," said Will. "I've restarted Reeva. It's our best chance of getting to him from down here—ten times more potent than a simple intercom voice."

Sue nodded her head silently. In a terrible state of numb horror, she watched the radar screen, watched that sleek load of expensive metal drop like a set of car keys and spin like a metal pinwheel in the sky.

"Miller, mobilize the emergency crews."

She closed her eyes, recalling data on gravity blackouts. Studies showed that pilots averaged twelve seconds of incapacity, twelve seconds of waking up in a dreamlike state, then two to four minutes before cognitive skills returned.

I didn't get to tell him...

She glanced at the radar screen again. All she could do now was wait. And hope...

Maybe he already knows.

WORDS OF POETRY circled in the darkness of Blackjack's unconscious mind.

Out to seas colder than the Hebrides I must go. Where the fleet of stars is anchored and the young Star captains glow....

His skin grew cold. So cold.

...the fleet of stars...

It was "The Dying Patriot." The poem that James McConnell had read at his son's funeral. Whit's funeral.

...where the young Star captains glow....

Now it was time, said a voice inside him. His time.

Now it was his turn to become the dying patriot, dancing on the edge of his father's sword.

The black bird was his black coffin.

He was flying up in it. Up and up, into the sky, weightless, disconnected. Now he would join the fleet of souls—the star captains...like Landson...and Whit...and countless others.

"Rodger..."

A voice.

"...wake up."

Now it was time...

"Warning. Rodger, wake up!"

A female voice.

But the darkness was pulling him; it wanted him bad, and he was willing to let it take him. Willing to finally join his brother...it was his duty to follow Whit...he always knew, since he'd been a boy...

"Rodger..."

Yet...there was something. Calling him.

"Wake up!"

Someone. A woman. A child. He should remember.

"Rodger, darling, listen to me..."

Yes. He knew that voice. Sue's voice.

"I need you. I love you."

They needed him.

"Listen to me. Wake up. Now."

Wake up?

"Fight for us, you damned cocky pilot! Fight!"

Blackjack blinked once, then twice; his eyes snapped open to find the world in chaos. He was falling like a stone from the heavens, the heavy machinery around him spinning violently in a terrible mind-bending cyclone.

"Warning," stated Reeva's calm, cool voice within his helmet. "Eject. Rodger, you must eject."

Eject?

"I'M GOING—"

"Captain," the lieutenant general advised Sue, "the emergency crews can handle—"

It was wasted breath. Simpson was talking to thin air. Sue Rigger had bolted from the room the moment she saw that the ejection seat had been activated.

Will was right behind her.

But Sue wasn't waiting for her brother. She wasn't waiting for anyone.

"Airman!"

The young ground-crew worker was just starting a jeep near the flight line. He looked up at the captain's call, raising his hand for an awkward salute.

"Forget that crap, just get me out to the crash site."

"But—"

"Now! That's an order, airman!"

The crash sight was disturbingly easy to locate on the flat desert floor. Miles away, billowing smoke plumed up into the cloudless blue sky, the flames of the Horizon wreckage looking like a yawning opening to hell itself.

She hung on through the bumpy ride. The jeep was off the airfield now, careening about fifty yards behind the emergency vehicles, but the site of the crash was still miles off.

Sue lifted a hand to her eyes, shading them from the strong sun. She searched the sky for any sign of the bright orange parachute, but there was none. Was he already down?

Her gaze shifted to the crash again.

God, did Blackjack even make it out? Were the instrument readings off? Had he been able to clear the canopy after ejection?

A thousand things could have gone terribly wrong, and now every one of the lethal possibilities ran through Sue's mind in a sickeningly efficient sequence.

She closed her eyes, trying to hold on to hope. Her fists were clenched so tightly, her nails dug into her palms.

When she opened her eyes again, she looked down at the three words scrawled on that scrap of paper. She held on to it now for dear life.

"Come on, Blackjack," she whispered. "Don't give up."

"Captain," called the airman over the loud rush of wind in the open jeep, "I see something."

Sue followed the airman's pointing arm. It was to the right of the crash site.

"Oh, please," she whispered, trying to make out the speck. "Go!" she ordered.

The airman jerked the wheel, and the jeep was gaining on the shimmering image on the hot desert floor.

Was it him. Or just a mirage?

The airman must have had the pedal to the floor. The jeep's wheels were eating up ground, rocketing them closer to that image. Sue strained her eyes, trying to get a clear view through the dirty windshield, but the wreckage's pluming smoke was now drifting across their line of sight.

"Captain Rigger!" called the airman. "That looks like a pilot...."

Sue's gaze found an image, appearing out of the dark, billowing smoke. It was shimmering in the desert heat, moving toward them across the dry earth.

"My God," she whispered, rising from her seat for a better look. She struggled to stand in the speeding jeep, her hands gripping the top of the windshield for balance. But what she saw left her stunned. She simply couldn't believe her eyes.

Blackjack was on his feet, limping toward them with fierce determination. His orange parachute was even rolled up under one arm, just as the manual said.

"You're damned right!" she cried. "That's a pilot!"

Chapter Sixteen

Sue was furiously pacing in the hall of the small Flatlands Base hospital.

"You'll wear out the tiles," warned her brother, sitting on a chair nearby.

"They can take it out of my pay."

The hospital was a small building and was used only for emergency treatment and short-term care. Anything more got a patient flown to a larger hospital. Sue was supremely grateful to hear that Blackjack would not be flown elsewhere.

The ambulance had been right behind Sue's jeep. It brought Blackjack straight here. For the past hour, Sue had been waiting, desperate for some kind of word. She was relieved when the doctor finally approached.

"We're going to watch him for forty-eight hours," said the middle-aged woman. She explained that Blackjack had suffered from some burns and bad bruises. Though he'd have a small facial scar by his eye and another few on his legs and chest, he was perfectly fine otherwise.

"May we see him now?" asked Sue.

"Sure, but don't stay too long. We've given him something to help him relax. He should get some sleep."

Sue glanced at her brother. Will smiled. "Go on in alone, I'll wait here for you."

She walked hesitantly into the white room. Blackjack's tall frame and broad chest were big for the hospital bed. He looked to be in fine living color against the stark white background, and she smiled at the sight of him.

His own dimples appeared at the sight of her. A wide, loving, happy smile began to stretch across his face.

"Hi," he said simply.

"Hi," she answered.

She moved into the room, next to his bed. "The doctor said I shouldn't stay long—"

"Did you read it?"

Sue met his intense gaze. She nodded silently.

"It's all I've got to say, I guess," said Blackjack.

"It's enough."

Blackjack reached out to capture her hand. "Except...maybe I do have a few more things to say."

She smiled and nodded.

"I've always loved you, Sue Rigger. I bet you didn't know that."

Sue felt pools of liquid forming in her eyes. "No."

"And," he continued, "I bet you didn't know the reason I hurt you. Back in North Carolina."

"Blackjack, you don't have to—"

"No," he said gently. "Let me."

She tightened her grip on his hand, and he interlaced his fingers with hers.

"I thought...that you'd be better off without me," he began. "That it would be better for you to love someone else...since I'd been planning on dying, like my brother."

"Like Whit?"

"I always figured it was my duty—"

"But...that's crazy."

"Yeah, I know. But only an oddball part of me thought that, Sue. I mean, I did manage to stay alive this long."

Sue shook her head in frustration. "Blackjack, I've been thinking a lot in the last hour, and I've come to the conclusion that... well, that maybe you were right—"

"About what?"

"You have to understand. It means the world to me to know you love me. That you love Max. But I'd rather have you around. Maybe love is too much of a distraction. I mean, I'd rather have you alive at a distance than dead any other way."

Blackjack's eyelids seemed to be growing heavy. The sedative was beginning to work on him.

"Don't give up on us, Sue," warned Blackjack. "I love you."

"I love you, too," she said.

"Yes..." he breathed. "I knew it."

"But, Blackjack, that doesn't mean... Blackjack?"

It was too late. He'd drifted into a drug-induced sleep.

"HE'LL COME AFTER YOU, you know," warned Will as he unloaded Sue's and Max's bags from the back of the jeep and placed them on the Las Vegas airport's parking ramp.

She had waited until the prognosis was good for Blackjack, then she arranged to take a week's leave. She loved Blackjack, loved him with all her heart, but she didn't want him making posttrauma confessions and drug-induced promises.

The best thing for both of them, she decided, was to carve out some breathing room.

"Will, just trust me," she said, trying to reassure her big brother. "Blackjack needs time to think. He's just been through a lot. So have I. Besides, Max misses Mom and Dad. Don't you, Max?"

Max was distracted by the people rushing in and out of the many glass doors of the commercial airport. "Yeah," he said absently. "I want to see Grandma and Grandpa. I want to show them my model planes."

Sue smiled down at her son. Max had chosen to take the models of the F-16 Falcon and the Stearman biplane—the ones that his father had helped him build.

"What did Simpson say?" asked Will, carrying the bags to a skycap.

"He understands that I need a week to get my head together. It'll be a whole new phase for the Reeva project when I get back. Wait till Rodger finds out."

She could hardly believe it, but Rodger McConnell had been promoted to the next rank up from colonel—brigadier general. His new promotion put him in charge of recruiting and training a new batch of pilots for Reeva's system testing.

"Hard to believe that clown's getting a star," said Will.

"I could say the same for you." Her brother was being promoted, as well, and making plans to marry Jane Cortez.

"Give my love to Mom and Dad for me," said Will, kissing Sue on the cheek.

"Sure, I'll tell them to make plans for a wedding soon."

"Whose?" teased Will.

"Just buy her the ring," she advised with a smile.

"WHAT DO YOU MEAN she's gone?" asked Blackjack, his voice dangerously low. He had just been released from the base hospital and was now confronting his commanding officer.

"Calm down. She's coming back. In a week," added Lieutenant General Simpson.

"Dammit!" Blackjack's fist connected with his commanding officer's desk.

"What's wrong?"

Blackjack glared at Simpson. "You ever been in a crash like mine?"

"Yes," Simpson said with a nod. "About fifteen years ago."

"Remember how it felt? After."

Simpson smiled slightly. "Yeah. I see your point."

Blackjack had never felt such a sense of urgency. He was alive. *Alive!* The demon had not won. And the reason was Sue. She *loved* him...and he loved her. And that's what had called him back from the darkness.

He knew the truth now—and it was racing through his veins like jet fire. The only reason he'd been living for his flying all these years was that he'd been *planning* on dying. But he wasn't planning on dying anymore; he was planning on living, and he'd be damned if those plans didn't include the woman he loved.

"I have no intention of wasting any more time. I've got unfinished business with that woman, and life is too short."

Blackjack leaned toward the lieutenant general with unwavering intent. "What airline is she taking?"

"Now, Blackjack—"

"What airline!"

SUE WAS RECLINING in her airline seat. Her eyes were closed. She and Max were well into the first leg of their flight from Nevada to Washington, D.C. Their first layover would be Kansas City.

"Mom, what's that?" asked the little voice beside her, his hand tugging lightly on her off-white suit jacket.

"What's what?" asked Sue on a yawn. Max had wanted the window seat so he could pretend that he was flying the plane.

"Mom!" said Max with a great deal more urgency. The tug was much harder this time. "Look!"

She opened her eyes and turned toward the window.

"Oh, good Lord. I don't believe it!"

At almost the same moment, the passengers near them began murmuring excitedly, "Hey, look out there," said a man in front of them. "Isn't that a jet fighter?"

"Hey, wow," said a child behind them.

The stewardess nearby was bending over the seats to get a better view of the F-16 Falcon that was keeping pace with the large Boeing 747.

Suddenly Sue heard the overhead speaker system clicking on. "Excuse me, ladies and gentlemen, this is your captain speaking. Is there a Major Susan Rigger flying with us this afternoon?"

"Oh, my God," whispered Sue, sinking into her seat in total mortification.

"Mom, that's you!" cried Max.

"Shh..." Sue said, trying not to attract attention.

"She's here!" cried Max, ignoring his mother, her cheeks flushed pink in embarrassment. "Here she is!"

The stewardess approached. "Are you Major Rigger?"

Sue nodded and the stewardess disappeared up the aisle.

Dreading the truth, Sue forced herself to glance out the small passenger window. She took a good look at the F-16 and cursed silently.

It was Blackjack, all right. His oxygen mask was off, and she could easily make out the square-jawed, handsome face, smiling broadly.

The click of the airliner's intercom sounded again. "Well, Major Rigger, I have an interesting message over our radio. It seems the pilot to our left there is looking for you."

Passengers on the other side of the large plane were now craning their necks to see the fighter jet.

"Brigadier General McConnell would like me to ask you if you'd consider being his wife."

Every single one of the plane's passengers was now in a tizzy. Whoops and hollers of startled amusement were sounding from the front of the plane to the back.

The stewardess returned and smiled down at Sue. "Well?"

Sue turned to her son. "Max, do you have a piece of paper?" she asked calmly. She looked up at the stewardess. "Tell the captain to tell the general to look in the passenger window over the 747's port-side wing."

"Yes, ma'am," said the stewardess.

"Here, Mom," said Max, handing his mother a big pad of blank white drawing paper. Sue reached down, grabbed a red crayon and scrawled three letters.

She leaned across Max and held the paper up to the window.

"What did she say?" asked a woman a few seats behind them.

"I don't know," said another voice. "Hey, does anyone know what's going on?"

Sue pulled the paper down and looked out her small window.

Blackjack's blue eyes were there, beyond the 747's wing. Those killer dimples were showing again.

I love you, he mouthed.

She returned the words, a deep feeling of happiness overtaking her. She knew he meant it. No man in a drug-induced haze could fly that thing.

"Mom!" cried Max. "What's going on?"

Sue leaned back in her seat. "Let's test your reading skills," she said to her young son.

She showed her son the paper.

"Yes," he read without pause. "Yes!" he shouted, climbing up on his seat to tell the whole plane. "Mom said yes!"

Sue wondered if Blackjack could hear the deafening sounds of screams and applause.

Maybe he had, she thought as she glanced out the window again and laughed. The F-16 had snapped up its flaps and was now performing a perfectly executed victory roll.

WHEN THEY TOUCHED DOWN in Kansas City, he was already waiting at the gate, a dozen hastily bought roses in his hand.

She was in his strong, loving arms in record time, her mouth against his, both of them happy beyond belief.

"Should we go back to Flatlands?" she asked.

"Hell, no. It's time I met your parents."

Epilogue

A few months later, the wedding was held on the Flying M Ranch. They were married outside, in the warmth of the setting sun, beneath a bower of roses and baby's breath. Wild Will was the best man, Curly Cortez, the maid of honor, their own wedding date set for early the following year.

Little Max was a heartbreaker in his black tuxedo, balancing two golden rings on a silk pillow, his German shepherd puppy sitting happily with the Butlers in the first row.

Sue's eyes took it all happily in. But the vision she was most taken with—the one that took her breath away—was that of her brave, blue-eyed pilot in full dress uniform, standing proudly by her side and promising his love.

The star on Blackjack's shoulder gleamed with a promise, too. He was now entering a new stage of his life—one that meant less risks in the air and more leadership on the ground. Sue's heart rested easily in the knowledge that this was his unfettered choice. He was finally ready to live for his son, for his wife—and for their future.

With the minister's pronouncement, making them man and wife, came the Air Force's own punctuation. A ceremonial overfly created a thrilling stir among their many guests as a tight formation of jet fighters roared magnificently across the wide blue sky above them.

After that, the party went on for hours, the celebrating for days—and long, pleasurable nights.

"I was thinking of setting up a home office in here," said Sue a week after they'd returned from their honeymoon. She had pulled Blackjack into the den at the back of the house.

"Home office?"

"I'll be needing some time off...and afterward I can use a modem to continue my work from the house."

"Why would you want to do that?"

She hugged him close. "Because...we're expecting."

"Expecting what?"

Sue just smiled up at him, waiting for him to catch on.

"Oh...oh! When did we...?"

"When didn't we?"

Blackjack's mouth glided onto hers in the gentlest, most loving of kisses. When he was done, he lifted his head, looking around the newly dusted and aired-out room.

"I guess that's about right," he said with a broad smile.

"What?"

"That you should be here. Working under the watchful eyes of Orville and Wilbur, and old Cal Rodgers."

"And you, I hope."

"You can bet on that," he said. "Just promise me one thing."

"What's that?"

"Let's never stop flying."

"I promise."

Then his mouth was on hers, and both were soaring once more.

UNLOCK THE DOOR TO GREAT ROMANCE AT BRIDE'S BAY RESORT

Join Harlequin's new across-the-lines series, set in an exclusive hotel on an island off the coast of South Carolina.

Seven of your favorite authors will bring you exciting stories about fascinating heroes and heroines discovering love at Bride's Bay Resort.

Look for these fabulous stories coming to a store near you beginning in January 1996.

Harlequin American Romance #613 in January
Matchmaking Baby by Cathy Gillen Thacker

Harlequin Presents #1794 in February
Indiscretions by Robyn Donald

Harlequin Intrigue #362 in March
Love and Lies by Dawn Stewardson

Harlequin Romance #3404 in April
Make Believe Engagement by Day Leclaire

Harlequin Temptation #588 in May
Stranger in the Night by Roseanne Williams

Harlequin Superromance #695 in June
Married to a Stranger by Connie Bennett

Harlequin Historicals #324 in July
Dulcie's Gift by Ruth Langan

Visit Bride's Bay Resort each month wherever Harlequin books are sold.

HARLEQUIN®

BBAYG

Yo amo novelas con corazón!

Starting this March, Harlequin opens up to a whole new world of readers with two new romance lines in SPANISH!

Harlequin Deseo
- passionate, sensual and exciting stories

Harlequin Bianca
- romances that are fun, fresh and very contemporary

With four titles a month, each line will offer the same wonderfully romantic stories that you've come to love—now available in Spanish.

Look for them at selected retail outlets.

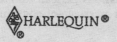

In Name Only

...because there are many reasons for saying "I do."

American Romance cordially invites you to a wedding of convenience. This is one reluctant bride and groom with their own unique reasons for marrying...IN NAME ONLY.

By popular demand American Romance continues this story of favorite marriage-of-convenience books. Don't miss

#624 THE NEWLYWED GAME
by Bonnie K. Winn
March 1996

Find out why some couples marry first...and learn to love later. Watch for IN NAME ONLY!

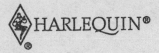